THE 14TH TALE

XANN-SHAPELLA SMITH

This book is a work of fiction. Any reference to historical events, real people, or real places are used fictitiously. Other names, characters, places, and events are products of the author's imagination, and any resemblance to actual events or places or persons, living or dead, is entirely coincidental.

Copyright © 2023 by Xann-shapella Smith

All rights reserved. No part of this book may be reproduced in any form or by any electronic or mechanical means, including information storage and retrieval systems, without written permission from the author, except for the use of brief quotations in a book review.

ISBN:

978-0-9992027-5-3

ACKNOWLEDGMENTS

For my family, who continue to volunteer in the workshop of my magical idea factory.

~ Like branches on an oak tree, our lives may grow in different directions, yet our roots remain as one. ~

PROLOGUE

The gate's shadow danced against the wall as the dust-filled beam of a flashlight cut through the darkness. Releasing the lock, the trespasser's hand took hold of the cold wrought iron. Without hesitation, he pushed open the barrier, unchecked by the gate's master. The swivel of iron against iron creaked out a foreboding song. Its cry met with disregard.

The faceless man in a dark suit aimed his light downward. His polished black oxfords reflected the light as they took turns leading him down the stairs. The stair's warning gave him no reason to pause as they creaked beneath his feet. Hubris drove his descent. Step by step, he continued until he reached the doors to the cellar, the purported home of a centuries-old secret.

With a turn of his open hand, the double doors opened in obedience to his command. The magical workroom lay bare before him. As he stepped through the entrance, his overpriced shoes pressed into the dirt floor, leaving evidence of his presence and the eventual pain of his encroachment.

Crude bookshelves laden with stacks of bound chronicles captured his attention. Searching the titles, his free hand moved from book to dusty book. His pace quickened with his desperation. "It has to be here!"

Bottles containing concoctions, tinctures, and tonics filled the vacancies between volumes, enticing brief moments of examination. Fighting his curiosity, he focused his search until he reached the last book. Clenching his fist, he held back his rage. The object of his quest was nowhere to be found.

Desperate, he turned to the mixing table and began ransacking the cluttered mess. His sweeping light lit several jars of mummified amphibians, the scent of scrub lands long removed. Viviparous lizards and newts jumped at him from obscurity.

Small pans of decoctions waited to be corked and wired. Herbs and medicinals dangled from strings while flower petals from the wilds of Cunnemarra dried on a rack. Elements ripe for the mortar and pestle obstructed his search. Bottles of volcanic ash from drifting Icelandic clouds waited in line for the scales alongside jars of dust mites and arachnids. The stench rising from a crock of animal hair soaking in a rancid solution turned his head.

His resolve prevailed once he caught a whiff of fresh air. A jar of wishbones appeared as the light swept back to the table. Not even the allure of a mystical recipe book was enough to quench his thirst. The prize he sought was beyond the simple magic of rudimentary potions. It held the key to power and wealth never before realized.

Pivoting in frustration, he found his footing as his light captured the reflection of a tapestry's golden threads. Encouraged, he slunk toward a small table tucked away in a dark corner. With a touch of reverence, he pulled back the hand-woven fabric, revealing the object of his quest: The *Book of Killian*.

CHAPTER ONE

A Porsche 911 darted in and out of traffic, chased by a silver unmarked police car. The squealing of tread against asphalt caused heads to turn as the Guards Red sports car worked to maintain traction. Blowing through a stop sign, the hardtop GT3 narrowly avoided a collision. The athleticism gained from the manual transmission and the power from the muscular engine put the driver ahead of the game. It was his race to lose.

A white police vehicle with blue markings followed unscathed. Its flashing lights and piercing siren alerted the shoppers in the sleepy business district to be on the watch. John Madsen, the young detective at the wheel, focused on the fugitive like an adversary in a video game. Scruffy locks of blonde surfer hair danced around his head as he weaved through vehicles, showcasing his driving skills and passion for the chase. Having an audience of bystanders elevated him to celebrity status, while the sounds coming through the open window provided the perfect soundtrack. He was the star of his own high-octane film.

He knew full well that the constraints of city driving were the only thing keeping the Porsche from leaving them in its dust. But he'd never admit it out loud. He loved the chase.

The opposite was true of Finn Donnelly, the seasoned Lieutenant Detective riding in the passenger seat, hoping he'd live to see forty-five. "My hair is still black. I hope to keep it that way."

"Pretty sure I saw a few grays when I followed you out of the precinct this morning." Madsen braked fast, then cranked the wheel to the right, narrowly avoiding the car trapped between him and the assailant. Refusing to give in to the narrow escape, he sped up, wishing he was driving his Dodge Charger.

"Pay attention to the road," Finn shot back as he casually ran his fingers through his hair, mimicking his partner's jab. "Gray hairs..."

Breaking for a random bicyclist, Madsen pressed the accelerator against the floor and changed his grip on the wheel. He'd lost valuable seconds. "I'll get him."

"Why couldn't this happen at the beginning of my shift?"

"I can slow down," joked Madsen

"You make me late for Ailee's swim meet, and you'll never see Sergeant." Finn removed his grip from the grab handle above the window to check his watch. "Fifteen minutes." His hand quickly returned to the handle as his partner took a ninety-degree angle, nearly sliding into a delivery truck. Finn could feel his sweat penetrating the cotton shirt beneath his navy blue, off the-rack-suit. Reaching for the knot in his green tie, he loosened it to help him breathe. Then he slid his hand down the patterns of swirling clovers for luck.

"Is Ailee feeling better?" asked Madsen, demonstrating his ability to multitask.

Finn slowly exhaled after the near collision. "We have another doctor's appointment tomorrow." Donnelly was a captive audience with a front-row seat to Madsen's action movie playing out through the windshield. "Watch it!" he warned as Madsen followed the Porsche through a farmer's market, barely missing the patrons and sellers fleeing the booths. "Look out, Madsen!"

The detective swerved, missing a woman carrying a large box to her car. A shiver down the driver's spine straightened his back.

Madsen had raised the stakes by following the perpetrator through a pedestrian area. "That was close."

"Too close," Finn warned as two patrol cars joined the chase. "He's headed for the freeway! Take Laden Street."

"I'll lose him!"

"Back-up's got him."

Madsen left the main road, drifting the corner. The Ford Police Interceptor had fewer obstacles to avoid once they entered a warehouse district and ran parallel to the chase. The Porsche's engine growled as it climbed toward its 9000rpm redline. Finn calculated as they sped across the intersecting streets with intermittent views of the Porsche. "One more block and you'll have him." With his car nearly maxed out, the young detective focused on the finish line. Finn remained calm, calculating a series of outcomes. "Take a right at the next intersection."

Madsen followed his partner's navigation, keeping control as all four wheels slid to the side. He continued down the street while Finn watched for obstacles, crossing his fingers for luck. With nowhere left to go, the young detective screeched sideways to a stop in the middle of the intersection. The driver of the red Porsche had no other option than to slam on his brakes, stopping inches from the detective's car. Thrilled by his catch, Madsen jumped out as the two squad cars arrived. Within seconds, the perp was blocked in from both sides and surrounded by policemen.

Finn breathed a sigh of relief as he loosened his grip on the handle, relaxed his crossed fingers and stroked his Irish tie. Choosing to watch through the windshield, he let Madsen have his moment. The look on his partner's face as he pulled the muscle-bound suspect from his car reminded Finn of himself before becoming a parent. Proudly, he watched Madsen cuff the bald assailant and turn him over to his fellow cops. The rant spewing from the suspect's mouth did not affect Madsen as he respectfully ran his hand over the Porsche's beautiful aerodynamic curves. Finn admired his cool head.

Twelve years ago, Finn would have been the one proudly hauling the suspect back to jail. Life as a single dad had humbled him. The thrill of the chase had been replaced by a more measured approach. Looking at his watch, Finn remembered his daughter's swim meet. "You got this, Madsen?" he asked, leaving the passenger side and circling around to the driver's side.

"Wish her luck."

"We're Irish."

Finn may have left Ireland behind, but his penchant for luck on the job came with him. Smiling, he jumped in and sped away, mentally mapping the fastest route to the recreation center.

For the students of Mr. Holt's freshman history class, being confined to a classroom on a partly cloudy day in May was testing every ounce of their discipline. As most of the class daydreamed of warmer weather, Ailee Donnelly slumbered on the pillowy pages of an open textbook. Her messy auburn hair covered the desk. Summer swimming league had begun, and the workouts were taking a toll. At least, that's what she told herself.

Fragmented facts of the Great Depression flowed in and out of her consciousness as she attempted to sleep. The teacher's pronouncement of dates, percentage rates and people's fates translated to a muddled fantasy in her mind. The pencil gripped between her thumb and fingers danced with each fidget while the dull sound of a marker thumping against the whiteboard provided the beat.

Until it stopped.

She could hear the distorted voice of her teacher getting closer, his volume increasing. Still, her eyelids refused to open.

"1933, Miss Donnelly."

"Hmm," she responded incoherently.

"1933."

Half asleep, Ailee's arm dropped from the desktop, taking a book with it. The noise of the book hitting the floor sounded like a starting gun at a swim meet. Ailee jumped up, expecting to be poolside. Instead, she found herself the focus of laughter and gibes. Adjusting her turquoise zip-up hoodie, she was never so glad to hear the final bell of the school day.

The teacher waited for her to collect her things and then gave her a final warning. "Being the best on the swim team won't matter if you fail my class."

"I'm sorry, Mr. Holt," she responded earnestly, wrapping her hair in a loose ponytail with the hair band on her wrist.

Recognizing the sincerity in her enchanting green eyes, the teacher changed his tone. "This isn't like you, Ailee."

Ailee watched him walk away, knowing he was right. This wasn't like her. She was an A-student and, at the young age of thirteen, captain of her swim team. The illness that had hijacked her life seemed to be chipping away at everything she loved.

As she left the room, Roger was waiting near the door, his head nearly meeting the top of the doorframe. He was tall for his age. The two friends merged into the flow of the crowded hallway, shoulders bouncing off shoulders as they walked toward their lockers. Roger was her periscope and path-maker when it came to navigating the overcrowded hallways of their junior high. "Don't let Mr. Holt get to you."

"He's right," she argued, stuck in her self-hosted pity party.

"They're not going to kick you off the team. You're faster than everyone."

The sound of multiple books hitting the hard floor caught Ailee's attention. Reaching down, she helped the younger student pick up the textbooks somebody shoved from her arms. Leaving the girl with a reassuring smile, Ailee pushed through the crowd of eager students to catch up with her friend. The struggle of swimming against the tide sucked the strength from her body. Falling against her locker, Ailee seized the moment for a much-needed rest. "I'm so tired."

"Are you drinking enough water?"

"I'm drinking like a fish." Ailee proved her point by taking a swig from her water bottle after opening her locker. "I can't even stay awake long enough to do my homework."

"Come over after the meet, and we'll study together," suggested

Roger, glancing at the familiar collage of waterfalls pictures decorating the inside of her locker door.

"I'll check with Dad if he shows up today."

"I've never seen your dad miss a meet?"

"He's a policeman," said Ailee as she took three textbooks from her locker and stuffed them in her pack before closing the door. "There's always a possibility."

Roger grabbed the strap of her backpack and flung it over his shoulder. "I don't want you wearing out before the meet."

"Too late," she replied. Sliding her hand into a zipped pocket on the outside of her pack, she removed a couple of protein bars and handed one to her best friend. Then she placed the straps of her swim bag over her shoulder as they headed toward the door.

Walking through the park between the school and the recreation center, Ailee noticed a woman in brown sunglasses spying on her from behind a maple tree. She recognized her from earlier that morning, still wearing the same knee-length, Aran cardigan she wore on the street corner near Ailee's house. Her oversized knitted hood concealed most of her hair except the loose braid draped over the front of her shoulder. The sage color of the sweater's yarn complimented her red hair.

Ailee stopped to take a closer look, prompting Roger to slow down. "What are you looking at?"

"The lady by the tree." Ailee turned back to Roger. "I think she's following me."

"What lady?"

"Right there." The woman vanished before she could get a second look. Ailee and Roger walked toward the large tree and found no trace of the mystery woman. With great interest, she scanned the people making use of the beautiful spring day. The park was alive with runners working out their stress, dog walkers glued to their phones and parents letting their kids play after school. The mystery woman in the sage sweater was nowhere to be found. "She was right here?"

"We're going to be late. Come on." Roger left the tree and walked toward the recreation center, thinking Ailee was right behind him.

Looking down, she saw a drawing etched into a patch of worn dirt near the tree's trunk. Bending to her knees, she took a closer look and then pulled back. Trying to remain calm, she pulled her fuchsia shirt to the side and looked at the birthmark on the front of her shoulder. It was the same shape: a Sessile oak tree leaf with nine protruding lobes.

Feeling her spine chill, she scrunched the opening of her blouse together inside her fist and held it tightly around her neck. She'd spent years wearing racing swimsuits, but the wide straps concealed most of her birthmark. The personal nature of the stranger's drawing induced a growing uneasiness within her chest. Her mind was abuzz with speculation as she scanned the park for the mystery stalker.

Pulling out her phone, Ailee noticed the time. The meet had started. She had to hurry, or her entrance into the competition would be forfeited. Quickly, she snapped a picture of the drawing. Satisfied with the digital photo, she picked up the artist's twig and scratched the rendering from existence. Mentally shaken, she took one more look around the park then hurried for the recreation center.

CHAPTER TWO

The pool facility was bustling with excitement when Finn rushed through the door. His timing couldn't have been better. Climbing the three benches to the top of the bleachers, he spotted his daughter leaving the bullpen. A crisscross wave of his arms let her know he'd arrived. Her confident approach to the starting platform gave him a reason to smile. He was impressed by the team's new teal-colored, mid-thigh racing suit and swim cap. The uniforms were brand new for the season. Finn knew his daughter must have had a say in the color since teal reflected the tropical water color palette she loved.

Ailee smiled at her dad with a reserved wave just before stepping onto the block and facing her lane. Her toned arms and legs reflected the countless hours she'd spent honing her skill. Swimming was everything to his daughter, and Finn knew it. Her goals were impressive for a thirteen-year-old. On the list were the Junior Olympics and Nationals. Finn took a deep breath as he watched her adjust her swim cap and lower her goggles. Just a month ago, he would have been cheering for a win alongside the other parents. Watching her bend into starting position, his only hope today was that she survive the heat.

Her dive from the platform was strong—excellent technique, as always. Finn rose to his feet as his daughter slipped beneath the water, both holding their breath.

The strength of her arms came into view as she re-emerged and powered down the lane. Freestyle was her stroke of choice. The cheering crowd grew louder as she separated herself from her competitors. The race was hers to lose. Flipping at the other end, she started back. Finn glanced at the pace clock. She was meeting her best time, and he worried she'd overdo it.

Ailee pushed beyond her fatigue until her hand slapped the concrete at the end of her 50 meter. Winning the race, she attempted to climb out of the pool. Halfway up, she fell backward and sank beneath the water.

Finn raced down the bleachers as he watched Roger dive in after her. The lifeguard followed. Together, they helped her out of the pool. Finn made his way to the other side as the volunteer nurse examined her. Crouching next to his daughter, he felt a rush of relief seeing her conscious and responding to questions.

Still a bit dizzy, Ailee made it to the team bench with the assistance of her father and coach. She purposely hid the fact that her head was still spinning and her heart was beating rapidly. She knew the outcome if her dad and coach knew what she was really experiencing. "I'll be fine. I just need a minute before the next heat."

"We're going home," announced her father as he stood up from the bench.

"The meet's not over!"

"I agree with your father, Ailee," said her coach. "You're out of the water till you find out what's wrong with you."

"You're benching me?"

"You're the best swimmer I've coached in years, but I won't risk your health."

"I'm fine!" Ailee grabbed her towel and stormed off the bench. She did her best to stabilize herself as she walked toward the locker room in protest.

"Thanks for backing me up," said Finn, waiting for the coach to rise to her feet. "We have another doctor's appointment in the morning. I'll keep you updated." Finn tossed a folded towel onto the wet bench and sat down as the coach walked away. Resting his elbows on his knees, he placed his head in his hands and breathed a sigh of relief. The bullpen announcer called for the next participants, and the meet went on as though nothing had happened. Ailee wasn't the center of everyone's universe, only her father's.

Needing a quiet place to think, Finn picked up his daughter's backpack, flung it over his shoulder and left the building. Waiting outside the door, he checked his phone for messages. As hard as he tried, he couldn't switch gears from Ailee to work. Looking toward the park for some form of distraction, he got more than he expected. Ailee's mystery woman, hidden behind brown sunglasses and wearing the same sage sweater, was staring straight at him.

Before he could make a move, Ailee threw the metal door open and walked through, stealing his attention from the stranger. Finn watched her pass by, ignoring his presence. When he looked back to the park, the woman was nowhere to be found. He chalked the sighting up to a haunting phantom from his past. "I got your backpack," he said, catching up to his daughter and removing the swim bag from her shoulder. Together they walked silently toward the car until the frustration brewing inside Ailee's young mind turned to anger. "I can't believe the coach is benching me!" Her pace quickened.

"That means no more practicing at the rec center either."

Stopping abruptly, Ailee confronted her father in disbelief. "That's not fair!"

"Who will jump in and pull you out if something goes wrong? Your aunt Gladys is no spring chicken, and you know I can't swim."

"How can you be a cop and not know how to swim?" Throwing up her arms, Ailee turned her back in protest.

"Quit changing the subject," demanded Finn, placing her swim bag beside to him. Reaching out, he turned his daughter back toward him. "We'll find out what's wrong, and you'll be back in the water before the next meet."

"You keep saying that!" complained Ailee, pulling away from her father's grip. Her sudden move sent her head into a spin. The dizziness that followed caused her to fall back against her dad. Feeling the support of his strong arms gave Ailee permission to exhale. "All the tests we've done have shown nothing."

Bending his head to his daughter's ear, Finn whispered a hopeful response. "This is a different doctor."

"And if they don't know?"

"We'll keep looking until we find a doctor who does."

Tired of the conversation and fleeting promises of hope, Ailee turned and looked into her dad's loving eyes. "And when we've used up all the doctors in the entire world, then what?" She knew the question was ridiculous and immature, but succumbing to a teenage mentality felt good.

Not willing to play her game, Finn gave it right back. "Do you know how many doctors that would be?"

"I'm walking home." Ailee lifted her swim bag to her shoulder and walked toward the street.

"You're not walking home. Ailee!" Finn tossed his daughter's backpack onto the floor, crawled into the car and watched her through the windshield. He wondered where his sweet little girl had gone. His peers warned him about the teenage years, but he never thought it would happen to his smart and driven daughter. Finn's thoughts drifted to Ailee's mother. For a moment, he allowed himself to cross the line he drew in the sand by secretly wishing she were here. He disbursed the thought as quickly as it arrived. The chance of her joining them after twelve years was nothing more than a pipe dream.

Shaking it off, he returned to the present. Finn gave Ailee a reasonable head start, then turned the key. The sound of Bach's Concerto in D Minor began where it left off, with the Adagio. The beauty of the melody, eventually supported by the harmony, brought the serenity he needed. His mother often told him as a child that he had music in him. He loved listening to her play the piano, watching her upper body move as the music carried her away to some distant somewhere. Putting the car in drive, he slowly rolled through the parking lot to the rhythm of the music, never losing sight of his daughter.

IT DIDN'T TAKE LONG before Ailee was on a quiet side street, leisurely cutting through the only neighborhood she'd ever known. She needed the space to process the many changes reigning down on her young life. Ailee could feel her energy waning as she calculated the remaining distance. Putting one foot in front of the other was her only option. Calling home for help was not a choice she was willing to make.

The familiar sounds of an approaching car brought the relief she had hoped for. Not that she would admit it. The strains of classical music from an open car window were music to her ears. One of her dad's old friends, Johann Sebastian Bach, was calming his nerves on the drive home. He had his favorite classical music selections and referred to them in his own way. Currently playing "Air on the G String," known in Donnelly-land as "Air Somewhere."

Looking back, she saw her dad approaching on the wrong side of the road. With a pretend eye roll, she kept walking, knowing he was driving right next to her. She refused to let him think he was right.

Finn could tell her strength was fading fast but she chose to play the game. He dangled his arm against the outside of the door, ready and waiting if she needed a hand to hold. "Want a ride?"

"My father taught me not to talk to strangers," she responded, focusing her eyes straight ahead as she struggled to stay vertical.

"Sounds like a wise man."

"He thinks so." More than anything, Ailee enjoyed the father/daughter banter they had perfected over the years. It allowed them to say what they felt without getting too emotional.

Finn upped the stakes. "Your Aunt Gladys is making her world-famous Irish stew." He waited for a response, tapping his hand against the side of the car in 4/4 time to the soothing sound of the orchestra.

"Even a policeman can get a ticket driving on the wrong side of the road," Ailee complained as the music softened her defenses. Her eyes began to well with tears from her roller-coaster day.

"Not if they're in pursuit."

Using humor to bring her back from the edge, Ailee stopped trying to walk and turned to her dad. "Now I'm a criminal?"

"You did steal my heart thirteen years ago," he said, pulling out his hanky and handing it to her.

"Almost fourteen." Ailee turned her head to wipe her tears.

"I stand corrected."

Placing her hands on the window seal, she leaned down and poured her heart out in one sentence. "I just want to be normal again."

He responded the only way he could to his extraordinary daughter. "You've never been normal a day in your life."

"You know what I mean," she argued.

"I'm open to giving normal a chance. At least for one night. Now will you get in the car?"

Ailee walked around the front of the vehicle, steadying herself by touching the hood. She tossed her swim bag on the floor, and collapsed into the passenger seat.

Finn pulled into the correct lane and parked along the curb. Shutting off the engine, he turned the key to the accessory position to keep the music playing. Once Ailee settled in, he reached into the back seat and picked up a tiny package. Engulfing it in one of his hands, he presented both fists. "Which hand?"

"What, am I five?" she smiled as she touched her finger to the top of his right fist. His surprises were always in his right hand. As a protector of the people he served, he wanted her to learn from a young age to make the right decision when faced with a question that could compromise her integrity.

"You'll probably always be five somewhere in my mind." Opening his hand, he revealed a small box wrapped in previously-used Christmas paper.

Ailee happily received the gift. "My birthday's not for eight days."

"Open it."

"Where have I seen this paper before?" she asked, knowing her dad's thrifty ways.

"Just open it."

Using her fingernail, Ailee lifted the tape, tearing the paper along with it. "Sorry," she joked about ripping the paper. Her teasing ended with the sight of a tan-colored, vintage jeweler's box. The corners were worn, and the Irish jeweler's inscription on the top had partially faded. Taking another look at her dad, she smiled in anticipation and then lifted the lid to reveal a delicate chain holding a sterling silver fairy pendant. Surprised by the nature of the present, her eyes returned to her father. "It's beautiful!"

Finn watched as his daughter rubbed her finger over the top of the antique pendant. It was round, three-quarter inch across, with a fairy engraved in the center. Above the fairy, the word Éire was inscribed, the Gaelic word for Ireland. The home of Ailee's ancestors. "I know how much you love your aunt's Irish folklore."

"You're Irish too, remember?"

"I live in the real world."

"Does it have to be one or the other?" she asked, opening the clasp on her necklace and then turning her back to her dad for help.

"For me," he answered, taking the two ends of the chain in his hands. "If my mum were here, she would disagree with me. This was her necklace. Her mother gave it to her as a teenager."

"Thanks, Dad." Ailee laid her fingers over the top of the charm, pressing it against her heart. "I love it."

"We better get home before Gladys calls 911 again."

"She does get a bit paranoid," agreed Ailee with a smile as she settled back into her seat.

"Her and the rest of her family."

"Dad," she argued, sitting back up. "Her family is my family."

"Half," responded Finn as he pulled onto the road. "Her family is half your family. The smaller half."

"A half is a half."

"And you say math's your worst subject. I expect an 'A' at the end of this quarter."

"Don't hold your breath." Ailee leaned her head back against the seat, basking in the after-effect of their banter. The extra walking had taken a toll. Not that she'd admit that to her dad. The fear she felt below the surface grew, gnawing at her gut. The woman from the park added another layer to the mystery she couldn't unravel. Another secret she kept to herself.

As the car pulled into the driveway, Ailee hoped for the normal night her dad had promised. Deep down, she had her doubts. The weaker she grew, the more hushed the conversations between her dad and her aunt had become. Could the only family she'd ever known be hiding something?

With her fingers still pressed against the fairy charm, she abandoned her suspicious thoughts. She was Irish, after all—a hundred percent. Luck was on her side.

CHAPTER THREE

Finn had expected more from the appointment with the new doctor. Unfortunately, it resembled the same experiences as all the others: checking her vitals and more blood tests. Standing in the corner of the room, he watched the nurse place the bandaid over the puncture site in his little girl's arm. His daughter was taking it like a champ. Finn, not so much. Opening the door to the exam room, the doctor escorted them into the hallway. "We'll contact you as soon as we get the results." His final words were all too familiar.

"Thanks, Doc." Ending the meeting with a handshake, Finn and Ailee made their way down the hallway of one of the many buildings on the Tufts Medical Center campus near Boston. "I have a good feeling about this guy." The words came quickly to Finn's mouth, but inside his chest, he felt the same ache he'd had for weeks.

"There's a swim meet this weekend," she mentioned as he paid his co-pay for the exam. Hoping the presence of other people would keep him calm enough to have a discussion.

"So you miss one," he responded, taking his receipt and thanking the medical receptionist.

Stepping in front of him, she planted her feet, hoping for further discussion. "What if one turns into two, then three, then four..."

"It's two days," interrupted her father. "Let's wait on the tests like the doctor recommended." Finn stepped to the side and opened the door for his daughter. Disappointed, she walked into the main hallway of the medical building, followed by her dad. Much to his dismay, Ailee refused to let it die.

"If I'm too sick to swim, then I'm too sick to go to school."

"Like that's going to work."

"It would if I had a father who cared," responded Ailee, attempting to guilt her father as they entered the elevator.

"I care so much... I'm going to drop you off right in front of the school door." By the time Finn won the argument, Ailee had turned her attention to her phone. Her fingers were texting faster than the elevator's three-story drop.

Leaving the elevator, they entered the lobby. Finn's smile faded as his focus shifted to a woman standing outside the glass entryway. Stunned by the sight of a person he hadn't seen in twelve years, Finn stopped as their eyes locked. The same woman from the park was still wearing the sage sweater. This time her hood was down, and a braid no longer constrained the red hair he'd run his fingers through so many times. Momentarily disabled by the collision of emotions, Finn waited for her to make a move.

Turning, she ran from the entrance.

Distracted by her phone, Ailee missed the sighting as she passed her father on the way to the door. "Are you coming?" she asked, turning back to him.

Rushing passed her, he blew through the door and onto the sidewalk, looking in every direction. He was desperate to find her. Jagged memories flashed through his mind as he searched the parking lot. Yesterday's phantom had become today's reality.

A taxi pulling out of the parking lot caught his eye. So did the woman's red hair catching the wind from the open window of the backseat.

Curious for answers, Ailee hurried out of the building, looking for what had captured her dad's attention. "What's going on?"

"We have to hurry," he yelled, grabbing his daughter's hand and running for the car. Finn unlocked the vehicle remotely, and they both jumped in and slammed the doors. They buckled their seatbelts as they drove through the parking lot. Ailee reached for the half-full bottle of water in the cup holder. The unexpected exertion of energy had stolen her breath. Taking a swig, she reacted to the water warmed by the car's heat, then placed it back in the cup holder and wiped her mouth. "Yuck!"

Finn pulled onto the street, turning left into the far lane. The blast from the horn of an oncoming car showed their disapproval.

"School's that way," noted Ailee, pointing in the opposite direction.

"We're taking a detour," responded Finn, following the taxi several cars back. Concentrating on his pursuit, he had no time or desire to explain the situation to his daughter.

Ailee could feel the adrenaline building as she moved her eyes between the windshield and her door window. Her dad was an expert at weaving through traffic, but she'd never seen him do it at such a fast speed. "Are we chasing a perp?" she asked excitedly, feeling more alive than she had two minutes ago.

"Where'd you learn to talk like that?"

"I'm the daughter of a cop."

Channeling his younger self, Finn weaved in and out of traffic, trying to catch up to the taxi. "I would never engage in a pursuit with a civilian in the car."

"This kinda feels like a pursuit," pressed Ailee with enthusiasm, riveted by the perturbed faces of their fellow drivers.

"I'll have you in class by third hour."

"I'm in no hurry," she quipped with a smile. "Take all the time you want." Ailee took a moment to study her dad's face. It was a rare occasion to witness her dad in his element. His control was impressive as he maneuvered through traffic. Still, she could see a concern on his face that she didn't recognize.

A red light put Finn farther behind. Wishing he was on duty with a siren at his ready, he could only watch the taxi get farther away. His mind raced while he waited. Why was she here? Why now, after so many years? He glanced at Ailee, fearing the answer. The light turned green, and he sped forward, the taxi no longer in sight. Hitting the 93, he located the taxi several cars up as they headed north. Once he switched to the 90, the freeway took them through the South Boston Waterfront area and across the Boston Harbor.

"Looks like we're heading for the airport," said Ailee, pointing to an overhead sign showing the exit for Boston Logan International. Promoting herself to the role of quasi-navigator was gratifying, and she wore her new position with pride.

Approaching the airport drop-off area, Finn found an opening and pulled to the curb. Ailee reached for the door but was stopped by her dad's insistence. "Stay here. If anyone asks, it's official police business." Then he tossed his sunglasses onto the dash and left the car. Ailee watched her dad run toward the door and disappear inside the airport. Reaching for her dad's department-issued sunglasses, Ailee placed them on her face and leaned back in satisfaction. "I knew we were in pursuit."

THE AIRPORT WAS an obstacle course of bodies and luggage, screaming children in strollers and business folks running for their flights. Stopping in the chaos, Finn looked for answers until his eyes rested on the international airline counter. Weaving in and out of oncoming travelers, he found the end of the line. Two customers waited in front of him, and only one attendant. He didn't like the math. Looking around, he located the departure screen across the lobby. Desperation pushed him through the crowd. He had to know why she was here.

Scanning the screens, he found the next flight to England. He looked for the ticketing counter of the airline about to depart. No line. He fought his way back through the crowd and approached the counter. "Your flight to England. Does it have a connection to Ireland? Is there a Molly Killian on board?"

"Passenger manifests are private, sir."

Finn pulled out his badge and slapped it on the counter. "The name's Molly Killian."

With a touch of nervousness, the ticketing agent scanned the flight information. "A Molly Killian has checked in for that flight."

"What gate?"

"C-29. It's in the final boarding stages," she said, watching him bolt from the counter, badge in hand. "You'll never make it!"

Finn pushed his way through the crowd until his eyes caught a TSA agent's location on a motorized transport. Approaching the agent, Finn pulled his badge from his pocket. "I need to commandeer this vehicle." A familiar face turned to Finn. "Not in my house, Donnelly."

"Tom."

"Late for a flight?" he chuckled robustly, happy to see his old friend.

"I need to get to C-29. It's an emergency."

"Official business or personal?"

"A bit of both."

"Get on." Tom weaved the transport through traffic as Finn counted the seconds. Finally hitting a long stretch, they made good time. His friend got him as close to the gate as he could. "Thanks, Tom, I owe you one." Finn leaped from the cart and ran toward the gate attendant. He reached the gate just as the door was closing. "I need to get on that plane."

"Sir, it's too late to board."

"I'm a police officer," he warned, hoping his status would make a difference.

"I'm sorry, Sir. The plane has disengaged from the sky bridge."

"I need to talk to someone on that plane." Finn presented his credentials and waited for the attendant's response.

The gate attendant took Finn's identification in hand and read the name. "One minute, Officer Donnelly." He walked to the ticket podium and picked up a pair of brown sunglasses with a gold frame and a cream-colored envelope. "The last passenger left this for you."

Surprised by the turn of events, Finn took the envelope and walked toward the large window. He recognized the sunglasses as the ones he left behind during his retreat from Ireland. Molly had bought them for him as a birthday present. They were his favorite pair of glasses and Molly's way of connecting him to their past. Placing them on his face, he stared at the plane as it pulled away from the gate. He wondered if she was staring back.

Finn studied the envelope and the graceful penmanship that penned his name. It was beautifully scripted. Her handwriting hadn't changed since he fell in love with her as a teenager. Cautiously, he unsealed the envelope and removed the letter. A familiar scent reached his nose, returning him to the bedroom of the small apartment they called home in Ireland. He imagined the piece of paper had rested on her vanity for days as she formed her thoughts. Deep inside, he suspected what it might say. Her inscription on the single folded piece of stationary confirmed his suspicion.

"Uh-hmm," interrupted Tom, clearing his throat.

Realizing his friend was waiting for him, he placed the letter back in the envelope and left the window. "You didn't need to wait for me."

"I can't have a rogue detective running amuck in my airport," Tom joked, hoping to ease the troubled look on his old friend's face.

"A good call." Finn sat beside him, safely placing the envelope in the chest pocket of his white shirt.

"I can stop the plane," offered Tom, knowing it was just a gesture.

"I got what I came for." Finn's mind was a thousand miles away as Tom pulled away from the gate. His past had come a-knocking, and he wasn't prepared to open the door. No one could reach the innermost part of his heart like Molly. She'd held the key for as long as he could remember. Finn thought he'd changed the lock years ago, but seeing her at the medical center and the smell of her scent on the stationary proved him wrong. Refusing to give in to the moment's vulnerability, he closed the door on the past and looked to the future.

AILEE HAD NEVER GONE SO LONG without a response to her text messages. Roger was in class, and she was bored waiting for her dad to return to the car. Reaching for the apple in the bottom of her bag, Ailee slowly pulled back empty-handed. A mischievous idea struck her mind. She was tempted to use her secret gift in public for the first time. The euphoria of taking such a risk cured her boredom. Ailee looked out the windows facing the sidewalk and waited for a break in the steady stream of travelers. Timing was everything.

Several years earlier, she eavesdropped on a conversation between her aunt and her dad about the Killian magic. Her father strictly forbade Gladys from using it in his daughter's presence or speaking of it. It didn't take long for Ailee to begin her own quest. Her ability to move small objects grew stronger with practice. So many times, she wanted to show her aunt the progress she'd made. The burden she would have placed on Gladys stopped her from sharing her success.

Seeing a break in the people passing by, she hovered her hand over her open backpack. An apple struggled to float through the opening but stopped inches from her hand. She tried to grab it while in the air. Gravity claimed it first. Determined, she checked the sidewalk and tried again. This time the apple made it to the palm of her hand. She celebrated with a victorious bite.

Surprised by the opening of the car door, she nearly choked on the large piece of fruit. Spitting the chunk of apple into her hand, she casually dropped it out the open window. Clearing her throat, she regained her composure. "Did you catch him?"

"Don't ask!" Finn fell into his seat, started the car, and pulled away from the curb.

Ailee could tell something was wrong by his agitated tone and the tight grip on the steering wheel. Studying the unsettled look on his face, she concluded that things did not go well at the airport. His grumpy response gave Ailee two choices: let him sulk or make him smile. "Why don't I buy you lunch to cheer you up?"

"You know it's illegal to bribe a police officer," responded Finn, still trying to sort through Molly's visit mentally. "We both have places to be."

Ailee nibbled at her apple, hoping to occupy her mouth enough to avoid saying the wrong thing. Sitting back in her seat, she changed her game plan to let him sulk. "Just trying to help."

"You're trying to get out of algebra," he argued as he pulled onto the main road and found a place in the traffic flow.

"Is it working?" she asked in a subdued voice.

The last thing Finn wanted was for his past to impact his daughter's future. The only thing he could control was the present. As a seasoned detective, he knew how to compartmentalize his emotions. It was time to de-escalate the conversation by offering an olive branch. "Is dessert included?"

"Yes," she smiled, sitting up and returning to the game. She couldn't resist following up with a wisecrack. "Donuts are cheap."

"Eat your apple." Finn's tense grip on the steering wheel eased as he merged onto the freeway. Ailee was the perfect distraction to his troubling prospects. It didn't take long for his daughter's apple crunching to be drowned out by her phone's playlist. Her choice of pop music over classical was acceptable thanks to the freeway's easy traffic flow. They'd be in Somerville before they knew it. Bach, Beethoven and Chopin wouldn't have to wait for long.

CHAPTER FOUR

Dinner was never missed and rarely, if ever, late at the Donnelly home. Gladys Killian would not have stood for it. She firmly believed that "laughter is brightest where food is best." She displayed her Irish sentiment in cross-stitch on the dining room wall. Three proper meals a day gave credence to her rule of thumb. Ailee never left for school without a homemade lunch in her bag and extra snacks for swim practice.

As Ailee's great-aunt, she took her motherly duties very seriously. The apron went over her blouse and skirt at dawn and stayed until time to enjoy a biscuit and hot tea before bed. Her one o'clock nap following a stroll through her latest romance helped her keep up with her grand-niece. The years were gaining on her, but her health was good. Using her knife, she scraped the last bite of stew onto her fork. Delicious. With the last of her bread, she wiped the plate clean. Dinner was complete. "Lamb stew's a heap tastier the second day."

"Was that the same stew as yesterday?" asked Ailee, swallowing the last bite.

"With a wee bit of dressin' up."

Picking up her plate, Ailee circled the table. "I'll do the dishes."

"You'll be doin' no such thing. Ya got a heap of homework t'finish up."

"Thanks for reminding me." Ailee kissed her aunt on the cheek and left the dining room. "Dinner was great," she hollered from the hallway. Ailee made it a practice to always get in the last word. Not an easy thing when you live with a couple of Irishmen.

Placing her hands on the table, Gladys lifted herself to her feet. Finn placed his hand over hers, drawing her gaze. Once he had her attention, he asked the question that had been plaguing his mind all afternoon. "What brought Molly to the States?"

"Ya don't be needin' me to tell ya, Finn Donnelly." Gladys pulled her hand from beneath his and stacked the plates. She already knew what his response would be.

"The test results will be back soon and we'll know more."

"They'll be no different t'the last," she assured him as she gathered the used utensils, carefully leaving the clean ones on the table.

"Says you," Finn shot back, leaving his chair and tossing his cloth napkin onto the table.

"Says the family."

"Your family."

"Ailee's family... and yours. Or have ya forgotten?" responded Gladys, placing her apron over her head and tying the back. She patted her hands against her perfectly styled hair. The white hairs had made inroads, replacing most of her dark brown hair.

"You may be her great-aunt, but I'm her dad." Pressing both hands on the table across from Gladys, Finn positioned himself for the debate.

"And Molly's her mum," she argued, motioning to the glass beside his hand.

He picked up the glass and moved it toward Gladys. Living in the States and working with the public had softened Finn's Irish accent. Engaging in the occasional passionate debate with Gladys brought it out again. After so many years of living under the same roof, an honest conversation style had developed between them. Free to bare their truths, they never took offense. "Just what would you have me do, Gladys?" whispered Finn, trying to keep his voice down. "Put her life in the hands of folks who aren't the full shillin'?"

"Bein' a wee bit eccentric's not a crime, Detective."

"A wee bit?" he asked with a sarcastic chuckle. "I left Ireland to keep Ailee away from the Killian nonsense, and now you have me throwin' her back into it? Head over heels, mind you."

"There'll be wigs on the greens if ya keep it up!" threatened Gladys, placing the glass on top of the plates. Tapping down her volume, she said what she thought would be the last word. "Time be at hand, Finn!"

"Molly and the rest of your kin have no place in Ailee's life."

"Why don't ya be askin' Ailee?" Gladys lifted the stack of dishes from the table and walked into the kitchen, Finn hot on her tail.

Removing the wedge from beneath the kitchen door, he allowed it to shut for privacy before laying down the Donnelly law. "You're not tellin' her!"

Gladys placed the stack of dishes on the counter with a thud, rattling the glasses. Turning to Finn, she looked him in the eye and took a deep breath. "Ya open your ears, Finn Donnelly, and ya open 'em wide!" She spoke with authority as she backed him across the kitchen, pressing his back to the cupboards on the opposite side. "Tis a week til her fourteenth birthday. The curse'll steal the life of that child in seven days."

"You know we don't talk of that, Gladys!" Breaking free from her fierce glare, Finn turned toward the window facing the darkness. "Not in this house."

"O', the great rules of the Donnelly home!" she shouted. "I've kept them for twelve long years," Gladys exclaimed in mockery, her arms flying through the air like she were performing an opera. She saw her five-foot-four, writhing frame reflected in the window facing Finn. He was getting it from both sides. For more than a decade, she'd kept the enormity of her Irish temper at bay for Ailee's sake. "If you think I'll let the lass die t'keep yer pride intact, yer not the warrior yer mum thought ya were!"

Gladys' words stung as they penetrated Finn's heart. The idea of letting down his departed mother was almost more than he could tolerate. The emotional storm stirring inside began to writhe like the belly of a volcano.

Stepping back to compose herself, Gladys patted her face with a tea towel and then tossed it over her shoulder. She'd been loyal to Finn's requests to keep the Killian family politics out of raising his daughter. It took some doing, and a whole lot of patience, but her adherence to his wishes had always been on point. She was there to be helpful to Finn and Molly, not divisive. Calmly, she continued her side of the debate as she prepped Ailee's study treat. "I made a promise t'my niece t'care for her daughter. I plan to keep that promise as long as she needs me." Gladys removed a cup and saucer from the cupboard and a jar of milk from the refrigerator. "Yer a good dad, Finn. Best I've seen. But yer goin' lose her if ya can't find the courage t'do what needs t'be done."

"Courage?" he shouted as he turned to face her. "I left my home. I left my country. I left everything I knew to give Ailee a life apart from all that."

"Ya can't outrun the curse," warned Gladys as she placed the saucer of cookies and cup of milk on a tray. "Ailee's only hope is t'return to Ireland, t'drink from the healin' waters. The holy well's the only way t'save her."

"Enough!" His emotional eruption threw him off balance. Finn caught himself against the pantry door as the strength drained from his body. Slowly, he melted onto the nearby stool, supporting his upper body by placing his hands on his knees.

Gladys wrapped her arm around his shoulder and quietly began her closing argument. "If the Killians are wrong, ya lose nothin'. But if we're right, Ailee gets t'live. Happily ever after."

"She should get that anyway."

"This is the path fate has giv'n her." Gladys lovingly lifted Finn's face to the light. "The lass grows weaker by the day. Start the journey while she's got the strength. She'll be needin' it. Ya both will." With that said Gladys picked up the tray and left the kitchen.

Finn mulled over Gladys' advice and warnings, then pulled out the letter from the airport. After caressing the handwriting on the envelope, he removed the note and re-read it. "Time to bring our daughter home. Molly." Never had such a simple sentence delivered such a powerful punch to the gut. He folded the letter and placed it in his pocket. Resting his eyes on the cookie jar brought the brief solace he needed. Sliding it to the counter's edge, he wrapped his arm around the jar and left the kitchen.

GLADYS WALKED through the open door into Ailee's bedroom. There was no happier place in the entire house. Entering her niece's room took her beyond the four walls of the Donnelly home. Posters of coastal seascapes, waterfalls, hidden lakes and magnificent sunsets over tropical oceans covered the dated wallpaper. Ailee's love of all things water was represented on all four walls. Even her child-like comforter displayed the pattern of tropical fish swimming above a coral reef. "Thought some brain food might be a help to ya." Placing the milk and cookies on the desk next to her, she picked up Ailee's school clothes from the foot of the bed.

"When did lace cookies become brain food?"

"Trust your aunt, Dear. Nurses know best."

She mimicked Gladys' Irish accent, and repeated one of her aunt's favorite sayings. "We'd all be worse without a nurse."

"So, you've been listenin' all these years, have ya?"

"Sometimes." She smiled coyly as a piece of cookie melted on her tongue.

Gladys put her niece's clothes in the hamper and then returned to Ailee's side. "Now, don't be studyin' all night. Sleep's good for the brain too."

"Sleeping is all I want to do."

"You'll be grand by mornin'." Gladys kissed Ailee on the forehead then walked toward the open door.

"Aunt Gladys?" Ailee looked at her aunt's reflection in the mirror above the desk. "Why did my parents break up?"

With her back to Ailee, Gladys drooped her head forward at the idea of opening Finn and Molly's can of worms. "That'd be a topic for your dad."

"You know he doesn't talk about her."

Turning back, Gladys held her position as she caught Ailee's gaze in the mirror. Hoping for an easy escape from the topic, she stalled answering with a question. "Have ya tried askin' him?"

"I've never felt a need to. I've always had Dad and you."

"And now?"

"Lately, I can't stop thinking about her."

With no good way out, Gladys settled into the extra chair near the desk. She picked up the framed picture of Ailee as a baby in the arms of her mother, Molly Killian. "For fourteen months, yer mum held ya, fed ya, rocked ya off t'sleep. There's a bond between ya."

"I don't believe that."

Ailee's words pricked Gladys' heart like the point of a sharp knife. "Don't ya be sayin' that, Ailee! Let alone be thinkin' it."

"She didn't love me," continued her niece as she turned her desk chair toward Gladys. "That's why she never came with us. They were married for ten years before I came along. I've done the math." Ailee took the picture from Gladys' hand and studied it for the hundredth time. "They were happy until I was born." Swiveling her chair back to her desk, she placed the frame in its usual place.

"The day of your birth was the greatest joy of your parent's life." Gladys wished she could share her vivid memories of Ailee's infancy, doted on by her parents. "It was a happy and lovin' time."

"Then why aren't they together?" she asked, taking a bite of her half-eaten cookie.

"I'll let ya in on a little secret." Gladys knew she had to change Ailee's pattern of thinking. "I have it on good authority... yer mum still cares for yer dad," Gladys whispered. "If ya ask me, yer dad feels the same."

Surprised by her great-aunt's revelation, Ailee wheeled her chair sideways, giving Gladys her undivided attention as she whispered back. "Is that why they never got divorced?"

Taking hold of Ailee's hand, Gladys realized she'd opened a door that would be difficult to close. So she did what Irish folk do best. Tell a tale. "When I was a wee girl in Ireland. Long ago. I'd lie in the lush grass of the small meadow near our home, countin' the geese as they soared overhead. Ya could hear 'em comin' before you could see 'em, callin' to each other with their high-pitched cries and honkin' sounds. Soon, they'd pass, high above and in all their majesty, flying in v-formation. It helped 'em keep an eye on each other. An odd number always made me sad. I'd tally 'em again before they got too far, hopin' I'd miscounted."

"What's wrong with an odd number?"

"That meant a goose had lost their mate. Like geese, some people are meant to be with each other for life and beyond."

"You really think they still love each other?"

Taking Ailee's hands in hers, Gladys looked into her niece's beautiful green eyes. "Neither of 'em has found a new mate, now have they?"

"Why stay apart all these years?"

"Maybe they're needin' to fly solo for a wee bit."

"That's not an answer."

Gladys rose from the chair and kissed Ailee on the forehead. "But enough."

"I hope you're right, Aunt Gladys."

"Ya ever found me t'be wrong?" Giving Ailee hope seemed the right way to end a difficult conversation. "I've got a busy day tomorrow, and you've got a heap of studyin'." Releasing Ailee's hand, Gladys started toward the door. Walking away released the sadness building inside her. Her eyes began to well up in sympathy for the little family she loved so dearly. She'd spent twelve years caring for them, and would give twelve more if it would make a difference.

"Goodnight, Aunt Gladys." Ailee reached for the glass of milk and her phone. Accessing the picture of her birthmark drawn in the soil, she wondered about the mystery woman in the sage sweater. Swiveling in her chair, she caught her aunt before she reached the door. "Do you think my mom's been keeping an eye on me... like the geese?"

Ailee's final question stopped Gladys in her tracks. "I got a notion yer right, Lass." Picking up Ailee's dirty clothes hamper, she hurried from the room. Closing the door behind her, she pressed the back of her head against it, needing a moment to collect herself. Turning toward the hallway, she came face to face with Finn. He was leaning against the wall and eating lace cookies from the jar. Wiping the tears from her face, Gladys had no energy left for another confrontation.

Eavesdropping on their conversation had softened Finn's heart to the point of tenderness. "I'll book the tickets before I go to bed." Wanting no response, he walked into his bedroom and shut the door.

"So, it begins." Placing her hand over her mouth, Gladys leaned against the wall. Her spike in emotions was at war with each other. Half wanted to shout for joy. She'd won the battle. The other half was fighting to hide the fear of what lay ahead. Gladys had grown up hearing stories of her Killian ancestors' tragic history. The loss of her father and her brother, Seamus, had made it personal. Finn had no idea the grueling journey he was about to undertake. Shaking off the ghosts from the past, she pulled herself together and headed to the top of the stairs. It would be a long night of preparation, beginning in the laundry room.

FINN SAT on the side of his bed, eating the last of his cookie as he listened to Gladys' footsteps grow faint. Another lace cookie found its way into his hand—his childhood remedy for all that ailed. He opened the nightstand drawer with his free hand and pulled out his laptop. A stream of yawns signified his desperation for sleep.

As promised, he began his search for airline departure dates and times. Finding a direct route was easier than expected. Within minutes, he located three seats together near the exit doors. They were the only unoccupied seats on the entire plane and his favorite location when flying. The pieces were falling into place as though they were meant to be. Not that Finn would ever see it that way. Before long, he had them booked on a non-stop flight to his homeland.

Lying back on his pillow, he felt a sense of relief. The knot in his stomach reminded him otherwise. Before he could drift off to sleep, the vivid imagery of carrying his daughter through a dark tunnel lit up his mind. For weeks, the same nightmare had kept him from a restful slumber. His conscious mind played it off as his subconscious dealing with an over-protective father's concern. Deep inside, he worried there might be more to it. The dream was more than just visual. He felt the life draining from Ailee's body with each step. The light at the end of the tunnel was always in sight but unreachable.

Expelling himself from his thoughts, he sat on the edge of the bed, refusing to think about what he feared the most. Unbuttoning his shirt, he walked into the bathroom, hoping a shower would clear his mind and relax his tense body enough to sleep.

CHAPTER FIVE

To Finn's surprise, the overnight flight had given him six glorious hours of sleep. No nightmares in dark tunnels, only Molly, visiting from years past. Facing his fear of the curse seemed to be releasing his mind from the captivity of his recent torment. Or maybe it was something Gladys slipped into the homemade herbal tea she brought with her and brewed on the plane. Either way, a calmness was slowly replacing the mental agony.

The recent sighting of Molly had stirred his emotions. He'd left his wife behind when he moved to the States, but it never stopped Molly from visiting his dreams. Whether derived from supernatural origins or his own subconscious, it was a bittersweet secret he kept to himself.

Leaving the airport in his rented Volkswagen Jetta, he circled the outskirts of Dublin, happy to avoid the traffic. The car's black color suited Finn's practical nature and stealth sensibilities. The last thing he wanted was to stand out. Inwardly, he felt like a traitor returning to the crime scene. Adjusting his rearview mirror, he saw Ailee staring out the window with wonder painted across her face. As much as he hated the idea of this trip, it was a fresh perspective to see Ireland through his daughter's eyes.

Hearing a sniffle from the front passenger seat, he knew firsthand what Gladys was experiencing. Her yearning heart was finally rewarded after years of separation. Pulling a pressed hanky from his pocket, he offered it over the center console. She gladly excepted his kindness and then turned to the side window to privately celebrate her homecoming.

Once outside Dublin's sprawling suburbs, the Irish countryside welcomed Finn back with open arms. The fog gave way to a partly blue sky, making their morning a beautiful and inviting sight. Despite the chill left from the clear night, Finn rolled down the window. The fragrance of dew evaporating in the sunlight sent him back in time.

Being raised by his grandparents gave him a less-modern perspective of his Irish roots. His gran was superstitious and his grandfather was pragmatic. He chose the route of his grandfather. That didn't mean the instinct to salute a lone magpie didn't pop into his head whenever he saw one. Irish superstitions were built-in from childhood, but he did his best to ignore them. Although he balked at the notions, arriving in Ireland on a sunny May morning was a rarity. Finn took it as half a sign that he'd made the right decision. A nod to his gran seemed appropriate. Turning off the highway, they followed the backroads, giving way to rural Ireland.

Ailee had a hundred questions, and Gladys was delighted to play tour guide as the time passed. Spotting a large mound of earth covered in grass and dotted with tall bushes, Ailee moved across the backseat to the driver's side for a better look. "Slow down, Dad!" Rolling down the window, she pointed in amazement to the hill in the distance. "Look, Aunt Gladys! A fairy mound. Over there!" Ailee grabbed her phone from the seat and captured the supposed fairy mound to send to her friends.

Laying the phone aside, Ailee pinched her fairy pendant between her fingers as the winding road slowly brought them closer to the ancient dwelling. In her young mind, there could be no better birthday gift than a trip to Ireland. She'd grown up listening to her great-aunt's bedtime stories of fairies and their fairy forts and gardens. "Tell the story again, Aunt Gladys," she pleaded. "Where the fairies came from." Ailee laid her head across her folded arms covering the window sill. The fresh air blew her auburn hair like a flag in the wind as she dreamed of far-off places. "Dad, slow down. We'll miss it!"

Checking the mirrors for any following cars, Finn pulled back on the accelerator to allow for the full experience. Admittedly, there wasn't much he wouldn't do for his daughter. Staring straight ahead, he was forced to become a willing participant in the perpetuation of Irish folklore. His eye-rolling and heavy sigh was lost on Ailee thanks to the noise from the open window.

Catching sight of Finn's mockery, Gladys couldn't resist a dramatic retelling of an Irish folktale. "I'd be only so happy to." Repositioning her body in a confined space wasn't easy at her age, but proper eye contact was a must when telling a story. Facing the driver's side of the car sent her voice directly to Finn's ear. As far as Gladys was concerned, turnabout was fair play. Silencing the local news on the radio, Gladys began her recitation. "More than a millennia ago, the Tuatha Dé Danann, were in the throws of their third and final battle t'control this Emerald Isle. The folk of the goddess Danu fought the invadin' Milesians by sword and with magic."

Finn pushed the back of his head against the headrest and rolled his eyes to the ceiling as the speedometer's needle slowly crept backward. In his opinion, the world of enchantment should stay where it belonged, between book covers that never opened.

Trying not to giggle at Finn's reaction, Gladys regaled with her rousing tale. "Givin' rise t'a magical storm, the squall rolled the length of the nine waves until it reached the enemy ship anchored at sea. Tossin' and turnin' against the wrath-filled waves, the enemy feared bein' swallowed up by the tempest's rage. Their adversary's retreat was all but certain until a Milesian poet rose to the ship's bow and serenaded the angry sea with a calmin' verse."

"Good grief," mumbled Finn beneath his breath.

"Victorious!" Gladys continued in rare form. "The Milesians oared their way back to shore and battled the Tuatha Dé Danann for the last time with blade and spear. For they truly believed in their ancient right t'this island of wonders."

Changing to a doleful tone, Gladys continued at a milder pace. "To the victors belong the spoils, and so it was with the Milesians. They apportioned our fair island as they saw fit. The conquerors drove the Tuath Dé to their new home beneath the ground while keepin' the surface for themselves. With the passage of time, the tribe of the gods evolved into the fairies that live in forts, forests and mounds throughout Ireland."

Ailee took one last look at the disappearing mound and then closed her eyes. "Maybe I'll meet a fairy for my birthday." It didn't take long for the yawns to arrive and drift her off to sleep. Gladys happily repositioned herself to a more comfortable posture, basking in the after-effects of a riveting narration.

The car increased in speed as Finn pressed his foot against the accelerator. The welcomed quiet allowed his thoughts to finally wander free of disturbance. Each dip through a valley or rise to a view took him back in time until he realized how much he missed his homeland. He'd worked hard over the years to suppress his longing heart, believing it was short-term. His original plan had him returning when Ailee reached adulthood. As time passed, however, he grew more content and settled with his life in the States.

ONCE FINN TURNED off the road, a long driveway was all that stood between him and his past. Impressions flooded his mind in no particular order, reason, or rhyme. Pulling up to the Killian family home, they sat silently until Gladys quietly proposed the next step. "Ya come when yer feelin' ready, Finn." She picked up her oversized purse and opened the door. "You'll be greeted with love. Ya know that." Her assurance was from the heart, and Finn trusted it.

The increasing pace of Gladys' steps made him jealous. He watched as the front door opened and arms embraced. "Welcome home, Gladys," he whispered. She'd given up so much to help him raise Ailee. Her sacrifice was one of legend. He wished he could feel the bounce in his step that he saw with Gladys. Memories of time spent at the Killian house washed over him. Here he had felt his greatest joy and his most profound sorrow. Good or bad, he was finally home and ready to face what lay ahead.

"Are we here?" His daughter's groggy voice brought him back to reality. Stretching her arms and twisting her back, she looked through the windshield. Oohs and Aahs came next as Ailee rolled down the window and stuck her head out to take in the entirety of the house. The two-level stone cottage with lace curtains in every window reminded her of something from a storybook. The clumps of moss growing on the northfacing stone added to the fairytale backdrop. The grounds next to the house were untamed compared to the manicured yards of her suburban neighborhood back in the States. Wildflowers sprang from the emerald-green grass swaying in the soft breeze. Star-shaped petals painted in blue-lilac danced alongside taller stems of yellow flowers on leafy spikes. She recognized the creamy yellow color of the primrose growing around the house's base. Ailee finally understood why her Aunt Gladys filled the house with primrose plants each spring.

Finn was envious of his daughter's unfettered view of the Killian home. He longed to go back in time and recapture the innocence, if only for a moment. Watching Ailee take in the grounds led him to a question already answered in the depths of her wide-eyed observance. "What do you think?"

"It's like nothing I've ever seen," she responded in a hushed tone as not to disturb the peaceful ambiance. "I still can't believe you brought me to Ireland for my birthday." Leaving behind her initial reaction, Ailee returned to her teenage enthusiasm. "Best birthday ever!" she shouted, placing some personal items in her backpack. "Are you coming?"

Finn hated withholding the valid reason for the trip but felt it was best under the circumstances. Even he was in the dark as to what would happen next. "I'll get the bags from the boot." Finn popped the trunk and walked to the back of the car as Ailee crawled out the other side. He watched her push her arms through the straps of her backpack as she slowly walked toward the Killian cottage. Tugging on the open collar of his white shirt, he straightened it beneath his grey sport coat. He had no idea what to wear for a first impression, and it almost made them late for their flight. He finally settled on dark jeans and brown leather shoes.

With luggage in tow, he followed the path with trepidation, the same path he used to run following his best friend, Quinn. He could never get to the Killian house quick enough as a youth. The tall Fuchsia hedge left of the house caught his eye. The pinkish-red blooms had yet to make an appearance, but it didn't stop him from recalling the secret hiding place of his first kiss as a young teenager. The flower's deep color would be forever synonymous with the color of Molly's lips. Turning to step through the door, he smelt the pungent scent of rosemary from the nearby plants. He could hear his Gran Donnelly reminding him to plant rosemary near his front door to keep evil away.

Gladys had left the door open, so Ailee walked in, followed by her dad with his arms full of luggage. The scent of the Killian cottage washed over Finn. He took a moment to distinguish the smell of stone minerals from the rock walls and recently polished hardwood. The smell of scones baking in the oven soon replaced all other scents. The familiar fragrances of his second home welcomed him like an old friend.

Anne, the housekeeper, hurried toward them. She'd been with the Killians for as long as he could remember. "Howya, Finn. And this beauty of a lass must be Ailee." Finn listened and did a bit of translating so Ailee could answer questions about the flight over.

Anne was as much a part of the family as any of them. As a young woman, barely twenty years of age, she'd had shown up on the Killian doorstep during an Atlantic depression that brought cold rain and strong winds. The power was out for miles. The glow of candles from the windows of the cottage offered a possible refuge from the weather, as well as the storm of her troubled life. Here a destitute stranger found employment, love and acceptance.

"They're waitin' for ya in the sittin' room." Anne lovingly wrapped her arm around Ailee's shoulder and led the way through the two open sliding doors.

Finn exhaled, then reluctantly followed. Turning the corner; his eyes followed the room's wall. He found the same beautiful paintings and antique furniture in the same place as the day he walked out. He wouldn't have had it any other way. His eyes finally came to rest on the matriarch of the family, Maureen Killian. Her welcoming smile brightened the room as always. Finn was happy to see that her rosy cheeks hadn't faded with time. In many respects, Maureen Killian was just as much a Grandma as his own Gran Donnelly, who raised him.

Taking in the rest of the room, he smiled at what would now be considered vintage decor. Handcrafted items covered everything from the windows to the furniture. Irish lace curtains and doilies, quilts and crocheted blankets were a big part of Maureen's legacy. Even their sweaters were hand knit with care and great skill.

Gladys lifted herself from the chair next to Maureen and placed her arm around Ailee's shoulders, moving her closer. "Ailee, this is my mum, yer great-gran."

"It's nice t' meet ya."

"Pleasure's mine, child." Maureen stood and gently wrapped her arms around Ailee, treasuring the moment. "We've been waitin' for this day." The smile on Maureen's face was not without a hidden sadness. The foretold day had finally arrived.

"Your house is amazing, Great-Grandmother."

"Gran is less a mouthful," she joked, sharing a wink. "Like me, this ol' house has seen better days."

"It so... magical," she added.

Shifting her focus to Finn, Maureen drove home a truth that Finn wanted nothing to do with. "There's a wee bit of magic in these old walls."

Reading the room, her aunt helped Ailee off with her backpack as she did every day after school. "Fancy a stroll t'the pond?" Gladys could feel Finn's temperature rising from across the room. The word 'magic' was forbidden in their Somerville home. Magic had become the default for everything that went wrong in his marriage. As impressed as she was with Finn's control, she still thought it best to give him and her mum privacy to catch up. "When yer blessed with a sunny day in Ireland, Ailee, you don't go wastin' it," said Gladys.

"Are there geese?" asked her niece.

"Swans too." Wrapping her arm around Ailee, Gladys escorted her toward the door.

"There's bound to be some ol' bread lyin' about," suggested Maureen as they left the room. "Anne'll see to it."

The housekeeper hurried from the doorway ahead of Ailee and Gladys. She had a bag of old bread waiting for just an occasion.

Finn and Maureen's eyes met again as they listened to Ailee's enthusiasm from outside the room. "We're really going to feed swans? Best birthday ever!" He used the time to study Maureen's belted dress, covered in a bright floral print and accompanied by a sweater. It had been her style for as long as he could remember. Hearing the door open and shut was the signal Finn was waiting for to share his displeasure. Protected by a row of luggage, he held his ground from across the room as he broached the subject. "We're here less than five minutes and you bring up magic?"

"T'was your daughter's doin'."

"You indulged her."

"Like it or not, all Killian women inherit a bit a magic on some level," said Maureen, firmly standing her ground. "Ya know it to be true."

"Not a word of it to Ailee," instructed Finn.

"This will always be yer home, Finn, but as long as I'm alive, I'll be runnin' it the way I see fit." Maureen took advantage of the door he opened to ensure he understood his place. "That includes the discussion of magic."

"I'm already regretting this trip," he lamented. The Killians had managed to keep their gift of magic a secret from Finn as he grew up. Even during their dating years, Molly hid it from Finn. It was a family secret, not to be shared with the outside world. Finn truly believed that Molly would have kept it a secret after they married if it hadn't been for the birthmark that appeared on Ailee's shoulder on her first birthday.

"C'mere then," signaled Maureen, motioning him toward her with a smile.

Finn moved the barricade of suitcases to the side and walked toward her. Before he could take her hand, she wrapped her arms around his waist. "Yer finally home where ya belong," she rejoiced, pulling his tall stature as close as the strength of her aged arms would allow. "Our fair warrior has returned."

"Don't start with the folklore," he pleaded light-heartedly, returning her affection in kind. The feel of her arms around him took him back to the day he lost his mother and father. Her loving arms held his small, shaking frame until his grandparents arrived. "The years have been good to you, Maureen." Pulling back, Finn looked lovingly into her eyes. "You're as much a beauty as I remember."

"Surely, yer thinkin' of Molly."

"I expected her to be here. Where is she?"

"It's a grand ol' day," said Maureen, changing subjects to avoid wading into waters she didn't want to tread. "Walk me t'the garden, Finn."

Arm in arm, they crossed the room as comfortably as if they'd seen each other every day for the past decade or more. Their shared embrace began to melt the walls Finn had worked so hard to build over the past twelve years.

The housekeeper made it to the door just ahead of them, opening it wide and anticipating a request.

"Bring a pot o' tea, Anne."

"Already brewin'. Scones and jam too." Anne picked up a light quilt near the door and draped it over Finn's free arm. "A bit chilly yet," she said with a loving pat to the quilt.

The housekeeper and confidant watched from the open doorway as they casually strolled down the trail toward the covered bench overlooking the pond. Having been privy to the family's many conversations over the years, she knew how much this moment meant to Maureen. The next chapter in Killian history had begun, and it would be her great pleasure to serve tea and scones during this momentous occasion.

Ailee's laughter filled the air as they approached the gazebo. No sound delighted her father more. The sweet scent of early-blooming woodbine turned his attention to the vines crawling up the trellis siding of the gazebo. The sight of the buttery yellow honeysuckle blossoms took him back to his childhood. He loved to chew on the sweet nectar-filled blooms as a kid. His mother encouraged it for their healing properties.

Sitting on the bench next to Maureen, Finn laid the blanket across her lap. Together, they took in the luscious landscape before them. "I'd forgotten how green the grass is. Has it always been this green?"

"Tis the Emerald Isle."

Reaching over, he tapped one of the white posts with his hand. "She's still in good shape."

"We had her top re-shingled, and Molly touched her up with a fresh coat of paint last autumn."

"A good place to pass the time."

"Molly's favorite," Maureen said with caution.

"I remember." Although it was midday, Finn vividly recalled the sunsets that used to paint the western sky and reflect against the pond. Even nature's splendor couldn't compete with the beauty of sharing those moments with the woman he loved. He could feel Molly beside him, her head resting on his shoulder.

The longing in Finn's eyes told Maureen everything she needed to know. The same distant look she saw when sitting next to Molly. "Has there been a day that's gone by that ya haven't given' her a thought?"

"What we had ended a long time ago."

"I lost the man I loved… far too soon." Maureen placed her aged hand over the silver locket resting against her chest. Her knobby knuckles covered the oak tree engraving. Her thinning skin was beginning to show the purple veins once hidden from view. It had been forty years since her husband held her young hand. "Not a day passes that I don't think of him."

Understanding a portion of her heartache, he took her hand in his and rested it above his knee. "Has she been by lately?"

"Occasional Sunday, gone by Monday."

"And the rest of the week?"

"That one's a rollin' stone." Maureen hated sidestepping Finn's questions, but according to Molly, it was too soon for him to see the big picture. Thankfully, he was an investigator by trade. Helping him discover the facts bit by bit would be better than unleashing the bombshell of truth.

"I thought she'd be here."

"When the time's right," Maureen assured him with a gentle squeeze of his hand.

"Right, for who?"

"For Ailee."

The sound of geese squawking while taking flight paused their conversation. Ailee stole her dad's attention with a wave from the bank. The commotion at the pond was the perfect respite from discussing Molly. Waving back, Finn returned to their conversation. "I didn't come back to drink tea, Maureen."

"Much can be gleaned from a friendly cup o' tea."

"I can't just sit around and wait."

"Saydee can help."

The sound of Saydee's name brought Finn to his feet. "There's no way I'm placing my daughter's life in the hands of Aunt Saydee!" Finn walked to the entrance and grabbed onto both posts to steady his reaction. The very mention of Saydee's name shot his blood pressure up twenty points.

"She's the keeper of the book."

"What book?"

"The *Book of Killian*. It's held the family secrets for centuries. Yer only other hope is Quinn."

Finn turned back to Maureen shaking his head in disbelief. "The only difference between Saydee and Quinn is that Quinn's been committed to an asylum."

"Yer talkin' about my daughter and grandson," rebuked Maureen. "Quinn was yer best friend."

Hanging his head in remorse, Finn knew he'd crossed a line. "I've missed him," he said, sadness dripping from his words. "Who Quinn used to be."

"He's still in there. Just a wee bit rattled."

"Wee bit?" Finn paused to collect himself before saying something he'd regret. "I just don't want Ailee involved in your family's... eccentricities."

"Like it or not, Finn, yer as much a part of this family as Ailee. Ya always will be."

"Why can't she have a normal life?" Finn's shoulders slumped beneath the weight as he returned to the bench. He hadn't felt this defeated since he left Ireland.

"Normal?"

"You know what I mean." Not wanting to discuss the topic of magic, Finn pulled out his phone to check his messages.

"Why must ya see magic as a bad thing?"

"Alleged magic," he insisted, unable to mentally process his partner's short text message he'd read several times.

"Call it what ya will. At the end of the day, it's still a family gift."

"It's not right for her." Placing the phone in his pocket, he rose from the bench and looked toward his car. Running was his natural instinct.

"Shouldn't that be Ailee's decision?"

"I'm her dad, Maureen."

"A wonderful dad you are." Slowly lifting herself to her feet, she approached from behind. "Ailee needs more than ya can give her."

"I won't let your belief in some ancient curse take her from me." Needing to end the conversation, Finn left Maureen's side and walked toward his daughter.

She knew very well what was weighing on his mind. He'd lost his parents in a boating accident as a child. The life jacket his mother placed on him saved his life. He was helpless to save his parents. Maureen's heart ached for Finn as she watched him walk toward the pond. He was a strong man who spent his life protecting his daughter and others from harm. Now the hands of her beloved warrior were useless against the hands of time.

CARRYING clean sheets fresh from the clothesline on the back patio, Anne quickly moved up the stairs. Ailee's needed her bed sooner than expected. She'd fainted near the pond, amplifying her need for rest. Grandma Maureen followed Anne at a slower pace, with Finn and Ailee bringing up the rear.

Using the handrail to steady herself, Ailee took it step by step. Collapsing from fatigue quickly brought her back to reality. Finn's arm, secured around her waist, gave her an added boost. The climb was challenging, but thoughts of swans kept her smiling. Her first morning in Ireland was a dream come true. Reaching the top brought relief as she followed her hosts into the bedroom.

Instantly drawn to a collage of random pictures, Ailee stopped near the vanity to look closer. She freed herself from her father's hold and lowered herself to the doily-covered padded bench. The photos surrounding the mirror told her story. "My whole life's on this wall." Leaning her elbows on the vanity, she smiled at the proof that her family cared about her.

Maureen approached from behind, staring at her great-granddaughter's reflection in the mirror. "It's been a treat watchin' ya grow."

"Did you do this?"

"Gladys sent 'em and yer mum pinned 'em up."

"My mom?" asked Ailee, happy to hear the revelation. "What's this?" asked Ailee, pointing to a silver pendant hanging from the side of the mirror.

"An oak tree pendant. The Killian family symbol. Yer mum left it for ya. It's a protection charm."

Gladys hurried into the room carrying a small glass of orange juice. "Let's get yer blood sugar up a wee bit." She placed the drink in Ailee's hand and waited for her to drink. It was a quick fix for helping people with diabetes after an episode. She had no idea if it would work for Ailee's situation.

"Is this my mom's room?" asked Ailee, swapping the glass of juice for a framed photo of Molly holding her as a baby. The same picture she had on her desk at home.

"When she pops by for a stay."

Without warning, Ailee started to faint, dropping the frame to the floor. The sound of glass cracking alerted Finn to the situation. He rushed to her side and caught her in his arms. Anne only had enough time to finish securing the fitted sheet to the mattress before her dad laid her down.

Once his daughter was safely in bed, Finn reached down and picked the photograph from the broken frame. He gently brushed any remaining shards of glass from the surface and placed it on the nightstand, then moved the fractured frame and its glass to the garbage so the ladies could finish the bed.

Needing some fresh air, Finn walked toward the narrow French windows leading to the Juliette balcony. Opening the glass doors, he stepped outside the room and placed his hands over the wrought iron banister. The sound of Ailee's weak voice added to the ache in his chest. "Is this my mother's pillow?" she asked as she breathed in the scent. Finn had never forgotten that scent. The fragrance floating in the air from the flowers below mimicked the perfume she once wore. Memories flooded his mind, taking him back to the happiest days of his life. He remembered them as though they were yesterday—the love, the laughter, the joy. The fact that he'd buried his memories so deeply over the years made the sudden surge of emotion painful. Conversation from inside the room drew his attention back to his daughter.

"A good nap'll have ya right as rain," said Gladys as they finished making the bed as best they could with Ailee in it. After a kiss on her forehead, Gladys and Anne left the room.

"I know I'm too old for a bedtime story," Ailee suggested, hoping her great-gran would take the bait. She needed a good distraction from her physical and emotional overload.

"Who's too old?" responded Maureen, followed by a guttural groan to express her dismay. "I drift off t'sleep beneath an open book each night."

"Aunt Gladys tells the best stories about Ireland?"

"That one's always had a gift for weavin' a tale."

"Tell me about this," said Ailee, lifting the fairy pendant from her chest. "It was my grandmother's."

"Mind me havin' a closer look?" Maureen took the charm from Ailee's fingers to examine it. "Yer gran had a lovely fairy garden. A small wooded area behind their home."

"Grandma Donnelly had a fairy garden?"

The mention of his mother pulled Finn from the balcony. Leaning against the door frame, arms folded across his chest, he listened as his mind traveled back to his childhood. Finn had forgotten about the fairy garden and the picnics he and his mother shared beneath the trees while his dad was at work. He used to love walking through the wildflowers with his hand in hers, her loose dress blowing with the breeze.

"Gladys is the one t'be tellin' ya tales," Maureen answered. "She inherited her father's touch for spinnin' a story."

"Please, Gran," asked Ailee. "I've named my fairy, Shaylee."

Needing to steady her reaction, Maureen clenched the quilt beside her and took a deep breath. "Where'd ya come up with that one?" she asked, astonished by the age-old name.

Finn noticed Maureen's reaction, pulling him out of the past and piquing his interest further. Hoping for more clues, he listened intently.

"I met Shaylee in my dreams," Ailee answered as though it were any other question.

"In yer dreams, did ya?"

"On the flight over," whispered Ailee, fighting to keep her eyes open. "She's waiting for me."

"Waitin' for ya?" Intrigued and slightly alarmed by the revelation, Maureen waited for an answer. None came. Leaning her arm over Ailee's waist, she looked into her eyes. "Where's she waitin'?"

"In a magical garden," she whispered. Abandoning her attempt to continue the conversation, Ailee closed her eyes.

Maureen lifted her eyes to find Finn staring straight back. "Who's Shaylee?" he whispered, sensing that Maureen knew something of the figure in his daughter's dream. He hoped she would part the Killian curtain for a glimpse.

"Who can know the things of dreams?" Even if she knew why Shaylee was visiting Ailee in her dreams, she wouldn't have been able to share it with Finn. It was too soon. Maureen kissed Ailee on the forehead before leaving the side of her bed. "Sweet dreams, Lass." Then she walked to the door, pausing to look back at Ailee before leaving the room.

The one thing Finn never doubted was the Killian's love for Ailee and himself. He entered the room from the balcony and settled into an easy chair next to the wall. Protection charm or not, he would stay nearby in case she needed him. The travel and emotional strain of the day had taken their toll. Within seconds he drifted off to sleep.

Ailee opened her weary eyes and focused on the photo of her mom setting on the nightstand. Using all her strength, she pointed her hand toward the picture and summoned it to her. Landing in her open hand, Ailee studied the details of her mother holding her as a baby. A feeling of contentment washed over her, easing the worry she felt about her health. She didn't understand the sentiment, nor could she explain it. But somehow, she trusted it. It wasn't long before Shaylee crept back into her dreams, guiding her back in time.

CHAPTER SIX

Aidan & Shaylee

Aidan Killian left his father's tiny, thatch-roof cottage on foot beneath a dark sky. Using a lantern to light his way, he carried with him a telescope of great value. The English nobleman who owned the estate had a passion for astronomy and enjoyed sharing his knowledge of the heavens with the son of his foreman. Seeing great potential in Aidan, the nobleman allowed him to borrow the telescope for the night.

Finding a stump for a chair, he lowered the wick in the lantern and set it on the ground. The stars were exceptionally bright, lending brilliance to the dark sky. Gently, he pulled the telescope from its case and raised it to the heavens, placing the glass to his eye. The shock of seeing the stars so close sent him backward onto the ground. Securing the telescope, he marveled at its power. Knowing better what to expect, he crawled back onto the stump and placed the scope to his eye.

Barely into his exploration, he heard a giggle come from behind him. Looking back, he saw nothing in the darkness. The giggle persisted, so he placed the telescope on the stump to investigate. It was well past bedtime, and all were asleep on the estate. He followed the direction of the giggle into the dark, leading him away from the telescope. There was nothing to be found. The snickering switched directions, now coming from behind.

A dark figure picked up his scope and began to play with it like a toy.

"Stop!" yelled Aidan, "Yer goin' t'break it."

"Break it?" she asked, confused by his warning.

"The lenses. They're glass," he said, surprised to hear a female voice. Her accent was nothing he'd heard before. Her words seemed to float on the air.

"Lenses?"

Aidan walked toward her, but she evaded his every move. Forced to play her game of tag, he wondered why a woman would be out so late and so far from home. He lost his mother at an early age, so he hadn't much interaction with the opposite sex. His father taught him to be a gentleman and expected it when they shopped in the village. Being polite on this night was getting him nowhere. Her laughter poked fun at Aidan's desperation. To her, it was a game; to him, consequential. He had to retake possession of the telescope. "T'isn't mine," he hollered, stopping to catch his breath. "Give it back. Please."

"Have you stolen it?"

"Borrowed."

"Then I shall satisfy my curiosity by borrowing it from you," said the young woman as she turned to leave.

"Wait! I can show you what it does," bargained Aidan, hoping she'd turn back.

Piquing her interest, she met Aidan back at the stump. "No tricks?"

"Ya have me word."

"Promise?"

"Sit with me."

Somehow, this mortal seemed different from the others she'd teased over the centuries. Intrigued by his kindness more than the telescope, she followed his direction, keeping the treasure wrapped securely in her arms.

Sitting beside her, Aidan reached for the telescope, but she turned away. "Trust me," he whispered in her ear.

"How can I?"

"Ya got t'trust me t'find out."

Turning back, she offered him the telescope to test his integrity.

Taking it firmly in his hands, he pointed it toward the sky. "Press yer eye here, like this," he said, illustrating how to use it. Leaning in, she placed her eye against the brass and peered through the scope. He expected the same surprised reaction he'd experienced—silence was her only response.

She slowly pulled away from the telescope and looked into Aidan's eyes. "How is it possible?"

Aidan took great pride in explaining the science of the telescope as explained to him. The technical terms were lost in translation. He began again, this time answering her questions. She placed the scope to her eye and peered at the stars in every direction. Her questions allowed Aidan to speculate and share his theories about the heavens. Together, they made up stories about the stars, giving them names, personalities and storylines. Their laughter filled the meadow as they relaxed into each other's presence.

Forfeiting his own exploration time, Aidan gallantly held the telescope until his arms collapsed from exhaustion. Placing the scope across his lap, the two sat under the night sky. "I got t'go," said Aidan, breaking the silence. "Got a full day of work startin' at dawn?"

"Work is important to you?"

"Helpin' me father is," responded Aidan, rolling the lantern's wick farther into the chimney. The light allowed him to see her face for the first time. Her stunning beauty was like nothing he'd seen before, causing him to pull back as he did with the telescope. The sighting lasted for only a second before she vanished. Utilizing the lantern light, he searched in all directions but to no avail. She'd disappeared without a goodbye.

Securing the telescope inside its leather carrying case, Aidan made his way home. Halfway there, he noticed a dancing light following him. It was rare to see a firefly in Ireland. He'd heard legends of the luminesce insects, but the closest he'd ever seen was a glow worm. And that was a rarity. Placing the telescope and lantern near the door to his father's cottage, he carefully tried to catch the mysterious creature in his hands. The clever light eluded him each time. Giving up, he watched the light flitter away, leaving Aidan with a puzzling notion to resolve in his dreams.

He woke early to return the telescope to his father's employer, just as he'd done with the books he borrowed on a regular basis. Educating Aidan had become a priority for the English nobleman. The hours Simon spent running the estate left little time for his son's schooling. The landowner and his wife *taught lessons in every subject. They saw his potential and wanted more for the young man.*

Exhausted from lack of sleep, Aidan's ability to keep up waned as the day progressed. Taking an afternoon break in the orchard, he bit into an apple and rested his back against a fruit tree. It wasn't long before he floated away with the delicate light he'd met in his dreams.

His father's call to supper woke him just as the sun set on the horizon. Pulling himself to his feet, he noticed the return of the firefly. Round and round he turned till he grew dizzy from his futile attempts to capture it. Leaning his hands on his knees, he steadied himself.

"Giving up so easily," spoke a familiar voice. He turned to see the mysterious woman from the previous night peering around the trunk of an apple tree. Twilight allowed for a more detailed study as she stepped into full sight. Her clothing style differed from anything he'd ever seen. The mingling of soft colors on a weave of sparkling thread cut through the low light of dusk. He wondered if she was real or a figment of his imagination. Her long hair, secured by a garland of what appeared to be tropical flowers, led him to suspect a different origin. "Are ya human or spirit?"

"Somewhere in between," she responded. "Can we play tonight?"

His father's holler grew more insistent, prompting Aidan's response. "Comin', Dad." She was gone by the time he turned back. "If ya can hear me, I'll be seein' you tonight.'" Leaving the orchard, he hurried toward the cottage to appease his father and his growling stomach.

The ethereal light fluttered out from behind the tree and then soared high into the evening sky. A breeze from the ocean swept across the meadow, causing the tall grass to sway melodiously as the light gracefully glided over the top. The wind patterns in the grass put on a show few humans would ever see as she traveled toward a grove of trees. The floating light transformed into her human form as she came to rest on a sturdy oak branch. With her legs dangling, she leaned against the trunk. She would wait for her friend to return.

AIDAN CONSUMED his evening stew and bread with the speed of ten hungry men. Leaping from his chair, he reached for a sweater before his father had finished half his bowl. "Where ya off to, Son?"

"Searchin' for fireflies," he responded, placing his hand on the latch.

"In Ireland?" Surprised by Aidan's quest, he passed along some fatherly wisdom. "A good night's sleep'll suit ya better."

"I won't be long," assured Aidan as he closed the door behind him. After leaping the fence, his fervor carried him across the pasture and into the far meadow. Out of breath, he arrived at the stump where they'd met the night before. There he waited, most impatiently. The waxing crescent of the new moon made it a bit easier to see than the previous night. The approaching clouds, however, meant their time together was dependent on the weather.

A distant giggle brought an end to his yearning as it guided him toward the nearby wooded area. Reaching the grove of trees, he stepped into the darkness beneath the mighty canopy of oak and ash. He could hear her playful snickers but chose not to follow into the forest's depths. "It's too dark," he hollered, hoping she would come to him. His wish was granted.

He watched in wonder as a lighted sphere floated down from the highest of limbs, growing in size with its descent. The large globe traveled into the forest, and Aidan followed the floating orb. The air cooled with each passing tree, chilling him through his woolen sweater. The scampering sounds of animals on the forest floor, competing with the churring of Nightjars, kept Aidan on alert. The glow of an owl's eyes bore down on him, driving him closer to the light with each piercing scream. "How much farther?" he enquired, maintaining a brave tone.

Rather than answering the question, the light vanished, leaving him victim to the dark. The forest animals sat tight, concealing their voices as they waited for the human's next move. Lost and alone, Aidan had no sense of direction and no light to guide him back to the meadow.

Relief came in the form of a whisper to his left ear. "Trust me."

"How can I?" he asked, mimicking her response from the night before.

"You have to trust me to find out," she whispered into his right ear, allowing her breath to warm his neck. Stepping back, she unfolded her fingers to reveal a round piece of limestone. Slowly it started to glow until the brightness encircled them. Attempting to slow his heartbeat, Aidan exhaled before turning to face his guide. Framed by the darkness, they allowed time to pass as they studied the details of each other's faces. The intimacy they shared surpassed words—a first for Aidan.

"My people call me Shaylee," she said softly.

"Yer people?"

The pattering of raindrops against the leaves fought for their attention. The harder they tried to hang onto the moment, the heavier the rain fell until the canopy of leaves could no longer protect them. Taking hold of her friend's hand, Shaylee ran through the forest until they reached a slab of rock protruding from the hillside. They settled into the small cave-like space beneath the outcropping. The glow of Shaylee's orb lit the stone walls, adding warmth to the cold rock as they listened to the rain.

The water began to pour from the edge of the overhanging rock, creating an enchanting waterfall between them and the forest. Concealed from the eyes of the world, Aidan and Shaylee waited out the storm. The soothing sound of the water settled their adrenaline, and they drifted off to sleep in each other's arms.

The songbirds serenaded Aidan from his sleep as they welcomed the dawn. The limestone rock his friend had used to light the way was lying next to him. Taking it as a memento, he hurried from the cave and eventually found his way out of the grove of trees. The wet grass soaked him to the bone as he ran through the meadow. His only hope of avoiding discipline was to crawl into bed before his father woke.

CHAPTER SEVEN

Ailee woke to the sound of lively voices from outside her window. She needed a moment to mentally adjust from running through the grass beside Aidan. Tossing her covers aside, she sat on the side of the bed and stretched her spine, surprised by the stiffness she felt. Then she rose to her feet and picked up the robe hanging over the bed's footboard. On sore muscles, she walked across the floor, unsure how the movement in her dream had affected her body. Reaching the narrow French windows, she pulled them open and walked onto the small second-floor balcony. The morning breeze was cool, causing her to tie her robe around her waist.

She could hear voices around the corner of the house engaged in a spirited discussion. "Dad?" she called, waiting for a response. It wasn't long before Finn walked into view. His button-up plaid shirt, neatly tucked into his belted jeans, matched the look he'd had for as long as she could remember. "Is everything okay?"

"Fine. Did you sleep well?"

"You wouldn't believe the dream I had."

"I'd like t'hear of it," said Maureen as she joined Finn below the balcony. "Fancy some breakfast before ya go."

"Maureen," softly reproved Finn. He was hoping to sneak away without Ailee noticing. A psychiatric hospital was no place for a teenage girl, especially in her condition.

"Where are we going?" asked Ailee, the secret out of the bag.

"Yer dad's off t'see Quinn."

"It's better if you stay with Gladys," strongly suggested her father, overriding Maureen's plotting.

"And miss the chance to meet my uncle?" Ailee disappeared from the balcony.

Frustrated, Finn turned and walked toward the car. "I told you I wanted to go by myself."

"That ya did," smiled Maureen as she watched him walk away. Making her way toward the house, Maureen met Anne waiting inside the front door. "Ailee'll take her meal on the road."

"Will she now?" Although subtle, Anne's accusatory tone was recognizable. She crossed her arms over her chest and leaned against the door frame waiting for further explanation for her employer's meddling.

"Settle yourself, Anne," she said. "It's just a wee nudge."

"And in what direction might that be?"

"Ailee needs to know her people," said Maureen. "Gettin' this clan together's like nailin' jelly to a wall." Stepping through the doorway, she muttered under her breath. "I'm a bit old for this." Anne took pleasure in being a fly on the wall. Leaving the door open, she smiled as she walked toward the kitchen to prepare Ailee a fried egg, a bacon rasher, and a slice of fried tomato with a side of toast.

Finn stopped the rental car at the iron gate and rolled down the window. The bronze plaque on the gate increased the knot size in his gut: Boyle Psychiatric Hospital. He hadn't seen Quinn in years. He remembered the day when his best friend was first admitted. It was half a lifetime ago and the beginning of a stream of involuntary commitments and outpatient sessions. Finn had no idea what to expect. This was the last place he wanted to be. Make that second to last. Seeking advice from Molly's Aunt Saydee was a frightening alternative. His thoughts turned to Ailee. "I shouldn't have brought you."

"I'm fine, Dad," she replied, sitting up in her seat and staring through the iron bars at the gray building in the distance. "I want to meet Uncle Quinn."

"This is no place for a kid."

"I'm a teenager, remember?" she responded, trying to wrap her untamed hair in a ponytail at the back of her neck. She only had time to brush her teeth and throw on a pair of jeans and a t-shirt with an applicable graphic: *Swim hair, don't care!*

Finn chuckled half-heartedly at his "grown up" daughter, then rolled down the window.

"What brings ya here?" came an official-sounding but pleasant voice from outside the car. The morning sun was behind him, silhouetting his large stature and making it difficult to see the details of his face.

"Visiting an old friend," answered Finn, lifting his hand to block the sun as he tried to make eye contact with the guard.

"Who's the patient?"

"Quinn Killian."

The security guard paused momentarily, then leaned down and looked through the window at Ailee. Physically, he looked like an overgrown boy scout, trustworthy and helpful in his pressed uniform and perfectly-combed hair. "Identification?" he ordered.

Finn recognized the change in the tone of the guard's voice after mentioning Quinn's name. The dodgy look in his eye gave Finn cause for concern. This was no boy scout. "Why do you need ID?"

"Protocol."

Under protest, Finn pulled out his American driver's license and handed it to the guard. "Would you like to see my police badge as well?"

"And her?"

"My daughter, Ailee."

Without a response, the man entered the security booth and picked up the phone.

Finn nervously tapped his finger on the steering wheel while his detective mind sussed out possible scenarios.

"What's he doing?" asked Ailee.

"Not sure. I didn't expect such tight security."

The guard returned to the open window and held out the license. Finn tried to take it, but the guard held onto it for a few seconds to show him who was boss. "Check in at the front desk and stay where yer told." He loosened his grip and stepped away from the car. Finn could feel the guard's gaze drilling into him as the gate slowly opened. He drove forward without a response or a second glance.

The large stone building was as grey as the backdrop of approaching clouds. Its concrete blocks and symmetrical windows screamed institution. The only flair to the building were the two triangular gables framing the entrance. The fog lifting from the grounds added a spooky mystique as Finn and Ailee pulled into a parking spot. "You can wait in the car if you like."

"Not a chance."

"The minute you start feeling weak or tired, we're out of there," said Finn, opening the car door.

As they approached the stairs to the entrance, Finn looked up at the clock tower in the center of the roof. How cruel to have a clock at a place where time stands still, he thought to himself. His perspective on time quickly switched gears to his own as Ailee moved passed him. Time was ticking by quickly, with less than a week to go. Shaking his head, he fought off thoughts of the curse. Staying grounded in reality was becoming more challenging by the hour. The door opened just as they reached the top step. A floral delivery man politely greeted them as he left the building. Grabbing the open door, Finn put his chivalry aside and entered the building before his daughter for security purposes. With uncertainty, they approached the nurse's station.

A female doctor in a white lab coat stood with her back toward them, doing paperwork, her elbow on the high counter. The recently delivered flower bouquet took up the work surface's center. Its lush display of bright blooms separated them from the doctor. A medical receptionist and a nurse clicked away on their keyboards.

"We're here to visit Quinn Killian."

A raised index finger was all he got in response before her hand returned to the keyboard. His experience with the security guard made it clear he had no clout once he entered the hospital grounds.

While waiting for the nurse to reply, Finn checked out the interior design. The taupe-colored wainscoting melted into the Classic Gray of the rest of the wall. An occasional pastel watercolor painting decorated the span between doors, bringing a touch of life to the dreary hallway. The polished and sterile vinyl sheet flooring reflected the ceiling's light. The design was exactly what Finn expected to see.

A feeling of familiarity washed over him. It was more than familiarity, but he couldn't put his thumb on it. He'd never been inside the building, yet somehow, he felt a connection. Searching the hallway for answers, he scoped out each orderly, nurse and patient. Turning his head in the other direction brought the back of the doctor's head into view through the flower blossoms and leaves. The twist used to secure her red hair in a low bun was exactly how Molly used to wear her hair as a nurse, rolled up from the bottom and pinned in place. Being in a hospital brought back all the times he'd pick his wife up from work. The familiarity suddenly made sense.

Finn returned to reality with the medical secretary's delayed response. "Our Chief Nursing Officer, Nurse Brón, will assist you."

"Brón," repeated Finn beneath his breath. "Sorrow, pain." Not the most comforting name for a nurse, he thought to himself. His Gaelic was rusty, but he recognized the word brón from language lessons taught at his mother's knee. His Celtic education continued alongside English when he went to live with his grandparents. Finn's fascination with the nurse's surname was quickly replaced by the echoing click-clack of a pair of wide heels marching toward him.

Nurse Brón's grey, business-style wool dress accentuated her tall and perfect posture as she pursued her target. The split-stand collar at the top of the dress elongated her neck, promoting a sense of command and authority. Finn felt an uneasiness as she approached. Her platinum blonde hair with streaks of red was fully contained at the back of her head. She greeted them with her long fingers laced together and without an ounce of expression. "What brings you to Boyle Hospital?"

"We're here to see Quinn Killian."

"And the reason for your visit?"

"I need a reason?"

"You do." Her definitive response echoed through the long, cold hallway.

"To break him out," smirked Ailee beneath her breath. Her nearly inaudible remark earned her a swift glare from Nurse Brón. "That was a joke," she added apologetically. She was surprised the nurse heard her comment.

"Threats do not amuse us."

"Sorry."

"Follow me," she responded sternly before turning and walking away.

"Threats?" Ailee whispered to her dad.

"Are you trying to get us thrown out?" he whispered with every ounce of seriousness.

"I can't believe she heard me."

"I can't believe you said it," muttered Finn as they left the nurse's station, fighting the urge to snicker.

Amused by their back and forth, Dr. Molly Killian turned to watch them walk away. Exhaling, she breathed for the first time since they approached the desk. The close proximity to her husband and daughter nearly overpowered her self-control. Every restraint she could muster was at attention. For twelve long years, she dreamed of being reunited with her family and holding them in her arms. But that dream would come at a terrible price.

Still, Molly smiled as she watched them walk side-by-side, Finn's arm loosely draped around Ailee's shoulder for support. Even with the passing of time, Molly's love for her daughter and the man raising her hadn't wavered.

The rational-thinking scientist within Molly soon replaced the melancholy. He should never have brought Ailee to this place, she thought to herself. "Careless!" Her breath carried the word from her mouth as she forcefully closed her folder.

Unable to walk away, she glanced over her shoulder. It felt like twelve years ago all over again. The beats of her heart increased dramatically as the distance between them widened. Her hand clutching the folder began to shake as she tightened her grip. Unable to get enough oxygen, Molly breathed deeply through her mouth. Grabbing at the bright scarf around her neck, she pulled the loop and slid it from her neck.

"Ya all right, Dr. Killian?"

"Just needin' some air." Pushing her way through the entrance doors, she ran down the steps and into the parking lot. Stumbling toward the visitor's meditation garden, she removed the restrictions of the lab coat. Molly knew exactly what was happening as she hid away. The experience of watching Ailee and Finn walk away triggered the onset of a panic attack. There was a time when Molly relied on a tonic brewed by her aunt to help with her anxiety. She hadn't touched it in years.

She fell to her knees and rolled onto her back beneath a hawthorn tree. The mayflower's branches swaying in the breeze helped slowly calm her, while the blossom's pungent odor acted as a distraction. Focusing on the white blossom flowers above, she waited for anxiety's grasp to let go of her heart. The wellspring of tears rolling past her temples slowed. Peace had come to her mind, but her strength was spent. Closing her eyes, she painted a picture of an imaginary future with her husband and daughter. The future she dreamed of before the curse.

CHAPTER EIGHT

Walking at a soldier's pace, Nurse Brón never wavered from the center of the hall nor turned her head in either direction. Her steps landed perfectly measured and succinct. As she advanced down the hall, the staff and patients scampered out of her way to avoid a collision. It was their responsibility to clear the way for the Chief Nursing Officer.

By contrast, Finn and Ailee's curiosity had them glancing through the rectangular windows of the hospital doors as they tried to keep up. The distraction made the long, dreary hallway less formidable. The large rooms were busy with group therapy meetings, exercise activities, meditation sessions, as well as art, music and craft therapies.

Approaching a set of double metal doors at the end of the hall, Finn could feel his heart beating faster. He had no idea what to expect or how Quinn would react. Would his childhood friend even remember him?

Leaving the building, they entered a grassy sanctum. The manicured yard was large, a quarter of an acre by Finn's best estimation. The secluded haven was surrounded by a high stone wall covered in moss and ivy. The contradiction between the tranquil grounds on the outside versus the lifeless color palette of the inside was not lost on the visitors. "Look at all the fairy statues," observed Ailee as she touched the fairy pendant lying against her chest. "They're everywhere."

"Don't get distracted," advised her dad, staring in the direction of the nurse's pointing finger.

"They look so life-like." Ailee peered into a nearby statue's eyes until the nurse yanked her away. Surprised by her lack of bedside manner, Ailee pulled her arm from the woman's tight grasp.

"Fifteen minutes. No more!" Nurse Brón said with a snap before returning to the building.

"Nurse Bully," murmured Ailee as she rubbed the bruised part of her arm. Getting no response from her dad, she turned to see him staring at a man in the distance. "Are you all right, Dad?" Ailee looked toward the older man in the oversized sweater that had captured her father's attention. He was shorter than she imagined, and his messy gray hair reminded her of a picture of Albert Einstein from a textbook. From what she could see, he was carrying on a one-man conversation while circling a fountain in the garden's center. His hands pushed deep into the pockets of his stretched-out, maroon jumper. "Is that him? Uncle Quinn?"

"I'd recognize that uneven gait anywhere."

"I thought he was wobbling because he's old."

"We're the same age," responded Finn. "He broke his foot as a kid. It never healed right cause he didn't want his mom to know what we were doing when he broke it. That's one of the reasons he rarely wears shoes." Finn left Ailee's side and slowly walked toward his old friend.

Ailee's imagination was intrigued by the mystery of what led to his uncle's broken foot. More than that, she liked the idea of her dad being mischievous when he was young. She strolled behind and waited for her dad to make contact. Even at a young age, she recognized the emotional impact of the moment. With Nurse Brón nowhere in sight, Ailee had unfinished business with each fairy she passed.

As Finn approached, he put forward his hand for a friendly shake. He waited in anticipation as Quinn studied his face. Without warning, Quinn's hands left his pockets and drew them together with a hug so tight he could hardly breathe. Finn hung on just as tightly, towering over him, basking in brotherly love. Their bond of friendship had survived despite Finn's decision to flee Ireland and those who loved him. "Forgive me, my old friend. I shouldn't have left without telling you why."

"Yer here now."

"All the years we've lost," uttered Finn as he pulled himself back to look into Quinn's eyes. "I did that."

"'If yer lookin' for a friend without a fault,'" began Quinn.

"'You'll be without a friend forever.' You always have an Irish proverb tucked up your sleeve."

"Welcome home, my warrior friend." Quinn couldn't resist pulling him close once again.

"It's good to be home."

"Warrior friend?" enquired Ailee as she approached, curious about a side of her dad she never knew.

"It's nothing," said her dad, opening himself up from their embrace.

"Spill," she demanded.

With a heavy sigh and tilt of his neck, Finn tried to downplay the topic. "My mom named me after a character from Irish Folklore."

"A warrior by the name of Fionn," inserted Quinn. "Greatest leader of the ancient Fianna."

"You wait till now to tell me this?" asked Ailee, finding a place to sit on the short wall of the fountain. "A warrior. No wonder you became a cop."

"Still policin', are ya?" Quinn lowered himself to the fountain's edge and motioned Finn to join him. "How'd you get so old?" he joked.

"I was about to ask you the same thing." Finn gave it right back like when they were kids. Taking a seat between Ailee and her uncle, Finn hoped to keep their conversation grounded in reality.

Quinn had other plans. Feeling somewhat secure after scanning the yard for spies and gremlins, he leaned into Finn. "I've been expectin' ya."

"Who told you we were coming?" asked Finn, playing what he thought was a game.

"My friends, the sídhe-folk," whispered Quinn.

"Sídhe-folk?" asked Ailee, sliding closer to her dad. Few things intrigued her young mind more than Irish folklore.

"Fairies," her dad clarified with a tone of disdain.

"That was before," he said, leaning closer to Ailee. Using his open hand to hide his pointing finger, Quinn directed their attention to the fairy statues scattered throughout the yard.

"Before what?" Ailee's interest was beyond piqued. Leaning in front of her dad, she waited in suspense.

Quinn placed his hand to the side of his mouth and shared his dangerous secret. "Before they got turned t'stone."

"Stone?" Ailee turned her attention to the two fairies in the fountain. "Is that why they look so real?"

"Ailee," Finn cautioned, trying to bring his daughter back to reality, but Quinn continued too quickly. "The fairy queen sent 'em to protect me," he whispered, drawing Ailee in deeper into his world.

"Fairy queen?" she asked, blown away by each new revelation.

Quinn pulled a small notebook from his pocket, worn from years of use. He licked his finger and started flipping through the pages. "I couldn't warn 'em in time."

"Warn them?"

"Ailee!" interrupted Finn. His caution did not affect his daughter. She'd traveled too far into Quinn's world.

"The witch's spells are powerful," continued Quinn.

"Witches?" Ailee tried to read the scribbled writing as the pages flipped by, full of diagrams and doodling.

Standing up, Finn separated them and took control of the conversation. "We're not here to talk about witches or fairies!" Turning back to Quinn, he lowered his voice. "We're here because my daughter, Molly's daughter, needs your help."

"Molly's daughter?" Quinn's attention switched instantly to the recollection of Finn's jaw-dropping news. Sliding the notebook back into his pocket, he rose to his feet. At full stature, he barely topped Ailee in height. After a quick finger brush of his messy hair, Quinn stretched out his hand to properly introduce himself. "Quinn Killian, Molly's brother."

"Nice to meet you, Uncle Quinn."

"Uncle Quinn. It's got an awfully nice ring to it," he responded with a friendly wink. "So nice of ya t'visit."

"We don't have much time, Quinn. Ailee needs to show you something." In response to her father's bidding, Ailee stretched open the neckline of her t-shirt to reveal her birthmark. Quinn's eyes enlarged as he unbuttoned his collar, revealing the same birthmark on the front of his shoulder: a Sessile oak tree leaf with nine protruding lobes. "Over again, startin' over again." Quinn pulled his collar together and slowly walked away in zigzag motions, uttering the same words. "Over again, startin' over again."

"Quinn? Quinn!" called Finn as he followed his friend away from the fountain.

Feeling faint from the rise in dopamine levels and their ensuing fall, Ailee decided to wait for her dad to return. She lowered herself to the fountain wall and stared at her reflection in the pool of water. Checking for onlookers, she decided to play with her magic. Twirling her finger above the water, she moved the water in different patterns until something distorted her designs. Looking toward the sky, she saw no sign of rain. Staring into the face of a fairy statue, she watched as a single tear rolled from the corner of her eye. "Dad?" Ailee looked to her father for help, but he was too far away. She watched as another tear dropped into the pool from the second fairy. "He's never going to believe this."

Across the yard, Quinn continued to spiral out of control. "I tried. I couldn't get to him," he babbled, pacing unevenly in all directions.

Determined to understand, Finn tried to keep up mentally and physically. "Get to who?"

"He told me t'wait."

"Who told you to wait?" Finn continued to plead for answers while pursuing Quinn's erratic course at the far end of the yard. Their child's game of Follow the Leader caught on with the other residents. Soon the yard was alive, with patients chasing each other around the grounds.

"'Close your eyes, Quinn.'" Consumed by the flashback, he continued to mimic his father's voice as he relived the worst day of his life. "'Drink from the well, Quinn.'"

Mentioning the holy well reminded Finn of Gladys' warning before they left the States. Trying to tap things down from the erratic behavior, Finn wrapped his arms around Quinn's shoulder and pulled him close. He needed to be the listening ear his friend once trusted.

"I didn't close my eyes," whispered Quinn, holding onto Finn like a lifeline to reality.

"What did you see?"

Pulling away, Quinn faced Finn with lucidity. "Life and death. One can't be without the other. No one can help my dad now?"

"Your dad?" Finn tried to piece together Quinn's riddle. "What happened?" Finn attempted to remember the facts of Quinn's father's passing. The official cause of death was an accident. The memorial was private—family only. Quinn and Molly's mother passed shortly after from a broken heart. That was the family's diagnosis.

"Over again. Startin' over again." Quinn began repeating the same blather, returning to his physical and mental wanderings and a world Finn did not understand.

The hospital's oasis had turned into a circus, with patients yelling nonsense at each other as they copied Quinn's game of tag. Frustrated and running out of time, Finn gently took Quinn by the shoulders and stared into his eyes. "Ailee's sick. She needs your help."

"She's comin'," warned Quinn. The look in his eyes showed the fear in his heart. "Find Molly."

Finn turned to see Nurse Brón on a direct path across the yard. Her speed seemed unnatural as she closed in on their location. Looking behind him, Quinn had created a safe distance between them. He was a scared prisoner, pressing his back against the stone wall, waiting for his punishment. Finn had brought trouble to Quinn's door.

Taking up the position between Finn and Quinn, Nurse Brón took control of the situation. "You will leave. Now!"

"What happened to fifteen minutes?"

"You're upsetting the patients."

"Five more minutes," he said, stepping toward her to test her resolve. He didn't get far. The force that knocked him to the ground was swift and powerful. Finn didn't see it coming. Before he could sit up, he was yanked to his feet by a couple of pairs of strong arms.

Held captive by two large orderlies, Nurse Brón approached without a hair out of place. "Leave on your own, or I'll have you and your daughter thrown out."

Finn weighed his options, and the numbers weren't good. Looking to Quinn for answers, he observed the slow turning of his head from side to side. Although his warrior instincts contradicted Quinn's will, Finn knew he could walk away. Quinn could not. For his friend's sake, he would yield. "Fine." Jerking his arms from their relaxed grip, he leveled a threatening look at his new enemy. He hoped it would be a subtle warning as he turned and walked across the yard. Leaving with his tail between his legs was not how he thought the visit would go.

Ailee motioned to her dad as he walked by the fountain, eager to share what she had discovered. "You've got to see this."

"Let's go!"

Ailee knew that tone. Staying was non-negotiable. She took one last look at the weeping fairy and then joined her father. "You're not going to believe what I just saw."

Obsessed with his mental investigation, Finn ignored Ailee's comments as he entered the building and stormed down the hall. "Something strange is going on here," he mumbled to himself.

"Exactly," replied Ailee. "Stone statues don't cry." She could feel her strength draining as she pushed to keep up with his pace.

"Nurse Brón is hiding something, and Quinn's in the middle of it."

Ailee tried again to tell her father about the magical event she had just witnessed. "I saw it with my own eyes."

Oblivious to Ailee's voice, Finn continued his self-serving rant under his breath as he left the building and walked to the car. "If she thinks I'm staying away, she's as misguided as her patients."

"Quinn was telling the truth," whispered Ailee as she walked through the open door, trying to catch her breath. The attempt to gain her father's attention had left her lightheaded. She stumbled down the stairs, gripping the railing for support until she ran short of pipe. She made it one more step before the ground started to spin. The overload of her imagination, combined with the rush down the hallway, had stolen her strength.

Arriving at the car, Finn reached into his pocket for the keys, still ranting from the humiliation he was dealt. "I'm coming back whether she likes it or not." Catching Ailee's reflection in the mirrored glass of the window, he rushed to her side as she fell to the ground. The impact of failing his daughter hit him like a truck. Taking her into his arms, he brushed the hair from her face. "Ailee. Talk to me, Ailee," he pleaded.

"The statues are alive." The words traveled on heavy breath as she sighed from exhaustion. Ignoring Ailee's impressionable nature, he slid his arm beneath her knees to pick her up.

Dr. Cyrus Boyle stood at the second-story window overlooking the parking lot. The departure of Quinn's unruly visitors had captured his full attention. With arms folded across his chest, he studied Finn as he scooped his daughter into his arms and carried her to the car. He observed as the father touched his daughter's feet to the ground, ensuring she could stand. Then he opened the passenger side door and helped her into the seat. The car's roof shielded his view, but Boyle imagined he was making her comfortable.

He watched intently as the father made his way back around the car. Curiously, the visitor stopped momentarily to stare up at the building. From his line of sight and the tilt of his head, Dr. Boyle concluded he was checking the time on the building's clock tower.

Unexpectedly, the stranger's eyes made contact with his on the way down from the clock. Boyle held his gaze, intrigued by how long the stare-down would last. As a psychiatrist, he longed to enter the outsider's mind, to unravel the secrets he held about Quinn. As a sorcerer of sorts, he hungered for a less orthodox examination. Winning the staring contest, Boyle smiled as he watched the stranger get in his car.

Nurse Brón entered the room with a gusto and approached the window, stopping just behind her boss. They both watched as the car pulled out of the parking lot. "His name is Finn Donnelly."

"And the girl?"

"His daughter. Ailee."

In frustration, the doctor ran the fingers of both hands through his dark wavy hair, revealing his M-shaped hairline and receding hair on both sides. "Why is he visiting Quinn?"

"He wouldn't say."

"They're coming for him. I can feel it."

"Quinn's secure within our walls," she argued, confident in her assessment.

Boyle turned from the window to his nearby desk. His swivel executive chair welcomed him back to its rich leather surface. "Any progress on the book?"

"I will find a way to read it."

"It needs to be done soon," ordered Boyle. "My gut's telling me he's after the same thing we are."

"I should have taken care of them in the yard," she pronounced regretfully as she walked toward the door.

"In broad daylight?"

"Who's going to believe the stories of a yard full of mental patients?" With her ego still intact, she left the office.

"There are other ways," he whispered as she left his office. Boyle entered his private laboratory through a secret door in his office. As a psychiatrist, lab work was part of the job. This lab went beyond science. Turning to his borrowed book of enchantments, he leafed through the pages. "Wrong season. Too much time. Missing an ingredient." Finally, he settled on the perfect potion. Reaching into a jar of gold dust, he scooped an ounce of particles into the palm of his hand. "We'll start with the lass."

AILEE PULLED herself up in the seat as a portion of strength replaced the frailty of her limbs. "Where are we?" she asked, staring out the window at the beautiful coastline.

Finn needed some time to think before returning to the Killian house so he took a drive to the coast. "Close your eyes and rest."

"What if I don't wake up?" she asked, her vulnerability laid bare.

Finn pulled into a scenic turnout and came to an abrupt stop. "Don't ever say that, Ailee!" Unnerved by his strong reaction, Finn left the car and walked toward the edge of the rugged cliff. The fierce wind coming off the sea helped clear the frustration from his mind.

With all her strength, Ailee pushed open the car door. The strong wind fought her every inch of the way. Keeping a hand on the vehicle, she used it for support till she got her legs beneath her. Looking at the distance between herself and her dad, she bowed to the wind's force and rested against the side of the car. Like most dads, Ailee's father had always been the strength in her life. He was changing as her illness progressed. Something was off, and deep in her gut, she knew it had to do with her. "We're not here for my birthday, are we?" she shouted into the wind as loudly as she could.

Not wanting to answer his daughter's question, he waited a moment before turning from the horizon. With enough time to think, he returned to the car to face his daughter. "Your birthday is what brought us here. Just not in the way you think."

"I need to know, Dad."

"Get in the car, and we'll talk," said her dad, prying the passenger side door open.

"I'm not moving till I know the truth!"

Leaning against the side of the car, Finn had no idea how to explain something he didn't understand himself. "Your illness is hereditary... in a way."

"In a way?"

"It has to do with your mother's side of the family and your birthday."

Becoming alarmed by how he danced around the topic, Ailee demanded the truth. "Am I dying?"

"No!" Finn faced his daughter and cupped her head in his hands. "You're not going to die!"

"Then what's wrong with me?"

Not sure what to say to calm both of their racing hearts, he stumbled ahead. "It's an illness that's been passed down through the Killian line."

"Illness... like Uncle Quinn?"

Finn's honesty poured from his heavy heart as he relaxed his hands from his daughter's face. "I wish I knew more."

Ailee's world changed in an instant. Needing some space, she leaned into the wind for support as she took several steps away from the car. "Is there a cure?" asked Ailee.

"From what I'm told."

She heard the uncertainty in his voice but continued to push for answers as she backed away from him. "Is the cure here in Ireland?"

"That seems to be the case."

"How long do I have?"

"We're going to find the cure," assured Finn as he followed her, step for step, watching the distance narrow between his daughter and the edge of the cliff.

"You didn't answer my question! How long?"

"I don't have the answers."

"Who does?" she asked, getting closer to the precipice.

"Ailee, stop!" Finn tried to grab her hand, but she pulled it back.

"You know more than you're telling me," she cried, continuing toward the edge. "Quit trying to protect me!"

Running out of things to say as well as ground beneath their feet, Finn grabbed his daughter and wrapped her in his arms. Her trembling frame shook from the chill of the cutting wind and the shock of his grim news. "It's my job to protect you." Looking down at the waves crashing against the jagged rocks made him sick to his stomach. Ailee needed his strength now more than ever and the truth. "If I knew more, I would tell you."

The security of her father's embrace would have to be enough. She knew he was doing everything he could to save her life. His return to Ireland was proof of that. At this point, her life was in the hands of a family she barely knew.

CHAPTER NINE

Enticing whispers drifted through the darkness of Ailee's bedroom. She tossed back and forth, fighting their call. The indistinct words became clearer as they pulled her from a deep sleep. "Ailee. Ailee." Disorientated, she made an effort to open her eyes. Her groggy mental state worked to piece together what was happening. Sitting up, she looked around the room but saw nothing. "Ailee." She heard it again. The voice came from the Juliette balcony. She wrapped a light blanket around her white sleep shirt and walked to the French windows. "Ailee." Moving the curtain aside, she saw the impossible. "I must be dreaming."

Two leprechauns sat comfortably on the balcony's railing, swinging their leather ankle boots. The vocal one wore an open red jacket, revealing his plaid-clad potbelly. His friend wore a green vest beneath his red plaid tailcoat, belted at the waist. Ailee rubbed her eyes, then took a second look. She'd grown up listening to her aunt's stories of these tiny creatures from Irish folklore. They were believed to be part of the fairy family. She never imagined seeing them in real life. Luckily, it was just a dream. Or so she thought.

"Ailee," he called again, flipping a gold coin off his thumb and catching it in the air.

THE 14TH TALE

Convinced she was dreaming, Ailee opened the doors. The breeze swept passed her into the room, lifting her white blanket like a cape. Her auburn hair floated on the currents of the wind, her face awash with moonlight. She appeared ethereal, not of this world. Her resemblance to royalty frightened the tiny creatures, but not as much as their master's wrath if they failed.

Summoning courage, the leprechaun in red plaid tipped his hat toward her. Then he flipped a coin toward Ailee, who caught it with both hands. Placing it between her teeth, she bit down. The coin was real.

"Come play with us, Ailee," said the tiny trickster in the tailcoat before standing on the railing and doing a jig to the beat of his friend's clapping.

Finding delight in his performance, Ailee began to clap along. She never imagined she'd actually see one of the little people. Ignoring her aunt's warnings to beware of their tricks, Ailee continued to enjoy his performance, joining in on the dance.

The dancing leprechaun's feet slowly came to a rest as his energy waned. He lifted his hat and used his forearm to wipe the sweat from his forehead. Still standing on the railing, he turned his back to Ailee and then looked over his shoulder. "Follow me, Ailee." Before she could respond, he leaped from the balcony.

Breathing in a sharp breath, Ailee gasped at his disappearance.

The second leprechaun turned on the railing, allowing his legs to dangle. "C'm with us."

Ailee watched him disappear as well. Thinking they'd both fallen to the ground, she covered her mouth in shock. Unable to quell her curiosity, she stepped onto the railing and peered over the edge. A sparkling slide composed of gold dust carried the leprechaun to the ground. She smiled in relief as she watched him dance with his friends at the bottom. "Try it, Ailee," whispered one of them.

"C'mon. It's fun," the rest said, bidding her to follow.

Ailee crawled over the iron balcony, securing the heels of her bare feet between the balusters. The sparkling slide enticed her to take a ride. The calls for her to let go continued until she loosened her grip and left the railing.

The sound of Ailee's scream woke Finn from an already restless sleep. Running from the bedroom, he arrived in his daughter's room to find the French windows wide open. Stepping onto the balcony, he witnessed what appeared to be Ailee lying motionless on the ground below. Her white sleep shirt stood out in the dark, as well as a white blanket lying nearby. The outside light came to life as the housekeeper ran around the corner of the house. Its pool of light stretched to the scene of the accident. Anne was the first on the scene below as Finn rushed from the room, his heartbeat thumping in his chest. He took the stairs in three jumps and ran out the door. "Call an ambulance!" he yelled as he ran toward his daughter. Anne returned to the house as Finn carefully checked her vitals. "Ailee? Ailee."

Maureen passed Anne on her way to the house. Her friend's worried glance gave warning of what lay ahead. The sight of Ailee lying unconscious beside her father slowed Maureen's approach. She sensed the presence of mischief. The smell of the grave lingered in the air, thick and dreadful. She shined her flashlight around the yard in search of answers. Nothing looked out of the ordinary. Collecting herself, Maureen placed her hand on Finn's shoulder. "Ailee?"

"She's alive."

Maureen breathed a sigh of relief. "We can be grateful for that."

"How could she have fallen?" Finn moved the hair from in front of his daughter's face as he tried to piece it together. "What was she doing on the balcony in the middle of the night?"

"Dark magic's in the air," she answered as Gladys ran toward them.

"Stop with the superstition!" As soon as the demand left his mouth, Finn found a gold coin lying on the grass next to Ailee's hand. He examined it closely beneath the light of Maureen's flashlight. The markings were like nothing he'd ever seen, causing his own superstitions to take root. Lifting the coin toward Maureen, he waited for her inspection.

"Superstition or not, that coin's not of our world." Before Maureen could take it for further analysis, the coin disintegrated into fine particles. The gold dust floated toward the night sky like a spinning helix. She followed it to the edge of the yard and watched it disappear into the firmament. "They know she's here," Maureen whispered, accepting the truth that Finn could not handle. A familiar ache engulfed her heart as she looked back at the terrified father slumped over his child, surrounded by Gladys and Anne. The difficulty of Ailee's journey just went from arduous to near impossible. Thankfully, they had generations of experience to glean from and the resilience and strength that came with the Killian name. Dawn would break in a matter of hours, replacing the darkness with hope.

FINN PACED the sterile white floor of his daughter's hospital room, each step keeping time with the ticking of the clock's second hand. With little time to get dressed, Finn donned yesterday's jeans and the wrinkled t-shirt he wore to bed. His mind moved rapidly, mulling over the previous night's events. He brought his daughter back to Ireland to save her life, not to endanger her further. Doubt flooded his mind. The more he thought about it, the more confused and irritated he became. The more aggravated he became, the faster he paced, searching for answers.

"They'll charge ya for new floorin' if ya keep it up," noted Maureen as she entered the room. "The longer you pace, the less time Ailee has."

"When she wakes up, we're going home. I believe that's best."

"Do ya now?" Maureen placed her warm cup of tea on Ailee's over-the-bed table and then made herself comfortable in the vinyl patient chair beside the bed. "Runnin' away again, are ya?"

"That's not fair."

"The Killian clan have dealt with unfair for fourteen generations. Yer just tippin' yer toe in it."

Stretching his arm along the top of the headboard, Finn studied his daughter's unconscious face. "I should never have tried explaining why we're here."

"Ya told her about the curse?"

"As much as I know, which isn't much." Finn returned to pacing the floor. "I don't know what to do, Maureen."

"Are ya askin', or are ya wallowin'?"

Relinquishing his pride, Finn pressed his back to the wall and prepared himself for what he didn't want to hear. "Asking?"

"Go t'Saydee. She'll know what t'do."

Before he could respond, Molly's image appeared in the window. Finn rushed to the door and threw it open, searching for the ghost from his past. Looking in both directions, she was nowhere to be found. "Did you see her? It was Molly. She was right here." Finn left the room before Maureen could respond.

Shaking her head in bewilderment, she reached for her knitting bag. Maureen needed the relief that knitting provided. A calm washed over her as she slipped the needle into the first stitch on the row. She'd lost count of the number of Aran jumpers she had knitted in her lifetime. Knitting the 'fisherman sweater' in all different sizes, patterns and colors had settled her nerves for years.

Her reminiscing was short-lived once Molly slipped through the door and closed it tight. Maureen watched with curiosity as her granddaughter pressed her back against the wall so no one would see her through the window.

"Aunt Gladys called. I came as quick as I could," she said, slightly out of breath. "How's Ailee?"

"Bumped her head good. She's got a concussion. Luckily, no bones are broken."

"Finn must be so angry with me," she said, covering her face with her hands. "How did this happen?"

"Best guess... a dream spell." Maureen laid her knitting on her lap. It was time for a serious talk. "Ya got him chasin' shadows."

The disapproving tone in her grandmother's voice was hard to accept, but it didn't deter Molly from sticking to the plan—her plan. "The time's not right, Gran."

"How much more time do ya need?" warned Maureen. "They know she's here."

"But do they know who she really is?"

"They did try to kill her. Saydee's protection charm was on the vanity. Gladys found it this morning. She's bringin' it by later."

"The vanity?" exclaimed Molly, bending her knees as she slid her back down the wall. "What good is that?"

"There's more. Finn told her the truth yesterday. What he knows of it." Maureen lifted the knitting needles from her lap and began working a row to ease her mind. "The girl's losin' hope. They both are."

"I shoulda been the one t'tell her," responded Molly, still crouched next to the wall, her head resting in her hands. "It shoulda come from a Killian." Looking up, she asked a question she already knew the answer to. "Why'd he bring her t'see Quinn?"

"I had some doin' in that. Finn's desperate for answers."

"He's not ready for answers." Rising to her feet, Molly stood ready to argue the point as she peeked out the window for signs of Finn's return.

"They need ya, Molly."

"I'm doin' everythin' I can for Ailee. And Finn."

"Your husband needs to know it."

She paced back and forth in front of the door and defended her actions. "I've got t'do it my way. Finn could never understand the world I'm dealin' with."

"He might surprise ya."

Finding herself in the corner of the wall next to the door, Molly moaned as she exhaled to relieve some of the pressure building in her chest. "Warrior or not, Gran, you know what he's like when it comes t'magic."

"I'm sendin' him to see Saydee," Maureen said decisively, expecting no argument from her granddaughter.

"She'll know what t'do." Molly agreed. Standing in silence, she took a moment to study her daughter from across the room. Her pile of regrets continued to grow in size. "I better get back to Quinn."

"How's my grandson doing?"

"His commitment hearin' is next week. I'm hopin', the mental health court will release him t'the care of the family."

"Home where he belongs."

"The secrecy spell is still keepin' him from revealin' the location of the holy well. I shoulda done it when he was younger. Boyle would never have heard of the holy well."

"You know what your Aunt Saydee would say."

"Quit boilin' ya cabbage twice."

"And your protection charm?" Maureen asked, mothering Molly in place of her own mother.

Molly lifted an oak tree pendant from inside her shirt. "Still workin'. Cyrus Boyle grows more powerful by the day."

"Borrowed magic. He's only as powerful as his master allows him t'be."

"He was once a good man. A good doctor."

"It's hard t'resist the dark powers."

"He's still Quinn's primary doctor. Makes it difficult for me t'treat him. I don't have access to his medical records either. No one does."

Maureen noticed Molly checking her watch for the time. "Quinn'll come back to us one day."

"I hope yer right, Gran." With a kiss blown from her hand, Molly reached for the doorknob. "Give my daughter a kiss for me."

"It's not that long a walk," said Maureen, motioning her granddaughter to the bed.

"It'll only make it harder t'do what needs done." Molly slipped out the door as stealthily as she'd arrived. Maureen returned to her knitting, trying not to think of how it would it end. Thankfully, Finn entered the room, bringing a change of thought. "No luck?" enquired Maureen.

"I don't get it. Her daughter's right here. Waiting to be helped. As a nurse, you'd think she'd be right by her side."

Reminded that he didn't know she was a doctor working at Quinn's hospital, Maureen kept it to herself. She'd secretly hoped that their paths would have crossed during his visit. Meddling in family business was a Killian attribute. "Molly's doin' all she can."

"Is she?" Finn approached the bed and the sight of his bruised daughter.

"Ya know what ya have t'do, Finn. Be the warrior of legend."

There was no escaping his namesake. Hanging his head, Finn took a deep breath and gripped the railing attached to her bed. "Tell me she'll be all right."

"She's in good hands. Go t'Saydee. She has what you need. The *Book of Killian*."

Torn between protest and compliance, Finn squeezed the stainless steel railing till his knuckles turned white. His quiet desperation compelled him to leave his daughter's side in search of answers. Kissing her forehead, he picked up his coat and left the room.

Maureen watched through the window as he walked down the long hallway—a lonely silhouette with the weight of the world on his shoulders. "Finn and Molly, two peas in a pod," she whispered. She understood Molly's reasoning for fighting the battle alone but disagreed with her assessment of Finn's readiness.

From the time he was a boy, Maureen delighted in filling Finn's head with the attributes of the legendary Fionn, who tasted the salmon of knowledge and instantly gained wisdom, bravery and enlightenment. Maureen had seen this same acuity in Finn's eyes while growing up. Finn's mother and father died far too young, so Maureen took it upon herself to continually remind him of his heroic potential. As neighbors, she owed his parents that much.

Molly also saw something special in Finn, the best friend of her twin brother. Maureen found solace in recalling her granddaughter's childhood crush that later turned to love. They'd been linked to each other from the time they were children. Even the span of the great Atlantic couldn't break the bond they shared. Resting her knitting needles on her lap, she gently took Ailee's hand in hers, hoping her loving touch would help to bring her back to them.

CHAPTER TEN

Turning off the main roadway, Finn followed the narrow dirt road through a stretch of field in need of tending. The low, blue limestone walls that bordered both sides of the road kept him from straying too far. Ireland's stone walls stood as monuments to their country's farming history. Rocks had to be removed from the earth to till the ground. Using these same rocks to delineate property lines was a practical use for piles of stone.

Flanked by oak trees, Saydee's Irish Georgian home appeared in the distance as he rounded a corner. Time and lack of professional maintenance had taken their toll. The high ceilings of the late 1800s dwelling made it taller than an average two-story home. The ivy growing up the walls partially camouflaged the house from view. Several chimneys protruded from the shingled rooftop like soldiers keeping watch. To the average passerby, the house would appear regal. Finn knew differently.

Leaving the car, he heard the sound of birds screeching overhead. Backing up, he noticed a murder of crows circling the rooftop. His mind drifted to Gran Donnelly's tales of the Morrigan, a trio of war goddesses who took the form of the blackbird to incite warriors on the battlefield. The last thing he needed today was to be incited by crows. Hoping it wasn't a bad omen, he walked to the door.

Once again, the astringent scent of rosemary loomed in the air. Disregarding the magical herb of protection as superstition, he knocked on the door. No answer. He knocked a second time. Pressing his thumb on the latch, he slowly entered the house. The only light in the room was from the open door. "Hello? Hello. Aunt Saydee?"

Needing more light, he made his way through the darkness, tripping over various objects till he reached the curtains. Dust flew in the air as he parted the drapes. Coughing from the particles, Finn turned to see a large painting above the mantel. The light hit it just right, bringing the characters to life.

He remembered the painting from long-ago visits with Molly. It still sent a shiver down his spine. The painting portrayed the powerful Rígan Lár, a fairy queen from the Otherworld, casting a spell on two young lovers. Somehow it was part of the Killian family's bizarre heritage—a story he chose to ignore. Before turning away, he noticed a familiarity in one of the faces. Moving around the cluttered coffee table, he came face to face with the young man's beloved. Her face resembled his daughter Ailee's. Jumping back caused him to trip and fall onto the nearby couch. A puff of dust surrounded him, triggering a second round of coughing. Retreating from the sitting area, Finn refused to look back at the painting. He would chalk the likeness up to bad lighting or the worry he felt for his daughter.

Walking toward the stairs, he noticed sticky notes of all different shapes and colors stuck to the walls and furniture. "Who lives like this?" Finn pulled a note off the end of the handrail. "Add dandelion root." Sticking the note back to the banister, he looked up and around the once majestic U-shaped staircase. A sound came from upstairs. Listening intently, he heard a faint voice. "Aunt Saydee?" No response.

Cautiously, he walked up the stairs. He'd never gone beyond the living room of Saydee's home, so he wasn't sure what to expect. The creaking of each step alerted him to the age of the wood and its years of use. The open doors lining the upstairs hallway provided the necessary light. The wall was lined with portraits: thirteen generations of

Killian men. He stared into the haunted eyes of each one as he passed, reading their names. Aged oil paintings led to black-and-white photos, and finally color. The second to the last portrait he recognized: Seamus Killian, Molly and Quinn's father. Next to Seamus hung an empty frame.

A raspy voice coming through an open door at the end of the hall diverted his attention back to Saydee. The dated hardwood of the second floor groaned beneath his weight as Finn followed the distant voice coming from the doorway. Finding a steep set of stairs to the rooftop, Finn climbed to the open hatch at the top. The hoarse voice was coming from the rooftop. Looking toward the sky filled with circling crows, he carefully pushed his head through the entry. What he found was different from what he expected.

The flat part of the roof was home to an extensive herb garden. Unconventional containers of all shapes and sizes cluttered the area, as well as a set of short rain barrels. Chipped ceramic pots, rusty buckets, dented coffee cans, biscuit tins, cracked pitchers, tarnished tea kettles, and mixing bowls containing chamomile, lemon balm, rosemary, thyme, feverfew, Saint John's wort, and milk thistle, to name a few. His expertise came from years of strolling through floral shops and the wilds of Ireland with Molly as his guide. In the recesses of his mind, he could see her picking a leaf from a branch and lifting it to her nose for further inspection.

A yell from the opposite side of the roof ended his walk through the past. He continued down the small path that snaked through her plant garden until he saw a pair of worn boots with light-colored knee socks bunched around the ankles. Peering around the large chimney, he discovered ropes securing her ankles to the flue. The possibility of Saydee being in trouble caused Finn to reach for his weapon. He found no gun and no holster. Stretching for a better view, he recognized Saydee's trademark style of brightlypatterned culottes paired with a handcrafted sweater. The 1980s fashion proved that the hostage on the roof was Molly's aunt.

Switching positions, he scanned the other side of the chimney for the culprits. No one was in sight. Burned-out candles reduced to piles of wax gave an idea of how long she'd been there. Finn watched as she jerked her head back and forth, up and down, tracing the position of each bird. "Ya keep circlin'. Ya filthy crows. Soon these old bones'll be ripe for the pickin'."

Finn pulled back and lowered his head between his raised knees. "If there were any other way," he muttered, knowing he had to rescue a woman who wronged him years ago. He told himself that now was not the time to dredge up the past. Ailee's future was his only thought as he stepped out from behind the chimney, ready to take on her assailants.

"Ya certainly took yer own sweet time, Finn Donnelly. All that remain are a hand full of days."

Finn moved quickly toward Saydee. Her unruly salt and pepper hair told her age as his fingers worked to unravel the rope knots binding her to the roof.

"Leave the ropes," she advised, her voice gruff from lack of water.

"They could come back at any minute," warned Finn as he cleared the candle stubs from beside her so he could kneel.

"Who ya talkin' about?"

"Whoever left you like this," Finn yelled, trying to understand Saydee's situation. "Why else would you be up here?"

"Lettin' nature take her course."

Finn looked at the crows as well as the approaching dark clouds. The last thing he wanted was to delve deeper into Saydee's world, but there was no other choice. "We have to get off this roof."

"I failed!" she cried to the heavens, shocking Finn with her outburst. "Strike me down!"

"Failed?" he asked, watching the sky for lightning bolts.

"I botched it."

"Botched what?" asked Finn, concluding that she was most likely her own captor.

"I've spent my life preparin' for the fourteenth and final tale."

"Final tale?" asked Finn, providing some separation from her madness by standing up and stepping away from her.

"As the keeper of the book," she said matter of factly.

Lost in a sea of crazy, he used the view of her home's surroundings as a distraction to maintain his fragile patience. "I'm listening."

"Shhh!" ordered Saydee. Carefully, she slipped her hand out of one of the ropes and caught a fly in her grip. She added the insect's carcass to a large pile of dead flies, then slipped her hand back into the rope. "They stole it while I slept."

Stupefied by what he witnessed, Finn had no words.

"Are ya listenin', Finn? The *Book of Killian*'s been stolen."

Her reference to the book piqued Finn's curiosity. Now they were getting somewhere. He squatted back down to learn more. "Maureen mentioned a family book of some kind."

"The *Book of Killian's* more than a mere book. It tells the tales of generations."

"Do we need the book to help Ailee?"

"We do, indeed."

"If you know who stole it, why not just get it back?"

Before Saydee could answer, an explosion rocked the house, knocking Finn off balance and over the edge.

"Finn? Finn. Where'd ya go off to?"

"Help!" he screamed from the roof's edge.

Saydee pulled her hands and feet from the bindings and crawled to the roof's edge. "What are ya doin', Finn?"

"Losing my grip. Hurry!"

She was too weak to pull him up, and there was no time to run to the basement for a ladder. Grabbing her oversized bag, she rummaged through the contents until she found what she sought.

"I can't hang on!" yelled Finn.

Extending her upper body over the roof's edge, she pulled the cork from a small vile and poured droplets onto his hands and arms. "This'll hurt. Not as much as slammin' to the ground, mind ya."

Feeling his fingers slipping, he let go with his right hand to get a new grip. The edge was out of reach. Calling out in pain, he tried desperately to hang on with one hand as his arms began to reshape.

"Let go, Finn."

Staring at her reassuring face, Finn realized he had no choice. He would trust in the one thing he hated more than anything: magic.

"Spread yer wings."

Small bones grew out from the bones in his arms, like limbs growing from the trunk of a tree. Feather's emerged from his skin as it stretched to its max. The agony of his arms changing shape pushed him away from the roof's edge. The pain of becoming a birdman was brutal, but his newly shaped arms saved him from a crippling fall.

Circling the parking area, he worked to control his wings as he floated on the air currents. The exhilaration of flight partially replaced the memory of the painful transformation. Never in his life had he felt such freedom. Catching a different current of air lifted him to new heights. He circumnavigated the house as Saydee watched from the rooftop. Looking down, he could see her cheering with both arms above her head.

Finn could see for miles. Brilliant green farmland divided by stone fences and the occasional home and shed. Brushing over the tops of trees, he felt the leaves comb his belly. The longer he flew, the more fearless he became. His view changed from earth to sky and back again as he rolled over and over. The thrill of flight escaped his mouth with hoots and hollers.

Eventually, the territorial crows joined Finn. Their coos and caws protested the stranger's impersonation of their kind. Taking turns, they began to dive-bomb their enemy. Fighting them off was useless so Finn focused on safely touching down. With precision, he turned his wings ever so carefully to guide his descent.

Landing with a forward-moving momentum, Finn took several running steps before stopping. He studied his wings and tried to wrap his head around what happened. It didn't take him long to return to reality. "So much for not getting sucked into Saydee's world."

Looking to the rooftop, he solicited her help. "Can I get my arms back now?"

"Not a bad test run, Finn!" Smiling, she pulled away from the edge of the roof. Searching the depths of her large bag, she located the proper vessel. An empty tin canister would be the new resting place for her impressive collection of dead flies. "Suppose it wasn't a total loss." Pressing the lid on tight, she placed it in her bag. With her thoughts humming with new hope, she would live to fight another day. It was time to go on the offense.

Trying to keep up with her mental to-do list, she headed straight for the purple coneflower. Pulling out a pair of small pruning sheers, she began collecting echinacea leaves for tea. "A cuppa will set me straight."

"Saydee!" Finn's voice boiled up the stairs and through the open hatch.

"Still so impatient." She stored her herbs and sheers in her bag, then climbed through the hatch and down the stairs. Finn was waiting at the bottom of the steep stairs, slapping his wings against the side of his thighs. Pointing them toward Saydee, he humbled himself enough to ask politely. "Please?"

"I'll whip somethin' up," she answered, walking through the doorway.

"Thank you." The blank frame on the wall still concerned Finn as he walked down the hallway. "This empty frame. Who's it for?" he asked, pointing toward it with his wing.

Molly had placed the family under a sworn oath to keep as much from Finn as possible. Saydee disagreed with her decision, but a promise is a promise. She turned and faced Finn. "The longer I stand here, the longer yer wings remain." Saydee turned and headed down the stairs.

Recognizing the pattern of deflection engaged by the Killian family, Finn gritted his teeth and followed her down the stairs, his long wings dragging behind him. He had better luck getting the truth from criminals in an interrogation room than his own in-laws.

Picking off a sticky note at the end of the banister, Saydee read it out loud. "Dandelion root. That explains it."

Finding the kitchen door askew on one hinge, Saydee shook her head in disbelief. "I hate it when dinner explodes." Even humor couldn't fix the situation. Struggling, she slid the heavy door to the side, allowing them to squeeze through the opening. The bomb site was worse than she had imagined. Standing in silence, they took in the aftermath of the explosion. The shredded curtains waved back and forth through the windows, now empty of glass. Pots and pans cluttered the floor while cooking utensils and knives were skewered into the walls.

The only thing still standing was the colossal iron pot resting on a burner in the middle of the kitchen. Seeing the pot's lid imbedded in the ceiling left nothing to the imagination. They had located the epicenter of the blast. A thick, rust-colored sauce covered everything. "I had a notion or two for this concoction." Saydee wiped her finger through a globule of sauce then placed it in her mouth. Her repulsion was immediate as she spit it on the floor. "It's got a wee bit of a kick."

Finn knew that it wasn't dinner cooking in the cauldron. With a smidgeon of sympathy, he watched her sort through the shambles of her kitchen on her way to the sink.

Wiping the sauce from a used cup, she filled it with water and drank every last drop. Her parched throat found relief in the saturation.

"Afternoon tea's on me," announced Finn, preempting an offer to cook.

"I'll get me scarf."

Before Saydee got too far, Finn reminded her of the glitch in the plan. "It's hard t'pay without fingers."

Taking a deep breath, Saydee sighed as her stomach growled. "Wait here! What I need's in my workshop." She left the kitchen and walked through the sitting room to a short iron gate. Pushing it open, she disappeared down the stairs.

Finn's body felt limp from the transformation and flight. He needed a place to rest that wasn't covered in orange-brown sauce. Walking into the sitting room, he sat in a padded rocking chair near a floor lamp. A bookshelf nearby held some surprising reading material: books on world travel. As far as he knew, Saydee had spent her life within the shores of Ireland. He never imagined she dreamed of far-off places. In front of the books at eye level, he studied what appeared to be Saydee's wedding picture. He had no idea she'd been married.

The glass on the frame was wiped clean of dust, unlike the rest of the picture frames and wooden shelving.

On top of the bookshelf, Finn saw a familiar photo amongst several framed pictures. It was his and Molly's wedding picture. His wings kept the frame at a distance. It was a simple occasion. Family, friends and neighbors gathered to wish them the merriest of life. Maureen's gazebo made the perfect venue, covered in May flowers and greenery. It felt like a fantasy, twenty-four years and a bit later. Allowing his head to fall back, Finn closed his eyes and returned to the dream.

A dream was also on Molly's mind but of a different sort. On the drive back from the hospital, Dr. Killian wracked her scientific brain, trying to think of a way to help Ailee return to consciousness. It didn't take long to transfer her thoughts to more mystical measures. She had to know if Ailee was still under the influence of the dream spell.

Rushing into her small apartment, she dropped her keys on the desk and picked up a framed picture of Ailee as she walked into the back bedroom. Flipping on the light, she opened the closet door to reveal her limited magical workroom. She'd been working with Saydee over the last several months to learn the way of dream spells.

Saydee disapproved of dream spells because of their invasive nature. At least, that's what she told her niece. She had a more compelling reason that she alone was privy to. Eventually, Molly talked her into it for Ailee's sake. She needed a way to get Finn to bring their daughter back to Ireland before her birthday. The idea of influencing him through his dreams seemed less combative than in person. No matter how hard they tried, their combined magic could not bridge the Atlantic Ocean. That's what they assumed.

Reaching for a bottle containing some of the potion left from their last attempt, Molly walked to the twin bed and sat down. She'd never attempted the spell without Saydee nearby to pull her back if something went wrong. She would risk it for Ailee.

Removing the cork, she knocked back a swig and then laid down. Turning her head, she faced the picture of Ailee on the nightstand. She focused intently on her daughter and then closed her eyes. It wasn't long before she sensed the potion's effects working through her mind.

A CRACK of thunder in the darkness led to the howling of the wind. She could feel the gale swirling around her like a dust devil. A blinding lightning strike destroyed the darkness, giving way to a sky filled with turbulent clouds. Molly found herself being devoured by a storm-tossed ocean. Before she could take a breath, a mighty wave engulfed her, carrying her under the water and flipping her hither and thither. Fighting her way to the surface, she searched in every direction until she saw Ailee battling her way through the tepid waves, freestyle.

Molly's tumultuous surroundings suddenly made sense psychiatrically. Relying on her training, the doctor began to psychoanalyze. Everything in her daughter's life had been turned upside down. Subconsciously, Ailee would go to where she felt the most in control: the water. The tempest represented the instability she was feeling in her own life. Competing against the storm was her way of finding control. Molly had arrived just in time. The mental energy her daughter expelled to fight the storm was slowing the healing process. The importance of getting her to more tranquil waters was paramount.

Swimming in Ailee's direction was time-consuming and laborious. After what seemed like hours, her limbs ached like she was halfway through an ultramarathon. Just as Molly would get close, a wave would bury her beneath the water. The span between them grew wider with each wave. Molly's strategy had to change. Saydee had warned her about the instability of using magic within a dream spell. Her advice was to employ it as a last resort. Molly had reached the point of now or never.

Focusing her thoughts, she called upon the friendliest problem solvers of the sea. Given their propensity to swim for deep waters during a storm, it was a long shot. The one thing she had going for her was the dream state and its endless possibilities. Hopefully, her magic would help it along.

Poking its nose above the surface, a good-natured dolphin used its whistle to communicate its agreement to help. Rubbing her hand over its bottlenose snout and up its melon was a sublime experience. Molly was an avid swimmer but had never experienced the dolphin's preferred habitat of warmer waters. Unintentionally, Ailee's dream had become a dream come true for her mother—one less thing on Molly's short bucket list.

Establishing a stream of communication between herself and the dolphin, Molly placed her hand over the lower part of its dorsal fin and pointed toward Ailee. The distance had widened even further since Molly took the time to call for reinforcements. The thrill of riding the waves next to a dolphin was freeing. The weight of her worries washed away with every shallow dive. Before long, the dolphin was swimming alongside her daughter with Molly in tow. Getting her attention was another story. "Ailee!" she yelled, trying to overpower the cracking thunder, howling wind, and Ailee's focus. "Ailee, stop!"

Losing the battle to the storm's roar, she reached over the dolphin as the waves heaved, trying to grab Ailee's wrist at the top of her stroke. Her daughter's wet hand slipped through her grip. It was enough to break her focus.

Pulling her face from the ocean, Ailee wiped the water from her eyes, only to discover that an amiable dolphin had hijacked her training. She felt a kinship as she rubbed her hand down the length of the creature's smooth skin. "Are you my spirit guide?" she asked, continuing to caress the mammal's rubbery hide.

Catching sight of a presence hiding behind the dolphin's dorsal fin, Ailee peered around to investigate. Surprised, she pulled back at the sight of Molly's face. "A mermaid," she cried out like a kid opening gifts on Christmas morning. Ailee watched in fascination as the mythical creature showed herself.

Molly's slicked-back, wet hair framed her alabaster skin, providing the perfect setting to showcase her green eyes. Her likeness to an imagined mermaid was striking. The enjoyment Molly felt from her daughter's childlike curiosity changed to a strange sensation in the lower half of her body. Trying to separate her legs became impossible as a transformation commenced from her waist to her toes. She was becoming the mermaid in Ailee's dream. Trying not to express her alarm, she kept focusing on Ailee as the alteration continued below the water.

"Why are you here?" Ailee hollered, her curiosity turning to suspicion.

"To help ya," called out her mom, concealing the sting in her heart from not being recognized. The thought of her daughter not knowing her identity was unsettling. Reminding herself that she was in a dream helped her cope with Ailee's innocence to her true identity and the change happening to her body. Uncertain of what the truth might do to Ailee's mental state, she eased into a therapy session with her daughter. "Why are ya here?"

"Keeping in shape for racing," she answered loudly. With wariness for their presence, she looked for answers in the dolphin's double-slit pupil.

"Ya picked a tough pool," observed Molly, yelling to elevate her voice above the crack of thunder.

Mesmerized by the moment, neither of them saw the tsunami-sized wave that buried them deep below the surface. The storm was reacting to Ailee's suspicions. Twisted like laundry during a wash cycle, Molly eventually used her new appendage to gain control. Searching the dark ocean for her daughter, she spotted her sinking into the depths. Using her mermaid tale and fin, Molly swam deeper till she came face to face with the lass. The silence of the deep seemed to have washed the cares of the world away, evidenced by her closed eyes and limp body. Taking hold of Ailee's hands, she used the power of her tail to speed them toward the light. The thrust of Molly's fin shot them through the surface and into the gale. Holding her daughter's head above the water, Molly had to act fast. "Ailee. Ailee!" Her screams brought her back to reality. "Are ya all right?"

"I think so," she tried to say between coughs as she wrapped her arms securely around Molly till she got her bearings.

Feeling her daughter's arms wrapped around her neck gave rise to a wave of emotion inside her heart. She fought for the right words. "You're safe, Ailee." Molly used her tail and fin to tread water in the churning waves, hoping their physical connection would steady the tempest. It was up to Ailee to calm the storm. "Talkin' would be easier in a calm sea," she whispered to her ear.

The force of the wind slowly began to lessen as echoes of thunder faded into the distance. The ocean waves returned to a rolling formation, bobbing Ailee and Molly through its highs and lows. The clouds parted just enough to allow rays of breathtaking sunbursts—a sign of hope.

Breaking through the surface, their dolphin friend shot into the air with all its splendor. Ailee loosened her grip on Molly to watch the dolphin celebrate. Within seconds, several other dolphins had joined in the show. The sheer joy in Ailee's countenance said more than words could convey. The fascination of watching them perform was therapeutic, to say the least. Ailee's spirit guides offered healing after the storm.

"Swim with me," requested Ailee, turning to her mermaid friend. Diving below the surface, her daughter kicked up her fin before completely disappearing.

Molly attempted to psychoanalyze her daughter's transformation into a mermaid and what it meant cognitively. Research regarding *dream rebound theory and the processing of emotions* cluttered her mind. Studies concerning *subjective recollections and repressed wishes* lit up her thoughts like newspaper headlines.

The textbook jargon monopolizing her thoughts ended the second she saw Ailee shoot through the ocean's surface with her dolphin friends. The image of sheer freedom blew her analytical mind. Watching Ailee spin about, her open arms cutting through the air, released a part of Doctor Killian that she'd locked away years ago.

Giving into her longing for simpler times, Molly dove beneath the surface and joined in her daughter's merriment. Swimming alongside her daughter washed away her troublesome burdens. Temporarily freed from years of worries about the curse, Molly felt like a kid again. Diving deep, building velocity, and breaching the surface was like nothing she'd ever experienced. They played together for what seemed like hours, exploring tropical coral reefs and hundreds of species of sea life. None of the ocean's wonders compared to spending time with her daughter.

Following Ailee's lead to the surface, Molly found herself in a fresh water lake at the foot of a beautiful waterfall. She watched Ailee pull herself onto a submerged rock, dangling her human limbs in the water. Joining her on a nearby rock, Molly found that her tale and fin had also transformed back to legs. The peacefulness of the waterfall allowed for quiet thought as Molly waited for her daughter to speak.

"You need to go," suggested Ailee.

As much as she wanted to argue the point, she knew pretending to be a friend in her daughter's dream couldn't last forever. "We both need to go."

"Quinn needs you." Ailee looked at her mom with total recognition. "Dad needs you too."

Ailee's dose of candor crashed down on Molly like an unexpected wave. The break in the dam flooded her mind with the reality of the curse, and its far-reaching tentacles. Feeling herself fading from the dream, Molly reached her hand toward Ailee, hoping she'd come with her. "Ailee, please."

She wasn't ready to say goodbye.

"I need a little more time," she whispered, fading from view. "I love you, Mom."

The sound of her daughter's final words echoed through the darkness. "I love you, Mom." Molly refused to wake. The tears forced their way out of the corner of her eyes and down her temples. The heavy weight of facing reality rested on her chest like a boulder. Although their time together was spent in a dream, she would cherish it for the rest of her short life.

The gift of spending time with her daughter beyond the confines of the curse became the motivation she needed. Opening her eyes, she let the tears flow. Her shirt and hair were soaked with sweat as she mopped her forehead dry. Walking into the bathroom, she turned on the shower and then stripped off her clothes. The steam from the shower camouflaged her breakdown as she slammed her fists against the tile. A decade of sobbing poured out like the waterfall of Ailee's dream.

CHAPTER ELEVEN

Singing and whistling an Irish children's song, Quinn limped along, attempting a jig as he made his way down the half-lit hallway, full from tea. *"So now I'm big, I've lots of sense, I'll keep my money and all my pence. I'll find someone t'play for me, I'll dance for my dinner and for my tea."*

Dinner was Quinn's favorite time of the day. Any meal was Quinn's favorite time of the day. His day revolved around eating time. Life in an institution didn't offer much else to look forward to. The game room and daily walks around the yard helped him pass the time, but the days were long. The worst days were therapy days, which seemed to be happening more frequently.

A light showed through the open door of his room at the end of the hall, perplexing Quinn. He always turned off his light and shut his door when leaving. Entering his room, he found Dr. Boyle sitting on his bed, still wearing his brown herringbone jacket with orange and red pinstripes over its matching tweed vest. Zeroing in on one of the vest's black buttons, Quinn avoided the doctor's eyes as best he could. Thinking if he moved slowly enough, Dr. Boyle wouldn't see him back toward the open door. That was not the case, as the door closed on Boyle's command.

"Such a pleasant mood. Tea must have been extra palatable."

"I always like coddle," he responded, pressing his back against the wall and slowly sliding toward the corner.

"Your favorite," said the doctor, using his calm and sympathetic therapy voice. "It reminds you of your childhood. It was your daddy's coddle you loved so much."

"Are we havin' a session?"

"Just a conversation. I brought another favorite." Dr. Boyle pulled out a box of chocolate-covered cherries from behind his back. "Do you want them, Quinn?"

"That'd be grand," he replied from the shadows.

"Come here then."

Quinn left the shadows and sat on the bed, leaving a healthy space between them. He took the box from Boyle's hand and placed it on his lap.

"How has the day been treating you?"

"Fine." His fear of Boyle took second place to the box of cherries.

"I heard you had some visitors yesterday."

Hearing the big hand click twelve, Quinn looked at the industrial clock. 6:00. Quinn had exceptional hearing. He placed the box of chocolates on his nightstand and opened the small drawer. Pulling out a deck of cards, he stood up to leave.

"Where do you think you're off to?"

"Six o'clock." Quinn folded his arms for protection, securing the cards within his grasp. "Time for a game."

"They'll start without you."

"I bring the cards."

"In this facility, I hold the cards." He watched with pleasure as his gravelly voice stopped Quinn in his tracks. "Now, sit down and eat a chocolate."

Quinn recognized his change in tone. He knew it was better to comply than face his ill humor. He opened the box, placed a chocolate in his mouth, and then sat on the bed, chewing nervously. His posture was perfectly straight, like a soldier waiting for inspection.

"Surely you want more."

THE 14TH TALE

Still chewing the first one, Quinn reached for a second and third until his mouth overflowed. Pulling the cards from the box, he shuffled them on the nightstand as he chewed.

Boyle waited for him to swallow, then continued his pursuit of answers. "Your visitors, Quinn. What did they want?"

"Finn's my old friend."

"And the girl?" Boyle slid next to him, closing the gap between them.

"I bring the cards," he said nervously, placing the deck safely back in the box.

"The girl, Quinn!" Boyle stood from the bed and hovered over his victim.

Frightened by his close presence, Quinn shoved a couple more chocolates in his mouth. His only hope was to play dumb and wait for Molly to rescue him.

"Are you trying to make me angry?" he whispered into Quinn's ear, sending chills down his spine.

Quinn shook his head to the opposite, his mouth too full to speak.

Boyle leaned closer, allowing his threatening whisper to carry into his ear a second time. "Do you want me to lose my temper?"

Quinn shook his head "no" as he continued to chew, juices running from the sides of his mouth.

"Why were they here? Tell me!"

Before Quinn could start his answer, Boyle swept his hand passed him, sending him through the air and pinning his back to the wall. With his victim suspended near the high ceiling, Boyle held his position.

The shock of his doctor's use of magic was more alarming than being suspended above the floor. Quinn was used to Boyle's mood changes but had no idea he dealt in magic. "Over again, startin' over again," mumbled Quinn as he stared at the distant floor.

"You know my rule about mumbling." Boyle walked toward him, staring up at his prey. He took great pleasure in the moment like a spider watching a fly caught in its web. "This used to be the Chief

Nursing Officer's room. Remember that, Quinn," he asked, returning to his sympathetic therapy voice.

"Let me down," he begged, searching the room for help while pressing his heels against the wall for support.

Boyle calmly continued his narrative. "I upgraded her living quarters so you could have a room with exceptionally high ceilings."

"Let me down. Please." Realizing his pleading had no effect, he attempted to strike a bargain. "I promise ya I'll be good."

"Face your fear of heights or tell me about the girl," snarled Boyle as he used his dark magic to slide Quinn over the plaster and slam him into the corner. Enjoying his power, Boyle reveled in making Quinn squirm.

Pressed against the ten-foot ceiling, Quinn reached his hands out on both sides, but there was nothing to grab. Drops of sweat fell from his forehead to the linoleum floor. "She... she has..."

"What does she have!" Losing what little patience he had left, Boyle slid his victim back to the center of the wall. "Tell me now!"

"Help me!" yelled Quinn, hoping his sister was still at work. "Help!"

Boyle upped the stakes by spinning Quinn head over heels. Gravity caused his pockets to empty. The protection charm fell from his shirt. Drunk on his own power, Boyle came face to face with Quinn in his upside-down position. Noticing the charm dangling from the end of a silver chain, he placed his hand beneath it. "No one's coming to help you." Ripping the charm from his neck, he gave Quinn one last chance. "Tell me about the girl."

"She has..." Staring into Boyle's brutish face, Quinn strained to hold onto the secret without the extra help of the charm. Boyle's eyes seemed as black as the buttons on his vest. His power was too much for Quinn's weakened state. "She has... the mark."

"The mark?"

"Like her Uncle Quinn," he whispered as he slid his shirt to the side, revealing his oak leaf birthmark.

Boyle turned away from Quinn as he processed the new information. "Molly has a daughter." He knew everything about Quinn but failed to delve into his sister's personal life. Dr. Killian's secret changed everything. Placing Quinn's charm into his vest pocket, he imagined the possibilities. The intrigue was short-lived as a loud knock pulled him from his mental reverie.

"C'mon, Quinn," came a voice through the door. "We need the cards. What's takin' ya so long?"

With a wave of Boyle's hand, Quinn dropped from the wall. Boyle stopped his free fall inches from impact. He couldn't risk an investigation into an accident without reasonable provocation. The panic of the fall rendered Quinn unconscious. Boyle allowed his body to rest in a slump on the linoleum floor.

Stepping over the crumpled heap, the doctor lifted Quinn's pillow from the bed and pulled out the large kitchen knife he'd placed there earlier. Knowing what the night had in store, he laid the blade on the floor beside Quinn's hand. Another outburst would prove to the courts that he wasn't ready to function independently in society. The chocolate-covered cherries would make sure of that. "Sweet nightmares." Boyle picked up the box of hexed chocolates and Quinn's cards, then opened the door. His appearance in the doorway surprised the residents.

"Dr. Boyle. We didn't know." The three men pulled back, slightly cowering in his presence.

Boyle gave them the answer they sought by presenting the deck of cards as a peace offering. "Quinn won't be joining you tonight. He's not feeling much himself."

Sheepishly, one of the men reached out and took the deck of cards from Boyle's hand. Wanting to check in on their friend, they waited for the doctor to leave.

"Move on!" ordered Boyle.

With only one direction to go, they turned in unison and left, each taking a turn to look over their shoulder.

Boyle watched them disappear at the end of the hallway. The power he wielded within his hospital was intoxicating but nowhere near enough. It would never be enough. The Killians held the secret to the motherlode. The key to solving the mystery had been under his nose the entire time: Molly Killian. Mixed feelings fought for relevance as he walked down the hallway. The pace of his heels striking the hard floor increased with each step. For years, he'd envisioned a future with Molly by his side. His advances, however, were always met with polite rejection based on their working relationship. Those days were over. He'd been rejected for the last time.

CHAPTER TWELVE

Leaving the local chipper with their fish-n-chip dinner wrapped up tight, Finn and Saydee walked toward a grassy sitting area. Finn ripped a corner off the top of the paper\ and pulled out a hot piece of potato. The mixture of salt and vinegar on a perfectly deepfried chip took him back to his childhood. "No one makes a chip like the Irish."

"Ta, Finn," responded Saydee, thanking him for dinner.

"Thank you for saving my life. And for my fingers," he joked, wiggling them back and forth.

"They're grand when it comes t'eatin'," responded Saydee as she came to rest on an iron bench. Finn sat beside her, taking in the view of the Gaelic Football field nearby. Finn recalled his love for the game and the club he used to belong to that occupied so many weekend matches. The extreme physical demands of the game made it unlikely he'd ever play again. At his age, cheering on his parish's club from the sidelines would have to suffice.

Saydee pulled a piece from her fish and placed it in her mouth. "Good batter. Fried up how I like it." She continued to eat, allowing Finn a few perfect moments before she got down to business. "I'm surprised ya came t'see me."

"It wasn't my idea."

"Ya still blame me."

"That's not why I'm here, Saydee."

"Hear me out."

"I've left it all behind," he said, turning his body away from her.

"Buryin' yer head in the sand, Finn, won't save yer daughter."

"What would you have me do, mull it over every day?"

"What ya should have done twelve years ago... listen."

"What would I have heard?"

Saydee wrapped the paper around her fish and chips and placed them on the bench beside her. She'd waited for this opportunity for more than a decade. It required finesse. "When the mark of the curse appeared on Ailee's first birthday, Molly came t'me with questions. I gave her the answers she needed t'protect her family."

Setting his dinner aside, Finn stood up to escape the conversation. He'd spent years trying to bury his angry feelings. The idea of traveling down the same road again stole his appetite. "I'm the one who protected Ailee by taking her away from all this."

"Ya think ya got all the answers!" said Saydee, growing impatient with his ignorance and lack of interest in the facts. "Ya think ya closed the book! Inspector Donnelly cracked the case."

"Molly should have come with us!" Finn shouted, turning back to Saydee, his finger pointing at her like a suspect in a line-up. "That's the answer."

She wrapped her hands around Finn's accusatory hand and pulled herself to her feet. "Love kept her here. Love for you, for her daughter, and for Quinn." She held her ground, waiting for Finn to open his mind.

"That's a strange kinda love." Finn attempted to pull away gently, but Saydee's grip was true.

"Sacrifice is the purest form of love," said Saydee with sadness. Releasing his hand, she returned to the bench.

"Sacrifice?" Finn joined her on the bench, finally willing to listen.

"Each generation is affected by the curse. Molly knows what needs t'be done. For years, she's placed herself in harm's way."

"Harm's way?" Taken back by the fact that Molly's life had been in danger since he left, Finn pressed for answers. "How?"

"Evil forces are at work."

"I need more to go on than that," enquired Finn.

"We've battled the forces of darkness for centuries. They'll do whatever it takes t'find the holy well."

"Forces of darkness?" Finn mocked her story as a fairytale as he rose to his feet.

Wiping his forehead in disbelief, he unleashed the next argument. "There are holy wells all over Ireland. What makes this one so special?"

"The healin' well's located where our world and the Otherworld converge. The Inbetween. It's protected by the fairy queen, Rígan Lár herself."

"Here we go," responded Finn, pacing back and forth, his head lowered to the ground. The last thing he wanted was more superstition.

"If evil forces discover the well, it'll be used for power and gain. Ailee's next in line t'drink from the well. Her life's in grave danger."

Continuing to pace, Finn tried to process the latest information. "So not only is Ailee dying from a curse, but evil forces are out to get her?" He wasn't proud of his mocking tone, but the topic of conversation seemed so ridiculous that it reduced him to his baser instincts.

"Molly's managed to keep Ailee a secret. All bets are off with her return t'Ireland."

"What about the book?"

"The *Book of Killian* tells the tale of how the curse came to be and each generation's journey to the well."

"Why would someone want to steal it?"

"It holds the map we need to the holy well."

"So these 'evil forces of darkness' have the map?"

"Won't do 'em any good til they find a way t'read the book. The pages are blank. Only members of the Killian family can see the writing."

"That buys us some time."

"Even now, they're cookin' up a spell t'render the book readable." Saydee rose from the bench as though she were entering a trance.

"They?"

"Dr. Cyrus Boyle and that witch of a nurse, Brón," she answered, staring blankly at the sun closing in on the horizon.

"A good description," agreed Finn, recalling their dust-up at the mental hospital. Finn needed more answers about the *Book of Killian*. "Can the book be compromised?"

"Dark magic's a powerful thing."

"That doesn't answer my question."

"Boyle thinks she serves him. He's got no idea what's awaitin' him."

"How do you know so much about her?"

"That'd be story for another day, Finn," said Saydee as she returned to the bench and picked up both their packages of fish-and-chips, and walked toward the sidewalk.

Getting out in front of her, Finn was unwilling to wait. "The day hasn't ended, and I'm still listening."

Saydee looked away from Finn as she opened the rawest part of her heart. She allowed Finn to see something beyond the eccentric aunt persona he'd known his whole life. "She's been a thorn in my side since I fell in love. We both wanted the same man."

"Did he choose her?"

"He fell in love with me," she answered, smiling at first, then changing her expression to sorrow. "For all the good it did him."

The silence that followed was enough for Finn to stop his line of questioning. He'd never seen Saydee in this light—a woman with a tragic past. She was the nutty hermit, influencing Molly with her wild ideas. His judgment had been sure and swift when he left for the States. Now, it would seem, she had a point. He never took the time to listen. His questioning of Saydee resulted in a mental probe of his prideful misconceptions. "I've been wrong about you. For that, I'm sorry."

The sincerity of Finn's humble apology touched Saydee's heart enough to break her promise to Molly. They were all on the same team and needed to start acting like it. "There's more t'be told about Ailee."

"Tell me."

Slipping her arm through his, she walked him down the sidewalk, giving him the rundown. "The curse falls on the first male child of each generation. Quinn never married, and Molly only had one child. A girl."

"Then why, Ailee?"

"The curse ends with the fourteenth tale, the fourteenth generation."

Finn pulled away from Saydee and came to a stop. With his guts churning, he turned to Saydee, hoping he had heard her wrong. "Ends?"

"Either the curse'll end, or the Killian line will."

"With Ailee." The news was sobering. Covering his mouth, he wasn't sure if he could take any more information. The idea of losing his daughter bent him in half, resting his hands on his knees.

Disregarding his fragile state, Saydee squatted next to him to share the plan brewing in her mind. She had to strike while the iron was hot. "Without the book, the only one who can help is Quinn."

Shaking his head back and forth in opposition, he turned to Saydee with a look of disbelief. "I tried talking to Quinn. He didn't make any sense. I don't think they'll let me near him again."

"So we break him out," Saydee said with every drop of her indomitable courage, then she turned and walked toward the car. She was a woman on a mission, and no one would stand in her way.

The idea of breaking into a psychiatric hospital straightened Finn like he'd just stuck his finger in an electrical receptacle. "That place is a prison!" he hollered after her as she crossed the empty street.

Reaching the car, she threw open the passenger side door as Finn hurried toward her. "Yer the namesake of a great warrior. Start actin' the part!" Saydee demanded as she got in the car, slammed the door and began munching on her chips.

Leaning his hands on the top of the car, he groaned from the reference. "I'll never outgrow it," said Finn, shaking his head at the warrior reference.

Rolling down her window, Saydee poked out her head. "Then grow into it! And do it fast! We've got preparin' t'do."

Walking around the front of the car, Finn maintained eye contact with Saydee through the windshield. Her sage advice was solid. He would need to embrace his inner warrior to save his family. To show his commitment, he stopped in front of the car and dropped out of sight.

Saydee stretched her neck to see beyond the car's bonnet, wondering what he was up to.

Slowly, Finn rose from the ground; his arms outstretched above his head like he was lifting an enormous boulder. Pretending to struggle beneath the weight, he strained his face and quivered his arms. His legs shook like an earthquake had taken control of his limbs. Then with a mighty lunge, he simulated throwing the massive boulder into the air.

Dusting his hands against each other, he walked toward the driver's side door, proud of his reenactment of Fionn, the ancient warrior who created the Isle of Man by throwing a large piece of land into the sea at his enemy.

Clapping her hands together, she applauded his performance as he crawled in behind the wheel. His change in attitude was a welcome sight. Feeling victorious, Saydee picked up Finn's packet of fish and chips and handed it to him. "Eat up."

"Thanks for the brutal pep talk," he remarked, eating the chips voraciously. Even cold, they were delicious. "What's the plan for getting Quinn out?"

"Thinkin' won't do the ploughin' for us," replied Saydee as she pulled apart a piece of battered fish. "I'll pack a bag."

"Are we staying overnight?"

"Different type of bag."

Ignoring the reference to her bag of tricks and potions, Finn retrieved a piece of fish from the paper and bit into it. He was committed to following Saydee's lead whether he agreed with her methods or not. "I hope you know what you're doing."

"Trust in yer family, Finn. We're Ailee's only hope." Saydee's words penetrated another layer of the wall he'd built around his heart. Brick by brick, his family continued their demolition, making inroads with their advances. It was time he joined forces for the greater good, even if it meant accepting the use of magic. He wasn't there yet, but the fact that he was considering it as a viable option showed his progress. With the acceptance of Gladys, he'd been raising Ailee by himself for twelve years. As proud as he was of his progress, no longer having to go it alone felt pretty good.

CHAPTER THIRTEEN

Dressed in matching black turtlenecks from Saydee's closet of vintage clothing, she and Finn snuck through the grove of trees surrounding Boyle's psychiatric hospital. The sky was partly cloudy, allowing them to see shapes with a small amount of natural light. Using flashlights rigged with green filters to cut back on the brightness, they made their way to the forbidding wall. Worn paths, most likely formed by teenage shenanigans, made their clandestine approach easier through the undergrowth.

Before long, they approached the stone wall designed to keep intruders out and residents where they belonged. Spray-painted graffiti on the fortification's lower part showed the trespasser's frequency. Looking to the top of the wall, Saydee and Finn mentally mapped out separate attack plans. The wall was taller on the outside due to the leveling of the ground within the walls. "It's like a fortress," whispered Finn.

"Tis a fortress," clarified Saydee, using her normal volume. "How's it feelin' bein' on the other side of the law, Inspector?"

"It's detective." Dropping to his knees, Finn removed his backpack and unzipped the top while revealing his plan of attack. "If I can get a rope over that large oak limb, we can shimmy to the top."

"Yer not sixty-plus years old with a bad back." Objecting to his plan, Saydee walked toward a nearby boulder and claimed it as her workbench. Facing the opposite direction, she could hear his grunts as he hurled the rope into the air.

"I can go it on my own." Finn continued to toss the rope into the air, missing the limb each time. "It's probably safer that way. Once I get inside it shouldn't take me long to find Quinn."

"Then I'll have two people t'break out," she whispered. Saydee didn't doubt Finn's physical capabilities, only his inexperience in dealing with the menacing powers guarding Quinn. Putting on a low-watt headlight, she began rummaging through her bag for the containers needed to work her magic. Examining each bottle's label, she selected a few from her bag and set them aside.

"What are you doing over there?" asked Finn, happy to have the rope finally secured to the limb.

"Levitation takes preparation," she whispered, thankful for Finn's preoccupation with the rope. Pulling out a small, battery-operated blender, she put in several ingredients and then opened the canister of fly carcasses. "How much do ya weigh?"

"If you're implying I can't climb this rope..."

"How much?"

"One sixty-five, give or take."

The 'give or take' gave her cause for concern, but under the circumstances, some lift was better than no lift. "Now for the piece de' resistance." Putting in the correct measurement of flies, give or take, she pushed the button and let it spin. "The magic of batteries." Using a funnel, she poured the gooey liquid into a bottle with a transfer pipette for a lid. Then she placed everything else back in her bag.

Turning around, she smiled at the sight of Finn trying his hardest to climb the rope. "For heaven's sake. We don't have all night, Finn," she whispered as she approached from behind. Sucking some potion into the pipette, she waited for Finn's feet to drop to the ground for the umpteenth time. Saydee applauded him for his determination, a special ops soldier in Ireland's Army Ranger Wing he was not. Unable to make it very high, his arms gave way again, and he landed on his feet. Taking advantage of Finn's brave failure, Saydee reached as high as she could and squeezed the rubber bulb of the transfer pipette, leaving a dollop of substance on his head that spread quickly. Finn turned to see Saydee holding a bottle in her hand. "Why is my scalp starting to burn?" Nervously, he reached up and touched his head.

"Possible side-effect."

"Side-effect?"

"One of the ingredients is a wee bit unstable."

"What have you done to me?" asked Finn, beginning to panic.

"It'll only be for a short time."

Before he could respond, his feet began to lift off the ground. Finn used his arms to steady himself as he worked to control his balance. "Saydee?"

"Hang onto the rope," she hollered. "We'll be needin' it on the other side."

"How do I stop?" asked Finn, close to the top of the wall.

"I measured for distance accordin' t'yer weight."

Without warning, the elevating stopped, leaving Finn at the mercy of gravity. Reaching out, he wrapped his arms over the top of the wall, hanging on with all his strength. "Sure. Let's use Finn as the test dummy," he muttered, struggling to get some leverage with the toe of his boot.

The ultimate mockery came as Saydee floated by like Mary Poppins with her carpet bag in tow. Landing in a sitting position on top of the wall, she waited for Finn to get a leg up and over the wall so he could join her. "Next time, no give or take when I'm mixin' a potion," she said, chastising him with her pointed finger.

Straddling both sides of the wall, Finn worked to control his reaction to Saydee's advice. Gathering his rope, he lowered it down the inside of the wall. "Should I expect any more surprises tonight?"

"All depends on what we encounter." Seeing Finn rub his burning scalp, she pulled a small tube from her bag. "Give me yer hand."

Skeptical of her motivations, he paused before doing as she asked. Offering up his hand, he watched as she carefully squeezed what appeared to be a lotion-like ointment onto his palm.

"Give it a rub. It'll stop the sting." As Finn followed her direction, Saydee looked down at the stone fairy statues scattered about the yard. The reflection of the night sky against the white stone caused them to stand out from the dark backdrop. "It's worse than I thought."

"What do you see?"

"More than Quinn is trapped within these walls." While Finn was rubbing liniment onto his scalp, Saydee took hold of the rope and slowly repelled into the hospital yard.

Caught off guard by her preemptive move, Finn watched from above while he waited his turn. Staring at the statues reminded him of what Quinn said about the stone figurines being his friends. Shaking off the fantasies of a broken mind, he took hold of the rope and shimmied to the ground. Staggering from the shock of seeing Saydee in her customized, modified pair of night vision goggles, he worked to find his footing. "Who are you, a member of the Irish Defence Forces?"

"I adapted 'em for the supernatural."

"As in... ghosts and goblins?" Finn's response was in jest. He didn't expect an answer.

"Keep yer eye peeled."

In a split-second, Saydee took everything Finn knew from his police training and tossed it out the window. "Can we put aside the strange reality you live in and develop a plan of action?"

"Just keep up." With carpet bag in hand, Saydee disappeared into the yard, moving from statue to statue to conceal their approach. Finn followed close behind with a new appreciation for her tactical skills. He didn't know much about her younger years. The idea of her working in special ops didn't seem so far off. Halfway across the yard, she noticed a light near the gate. She pointed toward it, using hand motions to share her plan with Finn. She waited for the guard at the entrance to turn his back, then signaled for them to run.

Making a mad dash toward the rolled-up door to the kitchen loading dock, they stopped next to the delivery truck. Signaling to Finn to stay put, Saydee watched for the truck driver to walk down the ramp with his dolly full of bags of potatoes and turnips. With the driver's back to them, she and Finn crept alongside the delivery truck, then squeezed through the space between the doorframe and the truck. Finding a hiding place in the adjacent laundry, they eavesdropped on the conversation while waiting for the driver to leave.

"Is the pot hot?" asked the delivery man.

"Ya won't be findin' it cold." The prep cook poured himself a cup of coffee. "It's a strange air tonight."

"Strange?"

"Eerie in a way," the cook explained, reacting to a shiver down his spine. "Stingy Jack must be on the prowl with his burnin' piece of coal."

"None of that. Still got me some road t'travel." Eagerly lifting an empty cup toward the prep cook, the truck driver showed his deep desire for the dark brew. Saydee and Finn watch from the laundry room's shadows as the strangers enjoyed their break in the hospital's large commercial kitchen.

"Last stop?" asked the cook.

"One more delivery and it's home t'the wife."

Walking toward the small table by the wall, the cook placed his cup down and gathered the loose playing cards into a pile. "Fancy a quick game of cards?"

"The usual stakes?"

"So long as Stingy Jack stays away."

Retreating further into the laundry, Finn desperately looked for a way out. The only other doorway led to the outside of the building—the opposite direction of where they wanted to be.

While Finn searched, Saydee remained calm, squatting near the opening to the kitchen. The cook's propensity for superstition was something she could work with. Having said that, a more practical option for accessing the rest of the hospital couldn't hurt. Turning to Finn, Saydee whispered a possibility. "Check for a laundry chute. Some of these old institutions still use 'em." Finn began searching for an access point while Saydee returned to her study of the kitchen. She needed more time to figure out her options.

While checking on the progress of the card game, she spied a rat scurrying between the boxes of produce. Recognizing the serendipitous nature of the moment, she pulled a small plastic squeeze bottle from her bag. After checking the label, she placed it in her pocket and pulled out a particular container of small Cotterite quartz pieces she'd gathered from a quarry in County Cork.

Sinking to the floor, she readied herself to get within striking distance. Crawling on her arms and legs, she moved between the wooden produce boxes like an obstacle course until she reached the bags of potatoes and turnips. Pulling out the biggest ones she could find, she drilled the metallic crystal pieces into the root vegetable's firm flesh by turning the jagged stones round and round. The pattern of pearl-lustered crystals resembled homely faces on the murphies and turnips. Setting them aside for later use, she continued to search every nook and cranny between the burlap bags, boxes and crates.

The sound of the rodent's nibbling caught her attention. Peering into a tight space, she found two rats gnawing on a carrot. Removing the cap from the bottle, she aimed and squeezed the liquid toward the rats. Bullseye! The rodents had no idea what hit them. Closing her eyes, she whispered a charge to the rats. Backing out of the tight crawlspace, Saydee returned to the laundry without being noticed.

"Over here," whispered Finn, loudly enough to get Saydee's attention as he pulled a rolling cart away from the wall. His flashlight revealed a myriad of spiders and cobwebs inside the opening, proving that the chute was not in use.

Saydee counted in her head: three, two, one. The explosion of screams and yells sent Finn back to the doorway. Saydee calmly followed.

Using broomsticks, the two men worked to end the life of the two high-strung rats as they erratically leaped about the kitchen like stars of an animated dance movie. As hard as the men tried, they couldn't get a direct hit.

"A rat's chasing them around the kitchen," whispered Finn. Looking at Saydee with suspicion, he shook his head at his gullibility. "So rats can dance now?"

"Imagine the luck," she replied as she watched with a smile while the rat continued his performance. As humorous as the show was, it wasn't driving the two men from the kitchen as she had hoped.

Saydee quickly whispered an incantation. Her spell fell upon the dressed-up root veggies waiting for their debut. Rising from the floor, the quarts implanted in the potatoes and turnips began to glow with a spooky radiance as the veggies floated across the room. The glowing eyes of the spud closed in on the two men. The cook's superstitious nature went into overdrive as he grabbed onto the delivery driver for dear life. "It's Stingy Jack's lanterns. Run!" The glowing veggies chased him and the driver around the delivery room and then into the yard. The sound of the truck ignition proved Saydee hadn't lost her touch. The truck driver had a fellow passenger for the rest of his route.

Finn looked to Saydee with wonder and disbelief. The night gave him a whole new appreciation for her abilities and talents. If she hadn't served in special ops, she certainly should have.

Responding with a wink, she hurried through the kitchen. Halfway across the floor, she relinquished the rats from duty and let them return to their supper. When they reached the door, Finn placed his hand on the knob before Saydee could grab it. "I'll go first. No telling what's on the other side."

Respecting his need to protect, she moved aside and allowed him to open the door. Just as he stepped into the low-lit hallway, he was body slammed into the wall by a force he didn't see coming. Finn ricocheted off the wall and onto the floor as the small figure continued down the hall at lightning speed. "Get away! Stay away from me!" he screamed.

Lying flat on his back, Finn recognized the voice of the man running down the hall. It was Quinn. Scared for his life, he looked back to see what was chasing his friend. The hallway was empty. Sitting up, he looked to Saydee for answers. "I didn't do anything."

"It's not you he's runnin' from," said Saydee, placing the extra strap to her bag across her body. "Thanks for goin' first." Stepping over his legs, Saydee ran after her nephew.

Confused by her response, Finn shook off the blunt force trauma and pulled himself to his feet. Keeping watch behind him, he staggered down the hallway. By the time Finn caught up to Saydee, she was studying her nephew's movements from outside the recreation room's doorway. Looking over her shoulder, he saw Quinn wielding a large chef's knife through the air. His shirt was torn and bloodstained. He'd done more damage to his own flesh than he had to the creature chasing him. "What's wrong with him?"

"He's under a dream spell." Grappling with the terror of a similar event in her own life, Saydee froze at the sight of Quinn using a kitchen knife to defend himself. The paralyzing effects of the flashback left her speechless.

"What should we do?" asked Finn, concerned Quinn would trip and fall on his knife. Getting no response, Finn took hold of Saydee's shoulders and turned her toward him. "We have to do something!"

"Best guess... he's bein' attacked by a troll," she said, fighting her way back from her disabling memory. "Quinn hates trolls."

"Trolls?" responded Finn, pulling a Swiss army knife from his pack. "I don't see any trolls."

"He does. Unless we break the spell, there's no tellin' the damage he'll do t'himself or us." Making her move, Saydee crawled beneath a nearby card table and opened her bag. "Distract him. I need time."

"Distract him?" Uncertain of his next move, he looked at the small blade on his knife compared to what Quinn was wielding. Folding the blade back into the knife, he placed it in his pocket and prepared to rush him like they were kids playing Rugby. As luck would have it, Quinn dove behind the couch before Finn could get a running start. Seeing an opening, Finn ran across the room and leaped over the sofa. Landing on all fours, he found himself staring down a knife blade pointed at his face. "It's me, Finn."

Pulling back his blade, Quinn's shaking hand kept it drawn. "Ya shouldn't be here."

"I'm taking you home." Finn tried to reason with him while respecting the knife pointed in his direction.

Rising to peer over the sofa, Quinn quickly retreated to his crouched position. "Run while ya still can!"

"Give me the knife, Quinn," demanded Finn as he reached for the weapon. "I'll protect you."

"The troll will kill ya!" Panicked, Quinn crawled backward and peered around the end of the couch. "I'll hold 'em off while ya run."

"There's nothing there!" No sooner had the words left his mouth than the couch in front of them soared across the room. "Run!" yelled Finn, finding himself a believer.

Seeking another cover, they fled their position. Finn dove over the couch on the opposite side of the room expecting Quinn to follow. Looking back, Quinn stood his ground, fighting with the vigor of a man in his twenties. "Run, Finn!" He was fighting to save his friend. Humbled by the sight, Finn searched the room for a way to battle the invisible creature. The presence of smoke alerted him to a possible fire. He watched in awe as Saydee triumphantly rose from the floor, her hands outstretched, controlling the milky white fog rising from her mixing bowl—her fierce expression showed her readiness for battle.

Swirling her hands around each other, she directed the mystical fog to wrap around Quinn like a boa. Once the mist had wholly encircled her nephew, Saydee released the lyrics of her spell on the wings of a familiar melody. "Fog, like songs of sweetest note, all around him gently float." She hoped the tune to the traditional Irish children's song, Báidín Fheilimí, would lull him off to sleep. It seemed fitting to battle dark magic with the voice of an angel.

The dark magic in Quinn's dream spell grew more savage in his fight against Saydee's counter spell. Quinn continued to swing the knife at the troll, slicing the air in every direction. Turning to and fro, he fought with the fierceness of a lion protecting its cub. In this case, his best friend. Quinn's knife grazed his arms and chest as he tried to cut the troll's strangling grip from his neck.

In response, Saydee raised the level of her enchanting voice as she caroled the words of her spell. "Take away his dream of fear. Let his thoughts ring calm and clear." Her skin took on a translucent shine as though she were channeling the mother goddess of the Tuatha Dé Danann.

Staggering and spent, Quinn refused to back down. He lunged awkwardly in every direction, brandishing his knife like a sword until he had nothing to give. Stopping in the center of the room, he raised his knife above him and pointed it at his chest. Losing the fight, he looked to Saydee in desperation. Finn ran toward him to grab the knife, but Saydee held him back with her magic. It took every particle of power she had to continue the spell while keeping Finn at bay. Her hand trembled from the exertion of holding him in place. Even with that, her beautiful voice continued to fill the room. "Release the knife with its dangerous blade. Go to sleep till the nightmare fades."

Quinn had to end the fight on his own, or the dream spell would continue until his demise. Quinn released the knife with a smile of gratitude to his protector and aunt. Finn watched it drop to the floor, landing point-down. Feeling Saydee's release, he rushed to Quinn, catching him in his arms. Laying Quinn aside, Finn pulled the knife from the floor and defended them from the invisible creature. "Is it gone!"

"It was only ever in Quinn's mind," whispered Saydee as she dropped to her knees from sheer exhaustion.

"But the couch?"

"Quinn's doin'," she explained, trying to catch her breath. "Dream spells are powerful. They affect a part of the mind we don't fully understand."

"Fully understand?" questioned Finn, tossing the knife aside. Finn lifted Quinn's unconscious body into his arms. "How is any of this understandable?" Walking toward a desk chair, he placed Quinn's limp, war-torn body in the seat. Using his pocket knife, he cut a strip from the curtains and wrapped it around Quinn's chest, securing him to the back of the chair. "Is he going to be all right?"

"Define, 'all right.'" Still on her hands and knees, Saydee gathered the tools of her trade and returned them to her bag. "We've got t'go." Offering her hand to Finn, he gallantly helped her to her feet and steadied her till she felt secure.

"There's another desk chair over there if you need it."

"It'll be a dark day when ya roll me away from a battle." Weakened but proud, she straightened her spine and walked to the door. Checking both directions, Saydee placed her bag's strap across her body and motioned for Finn to follow. Pushing a desk chair down the low-lit hallway posed more challenges than anticipated. The chair's five wheels seemed to each have a mind of their own, evidenced by its zigzag path. Finn fought to maintain control as he tried to keep up with Saydee. The sound of the chair rolling over the vinyl flooring made a stealthy exit nearly impossible. All they could do was run faster.

Nurse Brón threw open the door and stepped out of her room, holding a wine glass in her hand. She was just in time to see the dark figures disappear around a corner. Hoping to cut them off, she put her glass down and picked up a radio. Hurrying down an adjacent hallway, she called for security. The idea of a break-in or break-out was not happening on her watch.

As Saydee and Finn neared the exit door, the yard security lights lit up the hallway through the windows. "They know we're here," surmised Finn, stating the obvious.

"This is why I don't plan," remarked Saydee, putting her mind to the test as she peered into her open bag.

"What now?" asked Finn, expecting her to pull out a magic fix for their problem. Before Saydee could answer, Molly cried out from down the hallway. "C'mere!" Startled by the familiar voice, Finn turned to see his wife, Molly, waving them in her direction.

"Leave it to a Killian to be in the right place at the right time," remarked Saydee, hurrying toward her niece. "C'mon, Finn!" she hollered over her shoulder as she ran.

Grabbing the back of the chair, Finn swung Quinn around and pushed him back down the hallway. Concentrating on trying to control the chair temporarily held Finn's focus. The minute he came face to face with Molly, he slipped into interrogation mode. "What are you doing here?"

"Gettin' the three of ya out," she answered, signaling them to follow her through the swinging double doors.

"How'd she get in?" asked Finn, watching her through the glass in the doors as she ran through the cafeteria.

"Molly works here," said Saydee, opening the door as she passed. "We had to keep Quinn safe. And his secrets."

"What's your definition of safe?" he rebutted, putting his need for answers above their safety.

"C'mon, Finn!" Letting go of the swinging doors, Saydee followed her niece's escape route. Her words were enough to snap Finn back to reality. Realizing he was the only one left in the hallway, Finn pushed Quinn through the doors and into the cafeteria.

Molly waited for them to catch up then led them into a cleaning closet. "We don't have much time." Opening the closet door, she motioned them forward. Once inside, she turned on her flashlight and walked toward the back wall. "Help me, Finn." Finn cleared enough room to get to the wall by moving industrial-size boxes of paper products. Turning back to Molly, Finn shared his findings. "There's no way out."

"I discovered an old tunnel several years ago. It helps when I need to sneak in and out unnoticed." Molly squeezed passed Finn and placed her hand against the wall. A concealed door opened, revealing a set of stone steps.

"Well done, Molly," praised Saydee as she dawned her customized headlight and stepped through the doorway.

Finn leaned through the opening with his flashlight to inspect their getaway route. Seeing a set of stone steps, Finn knew what he needed to do. "Looks like I'm carrying Quinn."

Molly untied the piece of curtain fabric, holding her brother to the chair as Finn returned to help. "A desk chair?" asked Molly in jest. "Yer in a hospital. Ya couldn't have found a wheelchair?"

"It did the job, didn't it?" Hoisting Quinn over his shoulder was easy compared to controlling his disposition. "Ladies first."

Molly stepped through the opening, manning her flashlight and Saydee's. The rock stairs were steep so Molly crept down sideways, shining a light on both sides. "Are ya all right, Finn?"

"I've got him," reassuring Molly of her brother's safety.

"Take it slow," she advised. "No one knows of this passageway. We'll be safe for a while." The rock walls and stone steps were a shade slick from the moisture found in the damp tunnel. Molly made sure she found her footing before taking each new step. Going slow forced Finn to do the same.

"How long have you been a nurse here?" Finn used his free hand to steady himself against the wall as he followed Molly's light pattern.

"I began internin' while I was in med school. Once I graduated, I got a residency."

"A doctor?" Finn stopped. The news came as a shock.

"For some time now."

Her matter-of-fact delivery took him aback. Trying to hide his thoughts, he readjusted Quinn's body position as a distraction. While he was busy raising their child, she was busy advancing her career. Shaking off his disagreeable thoughts, he attempted to understand. "All that for Quinn?"

"Ailee's life may well depend on my brother."

"As hard as it is for me to admit, your daughter needs you as much as Quinn."

"Ya don't think I know that?" responded Molly, shining the light in Finn's face.

Blocking the light with his hand, Finn acknowledged his struggle. "I don't know what to think."

"What's takin' so long," hollered Saydee from the bottom of the stairs.

Lowering the light, Molly switched tactics as she continued her descent. "I caught sight of Ailee when ya came to see Quinn. She's beautiful."

"She got that from her mum."

"Her sharp wit came from her dad."

"We don't laugh as much as we used to."

Returning to the bottom of the stairs, Saydee tapped the toe of her boot against the hard floor. Her message to hurry up echoed off the walls. She knew they couldn't hide forever. The tunnel was feeling more and more like their sepulcher.

Once Finn and Molly reached the rock floor, their speed increased. The weight of Quinn's body over Finn's shoulder was beginning to take a toll. Relying on his inner warrior, he pushed through the pain in his back.

A junction in the tunnel stopped Saydee. "Which way?"

"Keep going' straight t'the cellar hatch," instructed Molly. "That tunnel leads to a boarded-up entrance t'the basement."

Once they reached the end of the tunnel, Saydee strained to push open the two flat doors above her. "Fresh air at last." Six steps later, she was free of the tunnel. Kneeling on the ground, she turned and offered her assistance to Finn.

Molly stepped aside for Finn to pass. "The trees'll provide cover for yer escape."

Taking the first step, Finn looked back at Molly. "Come with us."

"Not now."

"Why am I always asking, and you're always saying no?" Realizing the answer would never come, Finn carried Quinn up the steps.

"Finn," Molly called in desperation.

Hopeful, her husband turned back from the top.

"You and Ailee will laugh again," she promised before disappearing into the darkness.

Her last words to Finn were optimistic yet haunting. Finn stood his ground,

unable to move. He promised himself he would never reopen his heart, but the sight of Molly had melted the latch. He could feel it breaking all over again.

Needing Finn to focus on their escape, Saydee shut the cellar doors. "We've gotta go!" Her urgency ended his self-inflicted trance but did nothing for his heavy heart. Readjusting Quinn's limp body, Finn turned toward the woods and never looked back.

Isolated, Molly walked through the dark silence with painful memories as her only companion. She tried to ignore the constant ache inside for what felt like a lifespan, wearing a brave face for her family and herself. The same brave face displayed by generations of Killian ancestors. Every birthday, every holiday, Molly watched her daughter grow through pictures and swimming stats as she waited each week for letters from Gladys. For more than a decade, her heart ached from the separation.

The card she'd been dealt was cruel, but there was no turning back. She alone would save her family.

In agony, she poured out her heart, but the stone walls offered no comfort, only privacy. Turning off her flashlight, she sobbed in the darkness until she surrendered to exhaustion. Lacking the energy to move, Molly drifted off to sleep on the cool stone steps of what felt like her tomb.

CHAPTER FOURTEEN

Furious over Quinn's escape, Cyrus Boyle slammed his fist onto the workbench, rattling the beakers and trays. "First, we steal a book we can't read," he yelled toward the ceiling, fully expecting to be heard. "Now, Quinn's been stolen right from under our noses." Dressed in the same tweed suit he wore throughout the day, the doctor walked toward his bookshelf to compose himself. "Where's Molly?"

Nurse Brón approached from the open doorway to his lab like an apparition advancing from the shadows. The diagonal gathers of her black knit top, wrapped snuggly around her long waist, contrasted with her loose, wide-legged, black slacks. "Forget Quinn and Molly. It's the girl we need."

Unable to relinquish the betrayal, Boyle removed his suit jacket and threw it at a nearby chair. "How dare she hide a child from me?" he yelled, rolling up the sleeves of his white shirt.

"You can't blame yourself," the nurse said in a more soothing voice. The tactic of expressing empathy was a characteristic she knew nothing about. She continued undaunted. "Her aunt's secrecy charms are powerful."

"Wretched woman!"

Using a more personable approach was all she could think of to break Molly's hold over him. Releasing the two pins from her tight updo allowed her two-tone hair to fall across her shoulders. "She'll need to drink from the healing well soon."

"Who?" he asked, seeing Nurse Brón in a new light. It wasn't long before Boyle became mesmerized by the wheels of her cunning mind spinning in the pools of her eyes. The pleasure on her face furthered his interest. "What scheme are you conjuring?

The nurse continued testing her new theory, hoping he'd bite. She placed her lips near his ear and whispered just enough of her plan to keep him dangling from the hook. "The girl is the key to finding the well." Placing the palm of her hand gently against the doctor's heart, she crossed the line between business and pleasure. "It's pumping through her veins."

"I'm not following," he probed, his breathing labored.

"You will." Raising her hand to the knot of his necktie, she loosened his tie and unbuttoned his shirt collar. "Once we have her in our possession."

"Then it's only right we extend an invitation," he responded, hypnotized by her enticing touch.

Commanding Boyle's attention away from Molly gave the nurse great pleasure. She was his weak link. Stepping back from the doctor, Nurse Brón turned for the door. "I'll see to her invitation personally," she said, disappearing into the dark as mysteriously as she arrived.

Looking around the low-lit room, Boyle took a moment to cool his jets. After shaking off the nurse's bewitching influence, he walked from his lab into his office. Collapsing into his desk chair, he opened a drawer and pulled out a picture of himself with Molly. Years had passed since Molly stormed into his office to protest her twin brother's confinement to his facility.

YEARS EARLIER

Heavy rain slithered down the window, blurring Dr. Boyle's view of the parking lot as he watched for the arrival of Molly Killian. He waited with bated breath for the rush of adrenaline her outrage would deliver. Another destructive brawl in a local pub led to her brother's arrest. As his mental health advocate, he rushed to court after being summoned. Quinn's out-of-control behavior resulted in a ruling for involuntary commitment to the Boyle Psychiatric Hospital.

WATCHING *for Molly had become a weekly ritual for Cyrus Boyle. The worn spot on the hardwood floor would attest to his obsession. Quinn's therapy session took a backseat to his beautiful sister, who delivered him with exact punctuality. On Thursdays, he pulled out all the stops: best suit, planned topics of conversation and heaps of bedside manner. Still, his efforts were in vain. No matter how hard he tried, she kept a wall between them.*

She preferred waiting in the meditation garden near the entrance to the building, so Boyle rearranged his treatment room so he could watch her wander through the gardens. Quinn was never the wiser.

Her sadness amplified his attraction, drawing him into her sorrow. Her symptoms manifested themselves as a sort of melancholia. Quinn's revelation about his sister's grief from losing her husband stopped him short of that diagnosis. From a doctor's perspective, he understood the shock her mind was dealing with and the emotions it was creating. But the treatment wasn't his motivation.

Her vulnerability was intoxicating, and he used it to gain her trust slowly. He offered Molly nursing positions at his hospital and generous amounts of pay but each time, she declined. Boyle had all but given up when a phone call from the local magistrate about Quinn's behavior gave him a new opportunity. He hoped Quinn's confinement to his hospital would advance their relationship.

THE SOUND of Molly's tires screeching against the wet concrete relieved his longing. He watched her run from the car, the pouring rain blending with her tears, her heart pounding in her chest. He could feel her angst from the second-floor window. He'd already given orders to have her escorted to his private office, so he busied himself as he waited for the door to fly open.

"How could ya let this happen?" Molly's accusation flew across the room as she pushed past his administrative assistant.

Feigning empathy, Dr. Boyle rose from his chair and went to her aid. "I'm as upset as you are."

"What happened?"

"I'm still wading through the police report. I plan to examine Quinn later this afternoon."

"I need t'see him," she pleaded.

"He's been heavily sedated. We're letting him sleep it off."

"He was doin' so well," she said in disbelief as she turned away.

"Please, have a seat." Boyle led her to a dark leather loveseat in the sitting area. "I'll have someone bring you a towel."

"I'm fine," she responded, quivering as she stood beside the two-seat sofa.

"It won't help Quinn to see you like this." Boyle picked up a throw blanket and wrapped it around her wet shoulders, encouraging her to sit at the same time. "I have some hot tea if you're interested."

Molly watched him fill two dainty teacups and then add cream and sugar without asking her preference. He placed the cup and saucer in her hand and settled in next to her. "What can I do to help you through this?"

"I need answers."

"Of course."

"How long will he be here?" she asked, her trembling hand splashing a bit of tea from her cup.

Dr. Boyle used a linen to wipe the drops of tea from his pant leg. "I meet with the magistrate this afternoon. I'll know more then."

Placing the teacup on the tray, Molly leaned forward, covering her face with her hands. "I'm sorry." The fight to cure Quinn had gone on for years. Her battle fatigue was real.

"Don't apologize."

"Quinn's pain breaks my heart," she whispered through her tears.

Reading her vulnerability as a sign, Dr. Boyle placed his arm around her shoulder and pulled her toward him. She sobbed in the presumed safety of his arms. The euphoria he felt from being her knight in shining armor was better than any drug on the market. He couldn't remember the last time he felt so giddy.

After allowing for an acceptable amount of consolation, Boyle moved on to his next tactic. "Quinn tells me you've enrolled in medical school."

"Not sure why," she responded with a vote of no confidence. Molly pulled herself away from Boyle in search of a tissue. A perfectly folded handkerchief presented itself before she stretched for the box. "Thank you."

"You'll make a good doctor."

"I'm considerin' psychiatry. For Quinn."

Her revelation impacted Dr. Boyle like a kid on Christmas morning. Rising from the couch, he paced back and forth behind her while she wiped her tears and gained control. Boyle wanted a prestigious education, so he attended Oxford University Medical School for his Pre-Clinicals. He did his Clinicals at the John Radcliffe Hospital in Headington, Oxford, focusing on psychiatry in his fifth year. He returned to Ireland for his residency with lofty goals and a proper pattern of speech. "Several of the psych professors at university are colleagues of mine. I'd be happy to put in a word."

"That's kind of ya," responded Molly as she rose from the couch and returned his handkerchief. Sensing an overstep of boundaries, she returned to her independent mind. "I'd rather make my own way." With her composure salvaged, Molly walked toward the door. "I'll be back in the mornin' t'see Quinn."

As soon as she left his office, Dr. Cyrus Boyle was on the phone with his university colleagues. He couldn't resist the opportunity to ingratiate himself in Molly's good graces. He hoped his wheeling and dealing and the calling in of favors would create a deal even Molly's independent spirit couldn't refuse.

As PROMISED, Molly was waiting at the entrance when the medical receptionist turned the lock the following morning. She'd come prepared with her leather messenger bag full of documentation and notes regarding her brother's earliest treatments. "Quinn Killian's room number, please," she requested, approaching the nurse's station. With no time to do her hair, Molly tucked it beneath a plaid newsboy hat that matched her waistlength cape.

"I'll let Dr. Boyle know yer here." She dialed the extension before finishing her sentence, leaving Molly no choice but to wait. Within a few minutes, she saw him making his way down the long hall. Embarrassed by her lack of decorum during their last visit, she hoped to start on a fresh note.

"Quinn's finishing his breakfast. He'll meet us in the yard." Dr. Boyle turned to leave, expecting Molly to follow.

"I don't mind visitin' while he eats."

"Protocol, Ms. Killian, he won't be long."

"I prefer Molly."

Molly joined the doctor, walking side by side down the hallway. "What did ya find out from the magistrate?"

"He wants to re-evaluate after six months."

"Six months?" Molly stopped in demand of a reason for the length of time.

"The frequency of his outbursts has been increasing."

"I don't get it," argued Molly, allowing passage for an orderly driving a laundry cart. The security of the wall against her back helped to steady her position. "He's been improvin' for years."

"Having him here twenty-four/seven should help us diagnose what's changed." Staring at each other from opposite walls, they waited for more personnel to pass through with their various carts and beds. "The mornings are always the busiest. We'll have more privacy in the yard." Dr. Boyle led the way as he weaved through the traffic of staff. Molly followed closely, taking in the sights and sounds.

All the times she'd chauffeured Quinn to his sessions, she'd never been past the nurse's station near the front door. She preferred the freedom of the outdoors to the confinement of stone walls. By the time she reached the end of the hallway, she was finding it difficult to breathe. The time she spent visiting Quinn in a similar hospital years earlier had left an indelible impression. The relief she felt from seeing the doors open was liberating.

Surrounded by a high stone wall covered in ivy, the sizable yard was a peaceful spot where patients could connect with nature. Large trees growing on the outside of the wall supplied some shade. Molly's private anxiety began to melt into the solace of the grounds as she followed the doctor into the yard. The layout was simple: no yard art, no flower gardens, no statues and no distractions. An ornate stone fountain stood as the centerpiece, with several benches scattered about. The soothing sound of running water from the nearby fount helped to calm her nerves.

Dr. Boyle led her to a sitting area designed for meditation and thought. "It won't be long."

Molly accepted the invitation to join him on a cold, iron bench out of professional courtesy. The seat was wet with dew, so she tucked her wrap-around-cape beneath her before sitting. There was nothing she could do about her wet shoes. "Will my brother have access t'the yard?"

He leaned in to comfort her aching heart by holding her hand. "Of course. We encourage our patients to spend as much time outdoors as they like."

Daybreak's soft light gave a ray of hope to the grim darkness of Quinn's confinement. "Are the six months dependent on his progress?"

"It's mandatory. His progress within that period will determine your brother's release at the end of the six months."

Sliding her hand from beneath his grip, Molly reached into her bag and pulled out a small notepad and pen. "And visitin' hours?"

"Until we get a handle on what's triggering Quinn, visiting hours must be limited."

"He needs his family," she argued, rising from the bench and walking away. The delight Boyle felt from Molly's need for comfort increased. Jumping up, he followed her to the fountain. "As his doctor, my goal is to get him back to you as soon as medically possible."

"What can we do for him?" she asked, sitting on the outer rim of the fountain. Molly placed her messenger bag on her lap and wrapped her arms around it for strength.

"It's neither society nor your family's responsibility to create an environment where he can function." Boyle lowered himself to the fountain wall and turned to her with as much sincerity in his eyes as he could muster. "Quinn has to learn to live without being touched off, or at least be able to control the impact of certain triggers through therapy and medication."

"And ya think that's possible?"

"Based on his history, yes." The thrill of earning her respect by saying all the right things was a rousing way to start his day.

"I need t'be a part of his life."

"I have a proposal if you're interested." Boyle stood up to present his offer from a more powerful position. "Would a paid internship here at my hospital interest you while attending medical school?"

Her curiosity was piqued as she rose from the fountain to join him. "Doin' what?"

"What you do best. Nursing. Primarily." Slowly, Boyle took a step, hoping she would walk with him. "An educational internship would allow you to observe certain sessions, sit in on consultations and eventually participate in morning rounds. Take part in what we do as psychiatrists."

"Is that ethical?" she asked, walking next to him, her bag still wrapped in her arms.

"With signed consents and attention to patient confidentiality." Pausing before taking another step, Boyle assured her his plan was doable.

"And the university would be all right with an internship before completin' med school?" she asked with great hope.

"Consider it nursing duties with educational perks."

Emboldened by the idea of working near Quinn in a more prominent role was more than she expected. Turning to Boyle, the sparkle in her eyes expressed her gratitude. "That would allow me t'be part of his treatment."

"With limitations, but far more than just a visitor or a nurse."

"I'd like that, Dr. Boyle." Molly's joy increased at the sight of her brother sticking his head out the door and shielding his eyes from the sun.

"I'll clear it with my colleagues at university," said Boyle, distracting her from Quinn.

Turning back to Boyle, she cautioned him with a touch to his upper arm. "I haven't been accepted yet."

"Of course, Molly. We'll wait."

"Thank ya for everythin'," she said before returning her attention to her brother being led from the building by a large orderly. Seeing him in his robe, pajamas and bare feet took her back to visits as a young teenager. He'd preferred bare feet to shoes for most of his life.

Molly rushed toward him, embracing her twin brother with her whole heart. They strolled through the yard, trying to dissect the circumstances of his compulsory commitment. The death of their father fractured Quinn in a way that even the love of his family couldn't fix. As his twin sister, they had been in each other's lives since birth. One thing was for sure. There was nothing she wouldn't do to help her brother find his way back to their family. Nothing.

GRATIFIED with the result of his conversation with Molly, Boyle happily bounced up the stairs and strolled down the hall to his office. The hallway's fluorescent light cast his long shadow on the floor of the low-lit office as he stopped in the doorway. He briefly assessed the stranger, who had made herself comfortable in the chair facing his desk. The tight bun on the back of her head contained every strand of her platinum-blonde hair with broad red streaks. "Who let you in my office?"

"I did," said the mysterious woman, maintaining her perfect posture as she rose to a nearly six-foot stature. Dressed as though she were attending a funeral, she held a yellow-brown manilla folder in front of her. "The door was open."

The doctor couldn't argue the point. He'd rushed from his office when he saw Molly's car pull into the parking lot and couldn't remember closing the door. Sizing her up from head to toe, he felt a strange intimidation as he walked toward his desk. Sitting in his chair helped him feel more in charge. Pointing to the opposite chair, he invited her to join him. "Did we have an appointment?"

"An interview for the position of Chief Nursing Officer." Confidently, she sat down and laid the folder across her lap.

"Our current CNO's on holiday. She's due back Monday." Grateful for the call alert, he reached for his desk phone before it could beep twice. "This is Dr. Boyle." Realizing the severe nature of the call, he turned his chair ninety degrees to find some privacy from his interviewee's intimidating leer. "Broken! Both legs? What happened?" Taking in the grizzly details of her fall and ensuing damage, Boyle rubbed his forehead with his fingertips. Administratively, he weighed the gravity of his matron's long-term medical absence. "Keep me appraised."

Turning back, Boyle reverted to his professional tone as though nothing had happened. "It appears my Chief Nursing Officer was involved in an accident on vacation. The prognosis is positive."

"She's alive?" mentioned the stranger, seemingly surprised as she leaned toward the desk. Her eyes moved from side to side, mimicking the thoughts rushing through her head. "She has luck on her side."

"Thankfully so."

"Especially from that height," she whispered, tapping her long nails against the wooden surface of his desk.

"How do you..."

"I heard the other end of the conversation," she mentioned, leaning back into her chair and lacing her fingers together. "A third-floor balcony."

"Unnerved by her strange behavior, Boyle determined it was time to end their conversation. "Leave your CV with my secretary. We'll be in touch."

"Your hospital's in dire need of a permanent CNO."

"Temporary CNO," he corrected, rising to his feet and placing his hands on the desk as a barrier to further communication. "Internal restructuring will suffice for the time being."

"I came prepared for an interview, Dr. Boyle." Opening the folder on her lap, she carefully picked up her single-sheet resume and held it out for him to take. "The least you could do is have a look." She waited for him to return to his chair. Pursing her lips, she blew across the top of the paper as Boyle leaned forward to accept the CV. A fine dust of minuscule crystals left the form and entered his nostrils and eyes, causing him to nearly sneeze. Controlling the urge, he shook his head at the strange sensation winding through the connected neurons of his brain. Boyle rubbed his eyes, then returned to the conversation. "Allergies."

"My resume?"

"Let's see," he responded, scanning her list of past employment. "Your work experience is impressive."

"Unless you have any questions, I'll plan on filling the position first thing Monday morning," she said, rising from her chair. "I'll deliver my CV to your HR person on my way out."

"That'll be...," muttered Boyle, trying to access his fuzzy brain as he handed her the paper. "That'll be fine, Ms?"

"Nurse Brón will do." Stepping away from his desk, she turned back with some medical advice. "You may want to take something for those allergies."

Boyle watched her walk across the room like a model on the runway, her heels clicking in measured cadence. She appeared and vanished like a swift weather pattern, leaving a fog in his brain that he couldn't shake. Opening his drawer, he pulled out his allergy medication to battle his confusion. After consuming two pills and a glass of water, he swiveled himself away from his desk and closed his eyes.

CHAPTER FIFTEEN

Twenty-four hours had passed since Ailee's fall from the balcony, and still, she slept. Gladys sat crocheting next to Maureen, whose knitting project had progressed nicely. Putting her crocheting aside, Gladys stretched her body. "I think I'll walk down to the cafeteria. Would you like something, Mum?"

"Another cuppa would hit the spot."

"Aunt Glady?" called Ailee in a sleepy voice.

Gladys jumped from her chair and hurried to the bedside. "Ailee? Ya had us worried." Stroking her hair and squeezing her hand, Gladys let her niece know she was by her side.

"Where am I?"

"The hospital," answered Gladys. "Ya took a nasty fall."

"I don't remember."

"No bother, nothin's broken." Letting go of her hand, she poured her a glass of water as Maureen used the control to lift the back of her bed. No one was better at caring for Ailee than Gladys. She knew her wants and needs better than her own. "Drink up. Nurse's orders."

Taking the last swallow, Ailee placed the cup back in Gladys' outstretched hand. "Where's Dad?" she asked, trying to adjust herself to a more suitable position. The pain of her bruised muscles put an abrupt end to her attempt. Rearranging the pillows, Gladys worked to make her more comfortable. "He's takin' care of business. Don't be worryin' yerself."

"Business to do with me?" Ailee noticed the glance exchanged between her aunt and her great-gran. "I'm not a child."

"Gladys was headin' to the cafeteria," explained Maureen as she folded the top of her blanket into a straight fold. "Fancy somethin' t'eat?"

"I'm starving." Ailee looked at the clock. "Is it still open?"

"I have it on good authority they are. But only for biscuits and milk," said Gladys, walking to her chair to retrieve her purse.

"Are they as good as your cookies?"

Returning to Ailee's bedside, Gladys' treated the situation as though they were still in there Somerville home in the States. "Beggars can't be choosers."

"I'm so hungry, I'll eat anything."

Gladys kissed Ailee gently on the forehead and left the room. "That's my girl." Walking on sunshine, Gladys opened the door and left the room. The bounce to her step continued down the hall.

The bond between Ailee and her aunt warmed Maureen's heart. She'd watched the relationship grow with each letter and photo she received. To see it in person was a treat. Of Maureen's three children, Gladys, Saydee, and Seamus, only her son had children—a set of twins: Quinn and Molly. Gladys went the career route, putting her personal life on hold. She resigned from her career and left her homeland to raise her niece, Ailee. Maureen could not have been more proud of her daughter's legacy.

Sensing her granddaughter's restlessness, she pulled out a selection of reading material and arranged them like a fan for Ailee to peruse. "I bought some magazines and a book of cryptic crossword puzzles. Which would ya like?"

"Maybe later." She didn't want to cloud the images from her dream with frivolousness. The time she spent in the ocean of her subconscious was still very fresh. "Dad never talks about your side of the family, and he gets cranky when Aunt Gladys does."

Returning the magazines to one of her bags, Maureen sat down and took a deep breath. "As a wee lad, yer Dad was one of us. Always hangin' around the house, messin' about with Quinn."

"What about him and Mom?"

"Marryin' Molly just made it official?" she asked, picking up her knitting needles.

"How much did they love each other?"

Surprised by such a direct question, Maureen returned her needles and yarn to her bag without a stitch. The time had long passed for keeping secrets. Pushing herself from the chair, she sat on the bed next to Ailee. "Even as a boy, Finn would show up with a hand full of straggly wildflowers he'd picked along the way. Quite the romantic, that one."

"Mom's a nurse, right?"

"A doctor."

"A doctor," repeated Ailee in admiration. "What else?"

"She's earnest, t'boot. Too serious if you're askin' me."

"Too serious to deal with a kid?"

Maureen took Ailee's hands in hers and leaned forward. "Don't be sayin' that, let alone be thinkin' it. Your mum loves ya more than you'll ever know."

"I hate it when people say that."

"Say what?"

"'More than you'll ever know.' I want to know!"

"You'll be seein' her soon." Sliding from the bed, Maureen bent down and picked up her bag.

"I'm glad you're here."

"Likewise," said Maureen as she sat back on the bed and pulled a tabloid-type magazine from the bag. Opening the front cover, she turned it toward Ailee for a look. "Now, can I bend your ear t'the latest celebrity gossip?"

"Tell me the story of this," said Ailee, lifting the oak tree pendant from the nightstand where Gladys had left it.

"The oak tree's a special symbol in our family."

Ailee slid the gown off her shoulder, revealing the oak leaf patterned birthmark. "Like this?"

Standing up, Maureen rearranged her body position and then laid down next to Ailee. "There's a family tale that's been told for centuries."

"Like a fairytale?" asked Ailee, wrapping her fingers securely around the oak tree pendant.

"A real-life fairytale."

Ailee carefully turned on her side to face her great-grandma. The movement was painful, but she didn't want to miss a thing. Her imagination waited in anticipation.

"ONCE UPON A TIME, *more than three centuries ago, there lived a farmer named Simon Killian. Simon was an Irish commoner who worked hard as a tenant of his landlord, an English Nobleman. The plantation he worked on was large in size, and his landlord was good to Simon and his family. As the foreman over the other laborers, Simon was well respected in his job of raisin' cattle. The English landlord dwelt on his Irish estate in the spring and summer but spent his fall and winters in London.*

In those days, large tracts of land were being cleared of trees for farmin'. The wood from the forests was salvaged for lumber used in shipbuilding, wooden barrels for food storage and wine, wood to heat homes and for charcoal to be used in blacksmith fires and iron works. Most of the wood products were exported to England and beyond.

The tannins in the bark of the oak tree were used for tanning the cattle hides. Many oak trees died from being stripped of their bark. Ireland was once thick with forest. Legend has it that a squirrel could travel from the north of Ireland to the south without touchin' the ground. The deforestation was harsh and left Ireland nearly treeless. Fortunately, Simon's employer kept a portion of his estate forested for huntin' and recreational walks—a beautiful grove of oak and ash trees.

Simon lost his wife early in their marriage. Their only child, Aidan, was still a boy when she succumbed to her disease. Aidan grew into a fine young man, workin' alongside his father on the estate. At a young age, Simon recognized his son had a special gift. He could outwit, outthink and outguess everyone around him. He was so clever that no riddle, mystery, puzzle, question or quandary could baffle him.

As he grew into manhood, his gift grew stronger. Soon, word of Aidan's gift traveled throughout the community. Neighbors and strangers began to seek him out to solve their problems. News of Aidan's abilities eventually reached Rígan Lár, the fairy queen, who took an interest in the mortal. She saw his gift as a possible threat to the fairies and the Otherworld, so she passed an edict limitin' their interaction with mortals until Aidan's lifespan had passed. All of 'em observed the decree except one: a fairy named Shaylee. Shaylee and Aidan's friendship was too strong to sever.

Shaylee was a special fairy. She was the keeper of the key, a very important position handed down by Rígan Lár herself; because of this great responsibility, as well as the queen's decree, Aidan and Shaylee kept their friendship a secret. Hidin' away, they'd share their thoughts, their dreams and their deepest secrets. Before they knew it, their friendship had blossomed into romance.

Tragedy struck one day when Simon found Aidan ill in his bed. For several days, the father tried everything to heal his son, but he only grew worse. Aidan was all he had, and the thought of losin' him was more than he could bear. One night, in his feverish sleep, Aidan began muttering details of a secret holy well that could cure any ailment and a key that opened the gate."

"What's a holy well?" asked Ailee, pulling herself from the story."

"Wells with the power t'heal, t'inspire, or t'give a little luck. There are holy wells throughout Ireland, but the well in our story exists between our world and the Otherworld."

"The Otherworld?"

"A world beyond ours. Some say underground," explained her great-grandmother.

"In fairy mounds and forts, right?"

"Gladys taught ya well."

Ailee had already become acquainted with Aidan in her dreams, but she kept that a secret from Maureen. The continuation of their story was the perfect distraction.

"SIMON KNEW *the first step was findin' the key that unlocked the gate to the hidden well. That night, he left his home under the full moon of May, hopin' to save his son's life. He made his way to the grove of oak and ash trees. Sneaking through the trees, he watched for signs of life. He hoped the sidhe-folk wouldn't see him first. A faint sound of singin' and laughter caught his attention, so he continued deeper into the grove.*

Hidin' behind a large tree, he watched as a group of sidhe-folk danced and made merry in the moonlight. He noticed a key danglin' from a sash worn by a beautiful fairy. He'd found Aidan's friend and passage to the holy well. Sinkin' into the grass, he waited for 'em to fall asleep beneath the canopy of trees. Two hours passed before the merriment ended. Ever so quietly, he snuck toward Shaylee, removed the key carefully from her sash then crept away. His footsteps picked up pace as he moved through the forest, hopin' they wouldn't wake before he reached his house.

The warmth of their home felt good as he burst through the door and approached the hearth. The night was chilly, and he felt it to his bones. There were enough coals left to ignite more wood. He needed a safe place to hide the key in case they came for it. He pulled a wrought iron box from the mantle that a blacksmith had forged in the fire of friendship and inscribed it with the name Killian. He placed the key inside the box and put it on a small table as he settled into a chair next to Aidan's bed. He tried to wake Aidan to get directions to the holy well, but his sickness would not allow it. Findin' himself unable to stay awake, Simon closed his eyes just for a moment.

Back in the grove of trees, an uneasiness woke Shaylee from her sleep. Realizin' the key was missin', she followed the thief's scent to his home. She was surprised to arrive at Aidan's doorstep. She'd never been inside the thatched-roof cottage, so she opened the door slowly. Following the scent, she found Simon asleep next to Aidan's bed. She felt the presence of the key callin' to her from the iron box. She reached out to lift the lid, but the iron was so pure it burned her hand, causin' her to scream and pull back."

"How did the box burn her hand?" asked Ailee.

"Iron's like poison t'the sídhe-folk."

"Is she going t'die? They both can't die," said Ailee, sitting up in bed. "They're in love."

"It's just a wound," said Maureen, giving her the assurance she needed. "Sit back."

Ailee relaxed into the pillow, ready for the story to continue.

"The scream woke Simon, and he jumped from the chair. He had to think fast, so he proposed a deal. 'If you take me to your holy well and allow me to dip from its waters to save my son, I shall never return.'

'How do you know of the well?' Shaylee sat next to Aidan and placed the palm of her hand on his wet forehead. She could feel the life force draining from his body. His time was fleeting.

'He called for it in his fever.'

'Give me the key, and I'll return with the water.'

'How do I know you'll come back?'

'I give you my word.'

'Not good enough.'

'Aidan is my friend.'

'I'm his dad.'

'Mortals are not allowed to dip from the well.'

'I'll speak of it t'no one.'

'The laws of the Otherworld forbid it.'

'I promise never t'return.'

'Even so, it is forbidden.'

'Aidan's all I have. He's my world.'

Shaylee couldn't argue Simon's position. Over the past several months,

Aidan had become her world as well. 'I will take you to save Aidan on one condition.'

'Anythin'.'

'I must be the one to use the key and dip from the well.'

Questioning whether or not he could trust a fairy, he placed the iron box in a bag along with a leather water pouch, then strapped it to his back. 'The key will be in safekeepin' until we arrive at the well.' Beneath the moonlit night, Shaylee led the desperate father across the countryside. She wanted to pour her heart out to Simon, tell him of her love for Aidan, and find common ground in their trepidation. But neither one spoke a word. The only mortal Shaylee had ever known on such a personal level was Aidan.

Simon was in the same boat, having never seen or talked with a fairy. He recalled the stories told from childhood. The same folklore and myth that now entangled him. Desperate to save his son, he put aside the warnings taught to him as a youth. Shaylee was Aidan's only hope, and he would follow her wherever she led. Despite the moonlight, Simon had lost all sense of direction. She'd led him over hills, through clusters of trees, along cliffs and around boulders.

The light of the moon disappeared which told him they were in a cavern of sorts. Shaylee picked up a round rock that transformed into an orb, narrowly lighting the way. The light reflected off shiny objects as they moved through the deep cave, but the shadows kept the items hidden. Their footsteps echoed in the chamber, alerting Simon to the vastness of the space, making it easier for him to breathe.

Entering a tunnel surrounded by the protrusion of uneven rocks, their space shrunk in size. In his mind, Simon could feel the walls closin' in on him. Shakin' it off, he focused his eyes on the orb. Their speed increased as they grew closer to the well. Roundin' a corner, Shaylee stopped dead in her tracks. Simon came to a stop next to her, uncertain of what to expect. A woman stood in regal garb and jewels, as well as other sidhe-folk guarding the gate to the well. Shaylee lowered herself to her knees, and Simon followed. Their fate was now in the hands of the fairy queen."

Recognizing she'd said too much, Maureen moved from the bed and straightened her dress. "This may not be the best tale t'tell."

"Did they get the water? Did they save Aidan?"

A nurse entered the room, stealing Maureen's attention. "Someone's askin' for ya in the lobby."

"I'm not expecting anyone," responded Maureen.

"They insisted on seeing ya."

"It's the wee hours of the mornin'."

"I can send 'em away."

Maureen agreed to meet the visitor, seeing it as an opportunity to avoid the story's conclusion. "It looks like the endin' will have t'wait." Maureen followed the nurse out of the room.

Within seconds of leaving, Nurse Brón from the Boyle Psychiatric Hospital entered the room. Dressed like hospital staff, she pulled a vial of liquid and a syringe from her pocket and walked toward Ailee's bed. "Hello, Dear."

CHAPTER SIXTEEN

The reoccurrence of the same nightmare jolted Finn from his sleep. The dream was always the same: carrying his sick daughter toward the light at the end of a dark tunnel. Why couldn't he reach the end of the tunnel? The torment of losing his daughter returned with a vengeance. His return to Ireland was supposed to remedy the nightmares. He needed to check in with Maureen for an update on his daughter's status. His phone was nowhere to be found as he searched his pockets.

Sitting up, he felt the strain of his bent posture. After returning from Quinn's rescue mission, the chair was the first place he landed. Not the most intelligent place to sleep. Needing to move, he rose to his feet. Feeling the movement of every sore muscle, he stumbled to the window and parted the drapes. Dawn was breaking—a sign of new hope. At least, that's what he told himself.

No matter how hard he tried, he couldn't shake the vision of carrying Ailee through a dark cave. Nor could he leave behind the feeling that he couldn't save his daughter from her impending fate.

Rolling off the couch, Quinn hit the floor with a thud. Moaning and groaning, he pulled himself to his knees. Quinn examined his bloody, torn shirt and the bandages around his arm, looking to Finn for answers. "What happened?"

"Don't you remember?" asked Finn, searching his backpack for his phone.

"I was in my room. I needed the cards," he said, holding his head while crawling into the chair. His head was pounding—withdrawals from the dream spell.

"You weren't playing cards when we found you."

Looking around, he immediately recognized his cluttered surroundings. "Are we at Saydee's house?"

On cue, his aunt entered the room, dressed in a bright yellow pair of culottes with a matching scarf around her head. Saydee was ready and raring to go, carrying a fivegallon bucket in one hand and some clean clothes in the other. "Sorry, Quinn. Answers'll have t'wait." Turning to Finn, she quieted his concern. "It's rare to remember a dream spell."

"What about Quinn's medication?" whispered Finn. "Is he going to need something?"

"I'll take care of that," she said before dishing out the orders. "Grab the bag of oat feed next t'the stairs and take it outside."

"Feed?" asked Finn, still trying to grasp a morning that arrived too early while trying to find his phone.

"Why am I covered in blood?" asked Quinn, trying to remember.

"There's no use boilin' yer cabbage twice." The message was clear. Quit worrying about it.

Turning back to Finn, she continued her list and handed him a bucket. "Take this pale and fill it with water. You'll find a tap on the outside of the house."

"Are you sure he's going to be okay?"

"I need t'remove Molly's secrecy spell so he can show us the way."

"Molly's spell?"

"We'll be out when I'm done."

Finn picked up the bag of oats while trying to juggle the bucket and walked to the door. He glanced back at Saydee and Quinn, then left the room. The unexpected sight of a draft horse hitched to a mint-colored caravan greeted him on the other side of the door. He shook his head at the assumed mode of transportation. Parting the canvas curtain in the back, he placed the bag of oats on the floorboards and then walked to the water tap. "A good mornin' to ya," he said, greeting the horse while the bucket filled. He placed the lid securely on the bucket of water and lifted it into the back of the wagon.

Saydee and Quinn couldn't have timed their arrival better. Finn was impressed by his new appearance. The bloody clothes and his confusion were gone. "Help Quinn into the back," she suggested. Quinn happily crawled into the wagon with no need for help. Finn followed Saydee to the head of the wagon. "Up ya go," she said.

"I know nothing about driving a horse."

Smiling, she crawled onto the seat. "Good thing ya got me." Parting the canvas curtains at the front of the caravan, she tied them open with two pieces of rope. Quinn crawled to the oval opening as giddy as a school kid while Finn took his place next to Saydee. "Where did you get this?"

"Made a deal with a traveler," answered Saydee proudly. "Murphy's of good stock."

"Murphy?"

"The horse."

"Why aren't we taking my car?"

"It won't go where we gotta go," she said, handing him the reins.

"Where's that exactly?"

"Quinn's takin' us t'the key."

The smile faded from Quinn's face as Saydee spoke. "All you have t'do is lead the way." He choked back his fear with a nod, agreeing to be their guide. "Quinn and his dad were the last t'hold the key," mentioned Saydee, placing her hand on Quinn's shoulder to offer support. "The years have passed, but it's only yesterday for Quinn." Without the rest of the story, Finn's understanding was limited. He knew Quinn and Molly lost their parents when they were young but was never privy to the details.

With a tap of the reins, their journey began. Saydee showed Finn how to direct Murphy as Quinn pointed into the grassy meadow. The smell of early morning dew surrounded the wagon as they made tracks through the wet grass. It was the fragrance of freedom for Quinn, breathing it deep into his lungs. The countryside was rough and sometimes jarring, but the scenery was spectacular. Saydee kept the trek interesting for Quinn with stories of legend and folklore. The distraction was helpful. Although he'd never admit it, Finn enjoyed the tales as well. It helped the time pass.

With the slow rise of Quinn's arm, Finn and Saydee watched as he pointed to a lone tree in the distance. Finn followed his friend's direction as Quinn retreated to the back of the wagon and wrapped his arms around his knees. The last time he visited the mighty oak was the darkest day of his life.

Leaving the front of the wagon, Finn and Saydee opened the canvas covering at the back of the wagon. "Ya can do this, Quinn," advised Saydee. Using hand signals, she motioned him toward her.

"Do it for your niece," added Finn.

Quinn cautiously crawled from the back as Saydee removed a spade, a couple of pairs of gloves and a shovel. Quinn took a deep breath and walked to the trunk of the old oak. He began counting his steps in several directions as Finn and Saydee watched in suspense. "How much longer?" asked Finn. "I need to get back to Ailee."

"He'll find it."

"Twenty years is a long time. Things have changed."

"Not for Quinn," she said. "The key calls t'him."

Reluctantly pointing to his bare feet, Quinn finally revealed the location. Saydee gently took hold of her nephew's trembling hand and led him away while Finn put on his gloves and began to dig. The first foot or so was hard, requiring his full weight to drive the shovel into the rocky soil. Inch by inch, he removed rocks until he reached the rich soil beneath the surface. Except for an occasional root from the nearby tree, the digging went much faster. Eventually, he found himself waist-deep in the hole. The ache in his back gave him the perfect excuse to stop. He pushed on instead.

The deeper he dug, the more despondent he became. With each strike to the earth, he fought the cynical thoughts in his mind.

Needing a rest, he leaned back and wiped the sweat from his forehead. Watching Saydee and Quinn gathering wildflowers added to his discouragement.

With one look at Finn, Saydee recognized his low spirit and aching back. Leaving Quinn's side, she carried her bounteous armful of wild flowers to the back of the wagon and carefully placed them on a piece of canvas. They'd go a long way to restocking her supply. Pulling out a pocket knife from her bag, she walked to a nearby white willow tree and cut several strips of bark from one of its tender limbs. She slipped them into the pouch hanging from her waist, closed her knife and walked toward the dig sight. "No sign of it?"

"I'm digging a hole in the middle of nowhere based on the memory of a man we just broke out of a mental institution."

"If Quinn says it's here, then here it lies."

"What makes you so sure?" asked Finn. "Look at him. He can't even walk a straight line without being distracted."

"His mind may be fractured, but his memory's solid."

Trusting Saydee's assessment, Finn picked up his shovel and returned to the hole. He needed to keep his thoughts positive, so he engaged Saydee about the night before. "How did you know Quinn was under a... what did you call it?"

"A dream spell. The same thing that caused Ailee to fall from the balcony." Squatting down next to the hole, she continued to fill him in on her greatest foe. "It's a specialty of that evil witch and one she taught Boyle t'conjure."

Tossing a shovel of dirt on the pile next to Saydee, he asked another question before going in for another scoop. "Besides both of you falling in love with the same man," began Finn, recalling their conversation over fish and chips. "What did she do to you?"

"She murdered the love of my life."

Stunned by the steadiness of her response, Finn stopped digging and straightened up. His crime-solving mind needed clarification after being stunned by her revelation. "She murdered the man you loved?"

"And she used me t'do it." Standing up, she turned to look at

Quinn, picking flowers. She needed a moment to collect herself. "It was the night of our wedding day. I woke t'find my clothes soaked with his blood and my hand still clutching the knife." Saydee wrapped her fingers tightly around the handle of the spade as though she were still holding the knife. "Dream spells are powerful, and I was young then."

Speechless, Finn gripped the handle of his shovel as he tried to find the words to respond. "I'm sorry, Saydee. I had no idea." The more time he spent with Molly's family, the deeper he traveled into their tragic past. Molly had gone to great lengths to shield him from their heart-rending history. He was embarrassed that she thought he couldn't handle the truth. Recalling his constant complaining about her family's magic made him want to crawl into the hole he was digging.

Saydee sensed the difficulty he was experiencing, so she squatted down to look him in the eyes. "Since that dark day, I've devoted my life to my gift and the study of magic. The same magic that'll save yer daughter, Finn."

Shaking his head in agreement was all he had left to offer. Changing the grip on his shovel, he leaned into the hole and struck the ground. The sound of the cutting edge of his scoop striking iron changed the subject. Falling to his knees, he brushed the dirt away with his hands.

"Try this," said Saydee, handing Finn her spade. Looking back, she saw Quinn staring at them from beneath the shelter of the oak tree. Calm and poised, he waited for the fabled key to once again see the light of day. The ramifications were inescapable. No one knew that better than Quinn.

Rising with treasure in hand, Finn placed the iron box on the ground in front of Saydee. "It's in great shape for being buried so long."

"It's protected," said Saydee as she gently wiped the remaining dirt from the Killian name engraved on the lid. "I doubt Simon Killian intended his box t'become the conveyor of both torment and deliverance." Reverently, she lifted the cover from the box.

Noticing a pair of glasses lying inside, Finn picked them up for closer examination. "Quinn's glasses. He wore these when we were kids."

"Drinkin' from the holy well gave him his sight back," mentioned Saydee.

"What about the limp from his broken foot?"

"Healed. He pretends. Molly says it's part of dealin' with his guilt." With a trembling hand, Saydee picked up the chain attached to a silver pocket watch and pulled it from the box. Pressing it to her chest, she rested on her heels before opening the hunter's-case cover. Depressing the crown, the front of the watch popped open, revealing her brother's name: *Seamus Killian*. "I remember the day my father gave this to my brother," she whispered with melancholy in her voice. "They were happier times."

Quinn's shadow fell over them as he approached the hole in the ground. Reaching up, Saydee placed the watch in her nephew's hand and closed his fingers around the timepiece.

Seeing the leather pouch in the bottom of the iron box, Quinn started to back away toward the caravan. He kept his eyes glued on the box as though waiting for a wild animal to leap out and attack.

With an affirming nod from Saydee, Finn removed the pouch from the box. Still standing in the hole allowed him to use the ground level for a table and to be face-to-face with Saydee.

He untied the leather strap surrounding the rolled piece of leather and laid it flat. A large silver skeleton key caught the sun's reflection, momentarily impeding their view. Lifting it from its leather wrapping, Finn examined the handcrafted details. The bow at the end of the handle contained the design of an oak tree, gnarly and bent with age. Finn noticed an inscription along the side of the body connecting the bow to the teeth. "Can you read it?" asked Finn, handing it to Saydee.

"It's Gaeilge," said Saydee. "Have ya forgotten yer native tongue?"

"A little rusty."

"The gateway," said Saydee, tracing the inscription with her finger.

"Gateway to what?"

Holding it in her hand, she responded with sadness. "The key t'life and death for our family."

"What happened to Quinn and Molly's father?"

Before Saydee could answer, a thick fog rolled into the meadow, searching as though it had eyes. Quickly wrapping the key in its leather pouch, she placed it in the box and shut the lid. "We got t'go, now!" Rising to her feet, she picked up the box and hurried toward the caravan. Finn scrambled from the hole using the shovel for leverage. Keeping an eye on the approaching fog, he sped toward the wagon with a hand on his sore back.

Saydee stowed the precious cargo at the back of the wagon, far from Quinn, who was cowering at the front. Finn tossed a blanket over it and then turned to leave. Saydee stopped him. Reaching into the pouch hanging from her waist, she offered him a piece of white willow bark. "For the pain in yer back," she explained.

"You want me to chew on bark?" he asked in disbelief.

"It'll do ya wonders," she said, crawling into the back of the wagon. Rolling his eyes, Finn shoved the end into his mouth like a piece of licorice and circled to the head of the wagon. Climbing into the seat, he looked in every direction. The hard wooden seat wasn't doing his back any favors. "The fog's getting thick. Which way do we go?"

Saydee called from inside the wagon. "Murphy'll take us home."

With a tap of the reins, the horse walked into the fog. Finn could only hope that Saydee was right about Murphy knowing the way. Their lives and Ailee's depended on it.

Kneeling at the back of the wagon, Saydee removed the blanket and placed a second protection spell on the iron box to keep it hidden from dark forces. She covered the box and then crawled to the front to comfort Quinn. Wrapping her arm around her nephew, she sang one of his favorite Irish folksongs. The tender lyrics expressed with Saydee's sweet voice and perfect pitch relieved Quinn's anxiety.

Finn listened through the opening in the curtain, first with his ears, then with his heart. The lyrics were about family and hardship, two things the Killians knew well. The fog created a blank canvas for Finn's imagination as he pieced together the details he'd learned since he returned to Ireland. The picture was fragmented and missing information, but he was getting closer to the truth.

Finding the key moved them closer to the well—the healing well that would save Ailee's life. That's as much as he knew about it. They were making progress, yet the dark cave of his nightmare continued to plague his thoughts. It was a source of doubt that secretly weighed on his mind. Another thing weighing on his mind was his daughter's recovery from the fall. He hadn't heard from Maureen for twenty-four hours. He could only trust that she was in good hands. Yielding the rein, Finn gave Murphy the signal to lengthen his stride. The fog was letting up, and he had somewhere to be.

CHAPTER SEVENTEEN

Dr. Boyle entered his private chambers, followed by Nurse Brón. He stormed to the window and stared down at the parking lot. Kidnapping Molly's daughter was an act of war against the Killian clan. A move that left him a bit on edge. "They'll come looking for the girl."

"We can handle their tricks," she replied with arrogant confidence, holding her ground in the center of the room.

Turning back to face his supposed underling, he felt the need to impress upon her the importance of succeeding. "Ever since I learned of the Killian holy well, I've made it my life's mission to find it."

"All these years, and you still don't know its location," she responded, ensuring he understood his dependence on her abilities.

Her attempt at casting shade on Boyle ruffled his feathers. Coming face to face, he placed the blame squarely at her feet. "It was your job to break the secrecy spell. You're the one who has failed."

"You're lucky I came along when I did," she murmured under her breath, her duplicitous nature still hidden from her partner.

"Once we secure the location of the holy well, the possibilities will be limitless," he assured himself as he turned back to the window.

"And when we find it?" Using her powers behind his back, she rearranged the paintings on his wall with the movement of her fingers. She'd grown fatigued listening to his speech of self-importance.

"People will come from all parts of the world," he fantasized, staring out the window. "To be saved from the grips of death."

"What is the value of a human life?" she asked, completing the repositioning.

"Whatever I demand in payment." Boyle turned back to the nurse, making sure she understood who was in charge. "The well will be mine." Glancing at the paintings on the wall, he noticed something was off but couldn't put his finger on it.

"I'll prepare the girl for the procedure," she said, walking toward the door. "I suggest you prepare for visitors."

Stepping into the hallway, she closed the double doors behind her, clutching the handle. The temperature of the brass increased to red hot as the rage grew within her. Requiring immediate restraint, she soothed herself with the actuality of the situation. Dr. Boyle was still useful to the plan, so she would continue the game of cat and mouse until the day she no longer needed him. Walking away, she cooled her palm with her icy breath and turned her attention to Ailee Killian. "The possibilities are limitless."

THE HOSPITAL HALLWAY was alive with activity as Finn hurried toward his daughter's room. He'd been a detective long enough to recognize the signs of a crime scene without the presence of the police. Passing a group of worried nurses gathered around a hospital administrator on the phone gave him his first clue. His second clue was orderlies hurrying from room to room while frantic nurses ran passed each other with worry painted on their faces. Rushing into Ailee's room, Finn found the bed empty.

Confused, he walked toward the nurse's station. "I'm looking for my daughter, Ailee Killian." Before any of the nurses could answer, Gladys called to him from down the hallway. "Finn!" Maureen followed Gladys, and they met him halfway. Needing to catch her breath, Maureen let Gladys do the talking.

"Where is she, Gladys?" asked Finn, running his fingers through his hair. He was trying his hardest to hold back the panic manifested by his hands' inability to find a home.

"Ailee's missin'," admitted Gladys, patting her hand against her chest to calm her nerves. "I was called from the room under false pretense. When I returned, she was gone."

"How can she be gone?" Finn walked passed Maureen, looking in every direction.

"We've searched the entire hospital," added Gladys.

Turning back, Finn asked the obvious question. "Have you called the police?"

"The hospital may have," she answered. Taking a deep breath, she shared the last detail. "Molly's gone after her. She just left."

Finn turned on his heels and ran down the hallway, passing Saydee and Quinn without explanation.

"Where's he goin' so fast?" asked Saydee, catching up to her mom and sister.

"Ailee's been taken," answered Gladys as she pulled Saydee into their greatniece's empty room. Maureen followed with Quinn in tow, and they shut the door behind them. After a round of hugs, Saydee quickly filled everyone in on the events of the past twenty-four hours. The details were a bit untidy, but they got the gist. "Now, it's up to them," said Saydee, drawing their attention to the window overlooking the parking lot.

Maureen and Gladys gathered around for the show.

"My money's on Finn," said Saydee as they watched Molly get in her car and back out of her parking spot.

"Not if Molly has a say in it," added Maureen.

"How long before Molly tells Finn the truth?" asked Gladys.

"No one knows the truth till after it's done," answered Quinn from across the room. "No one."

Saydee walked toward Quinn and took hold of his hand. "C'mon, Quinn. Let's get ya home." Opening the door, Saydee led her nephew out of the room while Gladys and Maureen picked up their personal items. Catching a reflection of something shiny, Gladys pulled Ailee's protection charm from the sheet and held it up for Maureen to see. "I should of put it on her when I arrived." Gladys gasped loudly at the dereliction of her duty, covering her mouth to mask her dread.

"We haven't come this far t'fail," said Maureen, wrapping her arm around her daughter for added strength. "I wouldn't want to be the ones standin' between Finn and Molly and their daughter."

FINN RUSHED from the hospital entrance and into the parking lot, searching in every direction. He spied Molly, making the loop leading back to the exit. Sprinting toward the egress, Finn ran between cars, sliding across hoods and leaping short barrier walls as he tried to intercept Molly before she escaped. Just before she reached the exit, Finn stopped in the middle of the road.

Slamming on her brakes, Molly bumped her head on the steering wheel and bounced back. Taking a deep breath to collect herself, she shook her head as she rolled down the window. "What are ya doin'?"

"I could ask you the same thing," he replied, spreading his legs to shore up his base.

"Get out of the way!" she yelled from inside the car as the sound of police sirens grew closer.

"Why are you going after Ailee alone?" he asked, pressing his hands on the hood of her car.

"Get yer hands off the bonnet," she hollered, refusing to exit the car.

"You know where she is?"

"I've got a good idea."

"Let's get the police involved."

"And tell 'em what exactly?" Tired of yelling through the windshield, Molly threw open the door and left the car, determined to confront her husband. "That our daughter's been kidnapped by a witch and a psychiatrist who dabbles in sorcery?"

"We're waiting for the police to arrive."

"We'll never see her again if we do," warned Molly. "This requires finesse."

"By finesse, you mean magic."

"A certain expertise."

"Fine," responded Finn, walking toward the passenger door. "Use all the magic you want."

"What are ya doin'?" she asked, hurrying back to the driver's side.

"Going with you."

"It's too dangerous."

Leaning over the top of the car, Finn continued the argument. "I'm a cop. I'm good at danger."

"Not this kind."

"I can handle it."

"She's my daughter, Finn. I know how t'protect her."

"Now she's your daughter?"

"That's not fair."

"I've kept her safe all these years," said Finn as he opened the door to the car. "I'm not stepping aside now." Getting in the car, he shut the door and placed the seatbelt across his lap.

Molly joined him in the vehicle. After collecting her thoughts, she began with some ground rules. "We do this my way."

"It's your turf," he agreed, raising his hands to show his surrender.

Shifting into drive, she pulled onto the road just as the police cars rolled into the parking lot. "I'm the one who'll guide Ailee to the well. I'll make sure she's healed and safely returned."

"Why can't we both do it?"

"There can be only one escort."

"Why you?"

"The curse is my family's problem."

Swallowing twelve years of pride, Finn confessed with a simple statement. "Your family is my family."

"What?" she asked in disbelief, accidentally swerving into oncoming traffic.

"I was angry when I left Ireland," admitted Finn. "I had to channel it somewhere. The Killian family became the bullseye."

Confused by the unexpected direction of their conversation, Molly found herself off-balance. "What's changed yer thinkin'?"

"The last few days... I've seen the lengths your family will go to for one another."

"My family hasn't changed, Finn."

"I know," he replied, noticing a car about to pull out from a side street. "Watch out!"

Swerving to avoid a collision, Molly returned to her lane and the conversation as though nothing had happened. "Ya retreated from the fight, Finn!"

"Getting Ailee away from your family and the curse was the only thing I could think to do," he humbly admitted as he searched for a grab bar above the window.

"Not only did ya steal my daughter, ya stole my husband," she argued, accelerating far beyond the speed limit. "You and you alone made that decision. That's not how it works when two people love each other. My heart was in play all the same."

"I wanted you to come with us." Finn glanced at her speedometer and her one-handed control of the steering wheel. "I begged you!"

"I tried t'make ya understand, but ya wouldn't listen!" Molly's free hand flew through the air like she was conducting O Fortuna. "You were too focused on your fear. Ya couldn't see beyond Ailee's birthmark. Ya couldn't see beyond the curse."

Molly hit the nail on the head, and Finn knew it. With nothing left to argue, he stared out the window as they raced toward their destination. Finn had lived with his self-satisfaction for so long that he couldn't see the forest for the trees. Coming home had shaken his reality like an earthquake, leaving cracks large enough to see the light. He'd put the blame squarely at Molly's feet when there was no one to blame but ill-fated circumstances.

"I'm sorry, Finn." Molly's unexpected apology broke the silence. "I'm sorry we lost so much time." Choking back her feelings, she emptied the last of her heart. "I'll never regret lovin' ya."

Clearing his throat to fight back his emotion, Finn reached across the battle line and wrapped his fingers around his wife's hand, which had finally found rest on her lap. "Is it too late for us?"

The touch of his hand intensified her vulnerable state, taking her back to a time when that same touch calmed her nerves, kept her safe and held her tight. She could feel her defenses melting. She wanted to give him hope, but knowing what the next twentyfour hours would bring, there was none to offer. "We're gettin' close," she said, pulling her hand away and placing it on the steering wheel. "We need t'focus on Ailee," warned Molly, getting her head back in the game. "Just so we're clear… I alone'll take Ailee t'the well?"

Stunned by the reversal of subjects, Finn attempted to switch gears. "Why you?"

"You've done everythin' for her. Let me do this."

"Not everything," said Finn, hoping to recapture the moment they had just shared. "You brought her into this world."

"Into this mess!" Feeling the guilt of generations, Molly continued her plea. "Let me be the one t'save her."

"Before either of us can help her, we need to get her back. What's the plan?"

"I'm goin' t'walk through the front door."

Taking his turn at conducting, Finn shook his hands in the air. "I'm beginning to think your family doesn't understand the concept of planning when it comes to covert operations?"

"Ya mean 'our family?'" Pausing momentarily, Molly took pleasure in reminding him of his recent declaration of change. Then she got back to the non-plan. "I work here. Why wouldn't I walk in?" She turned off the road and prepared to flash her ID badge at the guard. "They're expectin' me." Without stopping, she drove into the parking lot of the Boyle Psychiatric Hospital and parked with the passenger side next to the meditation garden.

"I'll go around the back and use the underground passageway," said Finn. "Any idea where they're keeping Ailee?"

"She could be anywhere," Molly answered, popping open the glove box and pullin' out a flashlight. "I'll start in Cyrus' private chambers."

"Private chambers?"

"A fancy name for his library." After checking for battery life, she handed him the flashlight.

"I don't like the sound of it."

"I can handle myself," she said, clipping her ID to her lapel. "I'll keep him distracted while ya find our daughter."

"Distracted?"

"We're colleagues."

Turning to face Molly, he addressed the elephant in the car. "Why would a colleague take your daughter in the first place?"

Pulling a tube of lipstick from her purse, she applied a coat in the rearview mirror. "Dr. Boyle will stop at nothin' t'find the holy well."

Molly reached for the door, but Finn beat her to the latch.

Looking Finn in the eyes, she reassured him that she could handle herself. "My turf, remember?"

"I don't like you going in there alone," he whispered, staring back just as passionately. "Will you at least try to be careful?"

"'Careful' won't get our daughter back," she said before leaving the car.

Molly's departure left Finn at odds with his instincts. Molly going it alone went against his training and years of experience. But she had a point. This was her turf, magic and all.

Slinking from the car, Finn disappeared into the bushes, circling the grounds as covertly as possible. The evening twilight allowed for deeper shadows to mask his movement. Reaching the hatch to the basement, he opened one side and slipped down the steps, carefully closing the hatch overhead.

In the dark, he saw a distant light coming through the cracks of the boarded-up exit at the end of the tunnel to nowhere. Turning on his flashlight, he started down the tunnel toward the fissures of light. His plan to enter the building the same way he'd escaped with Quinn moved to plan B. The sound of scampering feet and squeaky voices alerted him to rats. Catching them in the beam of his light sent them scurrying away. Pointing the light at his feet unwittingly led him into a thick spider web that engulfed his face. Dropping the light, he feverishly wiped at his face, trying not to scream.

Once his face was mostly clear, he searched the stone floor but couldn't find the flashlight. Close to the tunnel's end, he continued without the light. Peering through the cracks between the boards, he saw a basement laboratory of sorts.

A weak moan drew his attention toward a concrete slab. His daughter lay strapped to the top. Slipping his fingers between the crack, he pulled against the boards with all his strength. It wasn't enough. The nails entered from inside the room. He tried kicking them off, but they wouldn't budge. He needed tools that would help him get through without a lot of noise.

Returning to the scene of the spider web, he got on his hands and knees and searched for the flashlight. He tried not to think about the wet, squishy things he was touching in the dark. Finally, his hand fell on the light. With a sigh of relief, he shook it a few times to make it operational. Getting to his feet, he hurried back to the main tunnel to the stairs that led to the cleaning closet.

He burst through the small door and searched the room for something he could use for leverage. Opening a toolbox, he found a small pry bar and a hammer. Before crawling into the tunnel, he looked to the door leading to the hallway. Molly was on the other side. The right choice took him back into the tunnel.

CHAPTER EIGHTEEN

Facing the intimidating double doors of Cyrus Boyle's private quarters, Molly took a deep breath. He'd replaced the single, more institutionally appropriate door three years earlier, removing the room's vulnerability. The new doors, with their reclaimed, oldgrowth wood, joined together by hand-forged, wrought-iron brackets, seemed impenetrable.

That same year, he relocated the administrative offices and remodeled the entire wing as his private domicile. After the remodel came the refurbishing. His penchant for the fanciful was straight out of Thomas Chippendale's eighteenth century designs: mahogany-finished Rococo-style furniture, curved in all the right places. His whimsical tastes were one of the last survivors of his dark evolution.

Before the double door installation, Molly accepted many invitations to join him in his library for post-work conversation, friendly banter and a nightcap. A friendship between peers had developed that was quite comfortable and therapeutic. The dark renovation of Cyrus Boyle changed everything.

Shaking off memory lane, she considered the brass door knocker, clenched in the jaws of an Oilliphéist, a scaly sea serpent from Irish folklore. Tracing her finger down the angry crease between the sea dragon's menacing eyes, she felt the inner courage needed to take on the human monster behind the door. There would be no knocking tonight. Pushing against the heavy doors, they turned on their hinges framing her perfectly beneath the door-jamb. The inside throw lock had been left open. He was expecting her.

The light generated by the large gas fireplace created mysterious shadows. Her eyes came to rest on Dr. Boyle, sitting in his favorite oversized leather armchair near the fireplace. His body covered the button-tufted back that gave the chair its charm. This is how she chose to remember him, reading a book by firelight at the end of a long day. Tonight, there was no book in his hand.

Stepping into the room, she passed by replicas of rare antiquities he could only dream of owning. Shadows danced against the wall-to-wall shelves, lapping at the books he once loved to read. A hint of sadness pricked her heart. Quickly, she dismissed the empathy. There was no textbook reason for his transformation, only evidence of dark powers at work. He'd crossed the line by kidnapping Ailee and there was only one way back. "I'm here for my daughter."

"I heard you were having a family emergency," he said, refusing to turn his eyes from the fire.

"Where is she?" asked Molly, slowly making her way toward the sitting area.

"All these years and not one mention of a child. Imagine how that makes me feel."

"Yer no longer capable of feelin'," she shot back, placing her hands firmly on the back of the sofa, using it as a barrier.

"You're wrong." Dr. Boyle turned to Molly, his voice dripping with artificial sincerity. "I feel sadness over the loss of our friendship."

"Ya didn't lose my friendship, Cyrus, ya traded it for what ya wanted more."

The truth of Molly's words was inescapable but Dr. Boyle couldn't see it. He demanded obeyance without question or debate. His lust for power had distorted his thinking. "Imagine my surprise when Quinn informed me about your daughter in one of our sessions."

"Through unscrupulous methods, no doubt."

"We each have our own approach."

"So much for the Hippocratic Oath."

"You misunderstand me, Molly," said Boyle, rising from the chair. "I don't want to cause anyone harm. Just the opposite. I want to heal people, all people. Access to the well will make that possible."

"Take me to my daughter." As Boyle moved toward her, Molly backed toward the door.

"Imagine having the ability to heal anyone of anything. It's a physician's dream come true. All these years you've kept it to yourself."

"It's not like that, Cyrus."

"Now that I have your daughter, I'm even closer to partaking of the healing waters."

"Give her to me!"

"Why don't we make a deal?" asked Boyle, grabbing Molly's wrist and holding her captive. "I'll give you your daughter if you rule by my side."

"'Rule by yer side?' Have ya lost yer mind?"

"I know what I want," he said, pulling her close. "I will have it."

Breaking free from his grasp, Molly saw Quinn's oak protection charm lying against his chest. Instinctively, she reached for it and ripped it from his neck. "Ya have no right." She turned toward the fortress doors, only to see them slam shut before of her. "Unless you brought help, I wouldn't plan on leaving any time soon."

Fielding a deluge of emotion, Molly found the focus she needed. "Ya may have sold yer soul for a hat full of tricks, but mine's the real deal." With that said, she impelled her arms toward the heavy doors. A powerful force blew them off their iron hinges and into the hallway. "I'll find her myself." Needing to give Finn time to find Ailee, she ran from the room, knowing Boyle would follow.

Enticed even more by the display of Molly's power, he did exactly as expected.

A drop of water fell from the ceiling, landing on Ailee's forehead, causing her to wake from a deep sleep. Through a fog, she surveyed the dark room with all its ghoulish shapes hiding in the shadows. She tried to lift her arms but realized they were bound to the cold slab beneath her. A prying sound drew her attention to the corner of the room. Weak from loss of blood and the effects of the curse, she drifted back to sleep before finding the source.

Inside the tunnel, Finn worked to pry the boards off the wooden frame near the bottom of the doorway. The sound of nails squeaking against the wood kept pausing his momentum. Wiping the sweat from his forehead, he continued until he'd removed enough boards to crawl through. Once inside, he scoped out the room for any threats. Out of habit, he again reached for his holstered gun, but there was no weapon or holster. He wasn't in Boston. He'd come ill-prepared for breaking and entering.

With pry bar in hand, he made his way through a messy collection of old medical equipment and ancient torture devices. This was no basement. It was a dungeon for torment. With his eyes focused on Ailee, he didn't notice the top board of an old wooden pillory unlatch itself and slowly rise from its base. The punishing device stood in the shadows, waiting for Finn to get within striking distance.

Finn continued toward his daughter, more confident with each step, until an unseen power impeded his rescue attempt. Twirled sideways by a force he couldn't see, Finn lost all control; his arms coerced into the two half holes of the pillory and his neck into the large hole. The top board slammed down, locking his hands and head into the device once used for public humiliation.

Finn fought with all his strength till the sound of footsteps striking the stone floor caught his attention. He recalled those same footsteps the day they arrived to visit with Quinn. He knew who was coming toward him from the shadows: Nurse Brón. "You better hope I don't get out of this thing," Finn threatened with the pry bar still in his hand.

A taunting laughter ricocheted off the concrete walls, causing a chill down Finn's spine. "Do your worst. People have tried for centuries," she boasted from the darkness.

"Show yourself!"

"Be careful what you wish for, Finn Donnelly. You just might get it."

"You won't get away with this," threatened Finn as his eyes darted around the room, searching the shadows and inanimate objects.

"Who will stop me? You?"

"I've called the police," said Finn, attempting to use his bar to pry open the restraint. "They'll be here any minute." Feeling the palm of his hand sizzle, he noticed the pry bar turning red with heat. Dropping it to the floor, he screamed from the pain of his melted flesh.

"I expect more from you than lies."

"Let me loose, and I won't disappoint," warned Finn, still reeling from the pain of his burn. Rattling the pillory, he attempted to break it free from its foundation.

"You're not going anywhere," she whispered, her silhouette appearing inches from his face.

"Aaaah!" screamed Finn, feeling her heavy breath against his skin.

"Neither is your daughter."

"Ailee!"

"Quiet!" she ordered, cutting off his yell by wrapping her long fingers around his throat. The points of her fingernails sunk into his flesh, drawing blood. "You'll frighten the child."

"You're no nurse," squeaked out Finn.

Letting go of his throat, Nurse Brón took his burned hand in hers. Within seconds, his burn was completely healed. "Who says I'm not a nurse?" Then she lifted her arm to the string hanging from the bare lightbulb on the ceiling. With a tug of the string, the light revealed a witch's frightening, twisted face, causing Finn to jerk back against the pillory. "Something wrong?" she asked, coming face to face as she licked his blood from her fingertips.

Terrified by her hideous features and the smell of death on her breath, Finn lost his only weapon: his words.

"I'm sorry," she said, displaying her decayed, gnarly teeth. "I forgot to put on my face." With a swipe of her hand, the witch's true identity returned to Nurse Brón's appearance. She dragged a tall stool across the stone floor and made herself comfortable inches from her prisoner. "WHO I am changes with a stroke of my hand," she said, caressing his cheek with the tips of her nails. "WHAT I am, you could never comprehend."

Finn stretched his neck as far as he could, but the tight clutch of the pillory made it impossible to avoid her touch. "I don't care what you are."

"Not yet," she warned, having more fun than she'd had in a long time.

"Is that a threat?"

"No, but this is," she said, pressing her mouth to his ear. "You're next, and I promise to take my time."

"Let my daughter go, and you can do whatever you want with me."

"I plan to let her go," said the nurse calmly as she stood from the stool. "If she's still alive after draining her."

Helpless to intervene, Finn rattled the pillory, trying again to shake it open. The lock refused to budge. He was a captive audience to his daughter's torture. "Ailee! Wake up!"

A large book flew across the room, hitting Finn square in the forehead and cutting the skin. "You're becoming a nuisance." Turning on a light next to Ailee, Nurse Brón picked up a plastic bag containing Ailee's blood. "Healthy veins," she noted, sticking a hundred-millimeter syringe into a secondary IV to extract a portion from the PVC blood bag. "I think we have enough to work with."

"Ailee!" screamed Finn as he desperately searched the room for some way to free himself.

This time the flying object hit from the other side, bouncing off the top of his head and making him a bit loopy. "Keep interrupting me, and I'll drain her dry."

"Dad?" called Ailee, waking from her sleep to see Nurse Brón hovering near her.

"I'm here, Ailee." Finn struggled again to free himself.

"What's happening?" Still fuzzy from the drugs, Ailee could see the outline of her dad trapped in the pillory.

"I'm just borrowing a little blood," answered Nurse Brón. "Be a good girl, and I might let your dad live. With a few alterations."

Looking around the room, Ailee spied an old metal bedpan on the table near the foot of the concrete slab. Summoning every drop of energy she had left, she used her magic to lift the bedpan from the table.

"Let her go!" screamed Finn. "Take my blood. You can have every drop!"

"Your blood is useless to me," she laughed, her shrill voice bouncing off the stone walls.

Focusing her attention on the syringe, the witch failed to see the launch of the bedpan. It knocked the syringe out of her hand, missing the witch by an inch. Her quick reaction froze the tube in mid-air. Securing the syringe inside her fist, she slowly rotated back to Ailee. "It seems you've found your Killian magic." With a wave of her hand, Ailee froze, her eyes wide open.

"What did you do to her?" demanded Finn, rattling the pillory.

"She needs her rest. Nurses orders." Using her long fingers like a comb, the evil witch ran them through Ailee's auburn hair, spreading it out on both sides. Sliding the palm of her hand down the side of her face, she stared into her open eyes. "The young are so impressionable."

"Get away from her!" screamed Finn. "Quit touching her."

The witch relished in the pain she was causing Finn. "Now that I know she's gifted, your daughter could be quite useful to me." Standing up, she picked up the syringe and walked toward the door. "With the right parenting, of course."

"You're not taking my daughter from me!" His scream fell on deaf ears as the door shut behind her.

Forced to listen to her evil laughter from outside the building,

Finn waited for it to fade into the distance. "Ailee," cried Finn. "Wake up, Ailee. Please, wake up!" Dropping his head, Finn exhaled in defeat. First, the curse took away his ability to help his daughter in the States, and now evil gave him a front-row seat to his daughter's demise. His only hope was Molly.

CHAPTER NINETEEN

Running down the low-lit hallway, Molly entered the kitchen and crouched behind a counter. She could hear Boyle's footsteps running toward the door. Closing her eyes, she hoped against hope that he would pass without pause. The slowing of his steps denied her wish. With precision, he walked into the kitchen and came to a stop. The sound of his heavy breathing slowed to an average pace. She knew he sensed her presence.

"It's only a matter of time before your daughter takes her last breath," he warned, setting her up for an ultimatum. Taking a couple more steps, he surveyed the kitchen for signs of Molly. "You can waste it by playing hide and seek, or save your daughter by joining forces with me." He walked closer to the counter concealing Molly, and placed the palms of his hands on the laminate. "Together, we could end all the suffering and pain. Our patients will be happy to pay whatever we ask for life-saving treatment. The Boyle Hospital will become world-renowned, and we'll be rich beyond our wildest dreams." Boyle leaned over the counter, peering down at his opponent. "Join me, Molly, and save your daughter. The choice is clear."

Molly's swing was swift and decisive as she rose from behind the counter. The fifteen-inch cast iron frying pan clocked her enemy in the side of the head with the force of a grizzly bear. The sound of his body hitting the floor was pure satisfaction. With skillet in hand, she walked around the counter, fighting the instinct to finish him off. "Clear enough for ya?" she asked, staring at his unconscious body. Dropping the pan next to his head, she grabbed the electrical cord to the large bread mixer, yanked it from the wall then wrapped it tightly around his wrists.

She walked out the door and stood in the hallway. Needing directions, she closed her eyes and listened. Her magical ability amplified the noises. Sounds from throughout the hospital came and went as she probed each room. Her search needed to go deeper. Focusing on her life-long connection with Finn, she engaged the full force of her heart to search for his thoughts. Tears ran from her eyes as she engaged every ounce of emotion. She could feel her physical strength draining.

The audible noise of the hospital finally withdrew, revealing Finn's thoughts. The overload of his mind entering hers was almost too much to bear. Except for Ailee's dream spell, she'd never used her power in such an invasive way. The very idea of it was wrong. She could only hope for his forgiveness. Pressing her back to the wall, she steadied herself as his thoughts engulfed her mind. His memories of their daughter and herself, of happier times, flooded her understanding. Communication in its purest form permeated her psyche. Trying to filter the information, she focused on finding a location. Images of being trapped in a cold, dark space caused Molly to cut the link to Finn's mind. "The basement."

With a slow start, she headed down the hall, her strength significantly reduced. Reaching the stairs, she clung to the handrail as she descended the three flights. Reaching the basement door, she found a padlock blocking her entrance. Leaning against the wall, she allowed herself the time necessary to renew a portion of her strength. Focusing on the padlock, she used her power to unlatch it from the door. The sound of it striking the concrete floor gave her satisfaction but weakened her even more.

Entering the dungeon, she first saw her husband trapped in the pillory. Throwing the stool out of her way, she rushed to his aid and began fumbling with the lock.

"Help Ailee," he pleaded, using his finger to point in her direction.

Looking over her shoulder, she saw her daughter lying on the cold stone slab, seemingly lifeless. Provoked by her daughter's suffering, she rallied every drop of power she had left in her drained body to shatter the metal lock.

The top bar gripping Finn's hands and head flew across the room. Freed from embarrassment, Finn followed Molly as she ran to rescue their daughter. Loosening the cords, Finn worked to free Ailee while watching Molly examine their daughter. "We have to get her to a hospital."

"I'm a doctor, remember?" Molly studied the IV in her arm, and the bag filled with blood. Carefully, she wrapped medical tape around Ailee's arm, securing the IV needle.

"What could they want with her blood?" asked Finn as he moved to the top of the slab to release her hands.

"Whatever the reason, it can't be good." Rising to her feet, Molly readied her daughter for transport by wrapping her in a blanket. "We need t'get her t'Saydee. Fast."

Hurrying around the slab, Finn approached Molly with a better idea. "The hospital is closer. They can help her."

Turning to face her husband, Molly ended the discussion. "Not with the things of my world."

"No offense, but I really hate the things of your world," said Finn as he scooped his daughter into his arms.

"Get in line." Molly placed the blood bag on Ailee's stomach, then secured it with her scarf.

"We can't get her out the way I came in," said Finn as he looked to the main entrance.

"Up the stairs. I'm right behind ya." Molly grabbed some bandages, gauze, and medical tape from the table and shoved them into her pocket. Turning to leave, she noticed a light coming from beneath a heavy towel at the back of the table. Removing the cover blinded her sight. She quickly cloaked the jar with the same towel and rubbed her eyes. She'd seen enough to understand the origin of the light. Putting two and two together, she vowed to make things right. Grabbing the covered two-quart jar filled with what appeared to be fireflies, she ran from the room.

Reaching the top of half a flight of stairs, Finn paused to catch his breath on the landing. Still unconscious, Ailee appeared lifeless in his arms. With renewed energy, he started up the next set of stairs. His lack of an exercise routine over the past several years was coming back to haunt him.

Molly pulled herself up the stairs using the handrail, rubbing her protection charm between her fingers for added strength. She could feel her energy returning with each step. It didn't take long to catch up with Finn as he reached the top.

"Whew," he exhaled, staring at Molly for support.

"We're close, Finn," she said, opening the door to the outside.

Feeling the hit of a second wind, he hurried through the open doorway only to be met by a flash of security lights along the wall at the back of the yard. Hiding in the shadows, they watched as security personnel entered the yard. "He must have tripled the guards tonight."

"What now?" he asked, praying the strength is his arms held out long enough to get Ailee to safety.

"We call for backup."

"It's about time we call the police."

"Not that kind of backup." Pulling the towel back far enough to remove the top of the lid, she prepared Finn for what was coming. "Get ready t'run." Opening the cover, she freed the lights from captivity. "Now!" Finn and Molly ran into the yard, flanked by flying lights.

"What's happening?" yelled Finn, trying to escape the chaos he didn't understand. One by one, the lights departed in different directions as Finn and Molly stayed the course. The feel of his legs turning to jelly worried Finn more than the disarray around him. He could feel his speed slowing and his arms failing. His best effort wasn't enough to outpace the guards gaining on him. The inability to reach the light at the end of the tunnel was becoming a reality. His nightmare was coming true.

Halfway across the yard, they still had a long stretch ahead of them. "Keep goin', Finn," encouraged Molly as she ran by his side. "Ya can do this." She continued championing him as she watched over her shoulder, waiting for reinforcements. Much to her relief, a cracking sound shot through the air, followed by a loud blast. Looking around, Finn saw one of the lights enter the chest of a fairy statue, then another nearby. Within seconds, the sculptures lit up from the inside, cracking open the concrete and exploding with a powerful force. The life force of the fairies had reunited with their bodies.

The fairies freed themselves from their stone prisons one by one as the detonations turned the yard into a battlefield. The guards were no match for the mythical creatures. Finn watched in disbelief as the fairies detached their utility belts and flew them up to the trees. Pants dropped to their ankles, and guns were the object of keepaway games. The rattled guards ran for their lives. Entering the parking lot, Finn had reached the peak of astonishment. "Who are you?"

"Just the girl ya married." Followed by a cheeky wink, she opened the door to the back of the car.

Finn gently laid Ailee on the back seat, making her as comfortable as possible, while Molly attached the bag containing her blood to the clothing hook above the window. Reintroducing the blood into her system would take time. Shutting the back doors, they hurried to the front seats. Pressing their seatbelt latches into the buckles; the two weary rescuers came face to face over the console. "You know what tomorrow is?" asked Finn.

"Our daughter's birthday." Molly started the car and headed for the closed gate. Her hands gripped the wheel with determination as she stared at the guard standing in front of the iron gate. His face showed the nervousness he felt from the lights and sounds coming from the yard. Still, he refused to abandon his post.

"I can take the guard out and get the gate open," offered Finn, reaching to release his seatbelt. "You get Ailee to Saydee's."

"There's no time t'stop," she said, summoning her power. Thrusting her hands toward the windshield, she blew the gates apart. Shocked by the gate slamming open, the guard ran to the controls.

Molly and Finn slipped through the wide opening and onto the highway before he could act.

Wiping the sweat from his forehead, Finn watched the guard through the back window until they were safely away. He'd never been so glad to say goodbye to a place in his life. What he'd experienced that night had changed his view of Ailee's fragile situation. The sight of his daughter's weakened body reminded him of the miles they had yet to travel before she was safely out of the woods.

Turning in his seat, he looked at his childhood crush, teenage sweetheart, and one true love. Her red hair was a mess of knots as it fell on her torn shirt. He finally understood her choice to stay behind all those years ago. She was protecting her daughter and preparing the way for her return. Tonight had shown him first-hand the depths she would go to for Ailee. The years she sacrificed were a gift of love to her daughter. Switching his focus to the road ahead, Finn hoped to hear of an actual plan. "What now?" he asked, assuming her mind had already mapped out their next move. "You were right about the hospital. Ailee's dehydrated. She needs some fluids."

"We don't have the time."

"Stay in the car with Ailee. I'll get what I need."

"Then what?"

"Saydee'll know."

Her answer wasn't what he had hoped for, but it sounded like the truth. "Is Ailee going to make it?"

"She has to," said Molly, using her free hand to point the rearview mirror at her daughter. In the blink of an eye, fourteen years had been reduced to twenty-four hours. She'd rehearsed the plan to save her daughter countless times, gauging for every possible scenario. In her head, it was as simple as one, two, three—tonight had proven her wrong.

Glancing at Finn, she could only imagine the processing taking place within his mind. A display of epic proportions had obliterated his simplistic understanding of magic. His bloody forehead and filthy clothes were evidence of his bravery. The mighty warrior she'd married so many years ago had finally returned. Fighting side by side

THE 14TH TALE

to save their daughter's life wasn't the reunion she expected. In hindsight, she wouldn't have had it any other way.

She was angry when he took their daughter from her homeland—the years had been lonely without Ailee and her husband. Ultimately, fleeing Ireland was the right move to keep their daughter's presence hidden from the forces of evil. She could see that now.

Wrapping her hand around Finn's, she communicated her gratitude without words. The drive would give them the time needed to recover from the physical exertion of their successful rescue.

HEARING loud noises from outside the building, Nurse Brón left her laboratory mixing table and walked toward the window at the end of the hall. Her pace increased as the intermittent flashes of what appeared to be fireworks lit up the dark hallway. She arrived just in time to see the last of the fairies burst from their concrete prisons and flee the yard. Chunks of stone strewn across the lawn were the only evidence of her captives. The sight of Boyle's security guards, wounded and in shambles, lit a fuse of anger that shattered the window pane, as well as some nearby beakers and glass trays. Thoughts of the fairies returning to the Otherworld increased her vengeance as she returned to the lab.

Returning to her stainless steel tabletop, she continued the process of treating Ailee's blood for proper use. Her plan to return to the Otherworld and exact revenge for her banishment had taken a hit. Knowledge of the entrance point had been removed from her mind as part of her punishment so long ago. Her only hope of re-entering the Otherworld was Boyle and the *Book of Killian*.

Biding her time, she pretended to be Boyle's lackey, doing his bidding as she waited for his plan to advance. That time was fast coming to a close. She would never have made it this far without his knowledge of the Killian curse. Catching her reflection in a large glass fragment, she saw portions of her true face exposed. The passage of time had sickened and twisted her body, corrupting her soft skin and once youthful presence.

With a swipe of her hand, she repaired her appearance. Her dark powers may have increased outside the Otherworld, but they were useless against her physical evolution. Turning back to the window, she watched the lights of the sídhe-folk disappear into the night sky. Distant memories flooded her mind.

CHAPTER TWENTY

Waiting in the wings of the forest grove, Deora watched the foolishness of the fairies as they danced through the grass—their frivolities on full display. Pulling her thick red hair over one shoulder, she loosely braided the cascading locks that hung to her waist. She preferred her hair somewhat controlled rather than at the whim of the night breeze.

"Another night of disapproval?" came a voice from behind.

Deora braided in silence as she waited for Braoinín's approach. "It's as though they've forgotten."

"Forgotten?" asked Braoinín, already knowing the answer.

"Who we once were."

"Must we live in the past to please you?"

"Where do we belong if not in the glory of our past?" she asked of her best friend and her queen. Her Rígan Lár "We were once a race of magical warriors." Deora pointed to the fairies dancing and laughing in the grove. "Look at what millenniums underground have done to us. Dancing in the night air for fear of being seen by the humans."

"Our days and our nights are what we make of them. The future has not been written."

"We have no future!" yelled Deora, her voice carrying into the grove.

"Silence yourself," the Rígan Lár ordered. "I will not have rain cast on their celebration."

"We still have power over the elements, Braoinín, or have your forgotten?" she warned. Moving her open hands in a circular motion, she lifted her arms to the sky, calling forth the rain clouds.

The fairies ran from the open grove at the sound of roaring thunder. Deora lowered her arms as the sound of raindrops began to fall on the leaves overhead.

"How would you have us spending our days and nights, Deora?" asked the Rígan Lár.

"In preparation." A lightning strike lit up the grove, followed by a mighty clap of thunder. She had the attention of her queen. "You and I once fought side by side. Our people defeated the Fir Bolg and the Fomorians."

"Yes, we fought side by side until we lost the final battle. Our past belongs in the past."

"Our past is our future. Why can't you see it?" The rainfall increased with Deora's fury until it became a deluge. Neither abandoned their ground.

"What would you have us do?" yelled Braoinín, elevating her voice above the storm.

Lifting the key attached to her sash, she held it between their faces. "We give them what they want."

"How will giving humans access to the healing well return us to power?"

"We've watched them for centuries. Their pain. Their suffering. Their sadness. What would they give to be freed from it all?"

Out of caution, Braoinín lowered her friend's hand holding the key and wrapped her hand around Deora's. "Have you spoken of this in the Otherworld?"

"You control the in-between, the entrance to the holy well. You're the queen of that domain. The rest of the kings and queens have their own territories to manage in the Otherworld."

"This is madness!"

"Think of it, Braoinín," tempted Deora as she allowed the key to fall to her side, safely held by her sash. "You and I hold the key to the future. The humans will gladly hand over what belongs to us in exchange for a cure for whatever ails. We'll be heroes as we drive them from our island nation and take our place on the surface where we belong."

Grateful for the rain's dampening effect on the sound of their voices, Braoinín stepped close to Deora. "As the keeper of the key, you must never speak of this again."

"I lay out a plan to reverse our fortunes, to right the wrongs, and that's all you have to say?"

"We lost the battle to the Milesians."

"But not the war."

"The war has ended!"

"For you, perhaps!"

"You know the price for a human to drink from the well," responded the Rígan Lár.

"Population control," she argued without an ounce of care for their lives.

With a twist of her hand, Braoinín stopped the rain and dispersed the clouds. "As Rígan Lár, I release you as keeper of the key."

Before Deora could grab the key, Braoinín held it safely in her hand.

"I've kept the key for over a thousand years," declared Deora.

"And look what it's done to you," whispered her friend. "Return to the Otherworld before this goes beyond a simple conversation." Transforming into a ball of light, the fairy queen lifted toward the canopy of branches and leaves, disappearing from Deora's view.

The grief she felt over the loss of the key and her friend's betrayal brought her to her knees. For the first time in her very long life, Deora felt isolated from her best friend and ostracized from her people. She no longer knew her own kind. The command to return to the Otherworld was a punishment. But for what? Her only desire was to return her people to their former glory. Crawling to her feet, she raised her fists to the heavens. "I will have my revenge!" Nothing but the echo of her voice responded. She had a decision to make. The sound of a twig snapping nearby would make the choice easier.

"Has it gone beyond a simple conversation?" The voice in the darkness was a familiar one.

"It has." Deora turned to face an acquaintance: the witch of the haunted forest. Her frightening, twisted face no longer shocked Deora, nor did the rancid smell of death on her breath. They'd dabbled together on occasion *when it benefited them both. The witch's magic was of a different source, but that didn't keep Deora from drinking from her tutelage.*

"The road diverges. Which way will you go?"

"From here on, I make my own road." Deora joined with the witch of the forest, leaving behind her people of the Otherworld. She bid goodbye to their rules and traditions with one last glance at the grove.

THE SOUND of a timer beeping brought Deora back to the present and her current life as Nurse Brón. Time was of the essence. She poured the blood mixture into a bag and then grabbed everything she needed for a transfusion. She tucked the book beneath her arm on her way out of the laboratory.

Following his scent, Nurse Brón located Boyle in the kitchen, still groggy from the wallop to the head. Untying his hands, she rolled up his sleeve and then placed a band around his upper arm to help locate a vein.

"What are you doing?" asked Boyle, struggling to focus.

"Hold still," she said forcefully as she inserted the needle into his arm, then quickly removed the band from around his bicep. Sticking the syringe's needle into the catheter, she delivered the blood mixture.

"Tell me we still have the girl?"

"A portion of her. I've adjusted for blood type. We'll know soon if this works," she said, untying the electrical cord from his wrists. "If I'm right, the book can only be read by those with Killian blood in their veins."

Struggling to get up, he pulled himself into a sitting position and leaned against the counter. The nurse crouched next to him and opened the *Book of Killian* together. "What do you see?" she asked as she removed the IV needle from his arm and applied a bandaid.

Staring at the blank pages, Boyle waited for the infusion to take effect. "It's not working."

"Give it time."

Using his thumb and index finger, he rubbed his eyes and took a second look. Random letters began to pop up across the open pages. He watched as they magically pieced together to form handwritten sentences. "The girl's blood worked."

Rising to her full form, Nurse Brón exhaled a sigh of relief. Retrieving the key that rightfully belonged to her was within her grasp. "What do you see?"

"Writing , but it's all just family drivel," said Boyle, skipping the 'fine print' of their experiences throughout the generations.

"Find the map," the witch insisted.

Boyle quickly turned the antiquated pages, surprised by the durability of the paper. Stopping briefly, he examined each generation's illustration. Deeming them absentminded doodles, he cast their importance aside in search of bigger fish. Page after page, he traveled until he reached a map at the center of the book. "I found it!"

Hand drawn centuries earlier, he traced the directions with his fingers. Nothing about the map made sense. "I doubt these trees and landmarks still exist."

"Keep looking," encouraged Nurse Brón, hoping a more modern map would appear.

The turning of the pages hastened until he found an updated version drawn in the twentieth century. "This map we can work with." Yanking on the page, he tried to rip the map from the book. It wouldn't budge. "Blasted book's indestructible." Enraged by the technicality, he tried again to pull the page from the hand-sewn binding.

"The book's protected," said the nurse. The entrance to the Kingdom of Idir is also protected. The knowledge of the entrance was wiped from her mind the second she turned her back on her kind. "Take a picture." She wanted desperately to see the map with her own eyes. She hoped a photographic copy would make it a reality.

Checking the quality of the phone's picture, Nurse Brón breathed a sigh of relief at sight of the map. "I love a happy ending."

"Since when he asked, closing the book and casting it aside like a used gum wrapper.

"When it's in my favor."

"Our favor," he reminded her as he crawled to his feet and walked out of the room.

"Of course," she agreed, appeasing his ego. She needed him for one last task. Picking up the book, she dusted it off and wrapped her arm around it. She would cherish the souvenir as a reminder of her triumphant return to the Otherworld.

Hurrying down the hall, they had little time left to make final preparations for their pilgrimage to the holy well. Her centuries-long wait would be over soon.

CHAPTER TWENTY-ONE

The early morning hours of their daughter's fourteenth birthday had Molly and Finn's insides in knots as they turned onto the dirt road leading to Saydee's home. A shared glance was the only communication they could muster as they faced the uncertainty of the day. The horse was already hitched to the caravan when they drove into the parking area. Lanterns lit the twilight as Saydee and Gladys placed baskets and bags inside the wagon.

"Looks like we're off-roadin' again." Turning to the backseat, Finn softly called to his daughter. "We're here, Ailee."

"It's time t'wake up," added Molly.

To the relief of her parents, Ailee opened her eyes and looked around the car. "Where are we?"

"You're safe, but we need to move," said Finn. By the time they left the car and opened the back doors, Ailee had drifted back to sleep.

Molly used an infrared thermometer to check her temperature and slipped a digital blood pressure cuff over her wrist. "Her vitals are improvin'." Finn scooped his weak daughter into his arms as Molly placed the blood bag and IV fluids on her stomach for transport. She'd absorbed over half of each, and Dr. Killian was happy with her progress. Taking advantage of the last moment he'd have alone with his wife before the family surrounded them, Finn used an old Irish saying to express his feelings. "'Two people shorten the road.' I understand that now. Together, we'll save our daughter."

Molly watched from the car as Finn carried Ailee toward the back of the wagon. Her husband's sentiment was genuine and from the heart. It would take the two of them to get Ailee to the gate, but only one of them could save her. Looking at the preset timer on her watch, she knew exactly how many hours, minutes, and seconds she had till the exact time of Ailee's birth. Taking a deep breath, she firmed her resolve to see it through to the end as she made her way toward the caravan.

Quinn was kneeling at the back of the wagon, waiting for his friend to place Ailee in his arms. Finn gratefully obliged. He watched as Quinn gently laid her at the front of the wagon on a bed he'd made specifically for her. Covering her with a warm quilt, Quinn tucked her in to keep her warm in the drafty caravan. Molly climbed inside to continue her daughter's medical care. Once she got the blood bag and fluids hung and checked the IV, she turned to her twin brother. Pulling his protection charm from her pocket, Molly placed it in the palm of his hand. With eyes full of gratitude, she thanked him for having the courage to be their guide.

Still carrying the weight of the world on his shoulders, Finn turned to Gladys, Saydee and Maureen. His eyes overflowed with uncertainty. He no longer had the strength or the will to hide his true feelings from his family.

"We're goin' t'save her, Finn," said Gladys as she hugged the father she'd assisted for so long.

"I've packed everythin' I can think of," said Saydee, lugging her heavy bag toward the wagon. Finn took it from her hands and easily handed it to Quinn to carefully place in the wagon.

Finn looked for a final morsel of wisdom in his oldest advisor. She'd been a constant in his life during his grayest days.

"There's no time for worry," added Maureen as she passed him by on the way to the wagon. "It's time t'do battle."

Finn accepted her advice as truth as he watched her join the rest of the Killians near the back of the wagon. "I see we're all going," observed Finn. "Is that necessary?"

Looking down from the back of the caravan, Quinn answered for everyone. "It's a long road that has no turnin'." His Irish proverb hit the nail on the head. After years of tradition, it was time the family broke the rules.

The sun caught Finn's attention as it broke through the darkness in the eastern sky. Walking away from the wagon, he stood in the center of the large yard and basked in the daybreak. It didn't take long for Saydee, Gladys and Maureen to join him. Once Ailee was comfortable and settled, Molly and Quinn joined them as well. Standing in a line facing the rising sun, they honored the day of Ailee's birth.

The quirky crew of scrappy fighters was peculiar at best, especially when it came to their unique style. They were a sea of sagging knee socks below bright culottes, skirts, and dresses, accompanied by handcrafted sweaters. The battle-worn members of the team stood in dirty jeans and ripped shirts stained with dirt and dried blood. With messy hair and weary faces, they made up the best chance of getting Ailee to the holy well.

"We're seven travelers making our journey on the fourteenth day of the mortal month of May," said Finn.

One by one, the Killians placed their hands on their oak pendants as they stared into the morning light.

Stepping behind Finn, Saydee laid a chain holding his own Killian protection charm around his neck. "Feel the strength of the mighty oak protectin' ya on yer journey." The reunion of Finn with his family had come full circle. Freeing himself from cynicism allowed his mother and Gran Donnelly's superstitious natures to wash over him as well.

"I'll make sure Ailee's wearin' hers," Gladys said, pulling the charm from her pocket.

After a moment of silence, they walked toward the caravan, united by heart, soul and duty. Finn made his way to the front and crawled onto the coachman's seat. A swish of Murphy's tale and a nod of his head told Finn he was ready. Parting the curtains, he checked to make sure everyone was aboard and comfortable. Then he turned around and picked up the reins.

"Do you fancy an extra set of eyes?" asked Quinn, sticking his head through the curtains.

"None better than yours."

A bit shaky, Quinn crawled onto the driver's seat next to his oldest friend.

Finn went one step further and offered him the reins, placing his arm around Quinn's shoulders for support.

"Maybe I could for a wee bit," he responded, taking the straps in his trembling hands. "Lead on, Murphy." The wagon pulled away from the house with a tap of the reins.

The lanterns in the back swayed with the caravan's movement as Saydee sorted and mentally cataloged the contents of her bag. She'd loaded it with as many enchanted tonics, tinctures, and potions as she could find in her magical work room. Better to be prepared than not. In awe of her sister's knowledge and abilities, Gladys helped the best she could. Saydee had committed her life to the study of her craft. Her own gifts had been put on the back burner while living abroad. To say she was rusty was an understatement.

Molly studied her aunts from the opposite side of the wagon, hoping they could keep Ailee alive long enough to drink from the well. Her condition had progressed beyond the help of modern medicine.

"Take her hand, Molly," whispered Maureen, sitting on the other side of Ailee. "She needs yer healin' energy."

Molly followed her gran's advice and took Ailee's hand in hers. The feeling was initially foreign, becoming familiar with each second that passed. Lying down on her side, Molly used her other hand to brush the hair from her daughter's eyes. Her memory of their shared dream spell was still fresh in her mind. She cherished the time they spent together, free of worry and care. It wasn't long before the wagon's movement rocked Molly to sleep. Her battle with Boyle and her sleepless night had left her exhausted. She would need the rest.

Saydee grew faint with the rising sun. Before closing her eyes, she noticed several stars still visible in the western sky. She found herself making a wish on behalf of her great-niece. Needing to rest for a moment, she drifted off to sleep next to Gladys, who, minutes earlier, succumbed to her heavy eyelids.

Settling in for the long haul, Maureen opened her bag and pulled out her knitting. She'd started a birthday sweater for Ailee in the hospital. A beautiful blue to represent the color of the Celtic Sea, south of Ireland. She heard her granddaughter moan as she wrapped the yarn around her first stitch.

"Gran?" Groggy and weak, Ailee's voice was a welcome sound.

"Welcome back, Lass," she responded, happy to see the light in her eyes. "Ya had us a wee bit worried."

"Why is my bed moving?" she asked, attempting to lift her head.

"We're in a caravan," answered Maureen, continuing to knit.

"Where's Dad?"

"He's driving with Quinn."

Trying to lift her arm, she found it embraced by someone lying next to her. "Who's holding my hand?"

"Yer mother. Shall I wake her?" asked Maureen, resting her knitting in her lap.

Stretching her neck to see her mother's face, Ailee recognized her from her dream. "She looks tired."

"It's been a long night."

"I'll just watch her sleep."

"A good idea," agreed Maureen, picking up her knitting and slipping a needle through a stitch.

"Gran?"

"I'm listenin'."

"Will you finish the story about Aidan and Shaylee?"

"When yer feeling stronger."

"I have to know how the story ends."

"I don't remember where we left off," said Maureen, searching for excuses to change Ailee's mind.

"Simon was pleading with the fairy queen, Rígan Lár."

"The memory of youth."

"They've been in my dreams since I arrived in Ireland."

"All right, then," said Maureen, realizing her great-granddaughter deserved to know the truth. Maureen began the story where she'd left off in the hospital.

"Simon knew his son's last hope was the fairy queen, so he fell to his knees, willin' t'do whatever it took t'save him. Kneelin' beside the brave father, Shaylee waited for the queen's rulin', knowin' she would adhere to the laws of the Otherworld."

Closing her eyes to use her imagination, Ailee found herself standing in the cave next to Shaylee. It didn't take her long to figure out she was witnessing the scene unfold in person. Once again, she'd been mentally transported back in time. Quietly she watched as Simon pleaded for his son's life.

"Only two things are required for a mortal to dip from the holy well," spoke Rígan Lár. "A key and a sacrifice."

"All that I have I give t'save Aidan."

"A life will suffice."

"A life?" responded Simon, shocked by the exacting terms.

"Consider your choice carefully," warned the fairy queen. "It may be your last."

"There'll be no considerin'," responded Simon, rising to his feet. "My life I freely give t'save my son. Promise me Aidan'll have a future."

"Your son will have a future." Rígan Lár watched as Simon pulled the iron box from his bag and removed the lid. He picked up the leather water pouch with the key in hand and walked toward the gate. The fairy queen and the others parted the way to let him pass.

Refusing to abide by the ruling, Shaylee stepped in front of Simon, placing herself between the mortal and the gate. "I am the keeper of the key. Allow me to open the gate."

"Grant him passage," ordered Rígan Lár.

"Give me the key, Simon," she whispered.

"My ruling stands!" roared the queen. "The mortal shall pass."

Shaylee argued on his behalf, continuing to fight for Simon. "He is a good man," she pleaded. "They are both good men."

"Let him be a man and make his choice."

Stepping out from behind Shaylee, Simon paused briefly. "Thank ya for savin' my son." Then he continued toward the silver gate. Sliding the key into the lock, he turned it to the left. Just as he pushed open the gate, a fierce whirlwind came from the tunnel's depths. The cyclone encircled Simon, spinning him toward the rock wall. His gut-wrenching cries filled the cavern as his body twisted with the force of the tempest. The whirlwind disappeared into the wall as quickly as it came, taking Simon Killian's body with it.

The cave stood in respectful silence following the deadly cyclone. The tragedy of the mortal's death crossed the line between worlds, touching the heart of each fairy present. Even Rígan Lár wished the rules designed to separate their two worlds were not so harsh. Shaylee placed her hands around the bars of the gate and laid her head against the silver. "I should have come alone." The cave's acoustics amplified her whisper, sharing her remorse with the somber spectators.

"Leave us!" ordered the queen.

Without question, the rest of the empathetic fairies transformed into lights and glided down the tunnel.

"You could have made an exception," said Shaylee, free to speak her mind without an audience.

"He is not of our world, and we are not of his."

"He trusted you."

"What happens to his son is not our concern," said the fairy queen as she removed the key from the lock and handed it to her. "You won't get another chance to be the key's guardian."

"You promised his son would have a future."

"He may still... but not by our hand."

"He won't live without our help."

"Then his son will die as all humans do." Declaring her final word on the subject, she changed into a glowing sphere of light and floated away.

The sight of Simon's stone effigy pushed her back against the cold rock. For the first time in her long life, Shaylee felt the ache of sorrow as she stared at him from across the cave—his every detail engraved on the rock. Scraping together enough courage, she walked toward the selfless father. "I should have told you... I'm in love with your son." The only response was the fairy queen's final words echoing in her mind. "His son will die as all humans do." It was a sobering thought that she'd never considered. Even if Aidan lived, his eventual death would leave her alone and heartbroken. "How cruel it is to be human," she whispered.

Cruel or not, she was in love with a man she could not live without. With new determination, she thrust her hand toward the ground, promptly retrieving the water pouch without taking a step. Defying the fairy queen, she opened the gate and ran down the long tunnel toward the holy well.

The light surrounding Ailee dimmed as she watched Shaylee travel down the long tunnel. The darkness soon dissipated, only to find herself standing beside the door of Simon's thatch-roof cottage. Ailee recognized it from her dream. Reaching for the door latch, she was surprised to see Shaylee's hand grab it first. The door flew open as she rushed into the cottage. Ailee followed.

Finding Aidan near death, Shaylee lifted his head and poured the water into his open mouth. Gently, she laid his head back on the pillow and waited for a sign. In all her years of existence, she'd never experienced such profound emotion. Her love for Aidan had transformed her heart.

"Shaylee," whispered Aidan, opening his eyes for the first time in days. "Is it you?"

"Aidan," she responded joyfully, taking his hand in hers.

"What are ya doin' here?"

"I brought water from the holy well," she explained, offering him the pouch. "Drink some more."

Drenched in his own sweat, he sat up and guzzled the water to quench his dehydration. Placing the empty bag beside him, he moved his feet to the floor, fully healed from the pain and fever that had gripped him for a week. "How can I thank ya?"

"You must leave this place," she warned, rising from the bed. "Tonight."

"What?" asked Aidan, confused by her answer.

"Quickly, Aidan!" she urged, filling a bag with food and supplies.

"Why?" Leaving the bed, he stripped off his wet nightshirt and searched for clean clothes. "I don't understand what's happenin'."

"By dipping from the holy well, I betrayed Rígan Lár. She will come for us."

"I'll repay her," promised Aidan as he pulled up his pants and reached for his shirt.

"Your father already did."

"Where is Dad?" asked Aidan, concerned by her tone. Taking hold of her hand, Aidan pulled her toward him and looked into her eyes. "Where is he, Shaylee?"

"There's no hope for your father, but there is for you. Leave now and never return." Handing him the bag, she started for the door.

Blocking her way, Aidan refused to let her walk out of his life. "Tell me what happened."

"I traveled a distance with a good man tonight. A man who loved his son more than his own life." She watched as her words pierced Aidan's heart. Growing weak in the knees, he fell against the door frame. Taking him in her arms, she held him tight until his strength returned. "He wanted a future for you. So do I."

"Don't leave me, Shaylee," he pleaded. "I'm all alone."

"It'll be worse if Rígan Lár finds us together."

"Ya brought me life. I can't live without ya," implored Aidan as he stared deep into her eyes. Running his fingers through her hair, he leaned in to kiss her.

"If we do this, two worlds will collide," warned Shaylee. "It will be felt far and wide."

"Let it be." After months of resisting their passion for fear of discovery, they abandoned their harnessed restraint. Time stood still while they manifested their love for each other with a passionate kiss. The earth rumbled beneath their feet as the forces of nature declared their union to both worlds.

Shaylee pulled back from Aidan and stared into his eyes. The beauty of what they shared faded with the drenching wash of imminent doom. "She knows. You won't have another chance for escape."

"Come with me."

"No!" she cried, stepping out of the house. "I must return to the queen."

"Ya can't face her alone." Aidan stepped from the doorway and took hold of her hand.

"I'll try to reason with her," she said in an attempt to alleviate his concerns.

"T'is mine t'reason," he argued.

"Your father gave his life for you. Don't throw it away."

Pulling her close, he looked into her eyes with every ounce of sincerity he could muster. "We belong together."

"I love you, Aidan, but I'm not powerful enough to protect us from what's coming." Turning from Aidan, she felt the menacing force of a tracking-breeze sweep past her. Shaylee closed her eyes, readying herself for what was to come. She knew the fairy queen's judgment would be swift and void of mercy—an example and deterrent for all the fairies. Reaching back, she wrapped Aidan's arms around her waist. "Hold on." She'd done all she could for the man she loved, and now they would face the consequences together.

The wind enveloped them, slowly spinning the couple off the ground and away from the cottage. Aidan held on tight as the whirlwind carried them through the air, pushing him beyond the extremity of his mortal understanding. The manifestation of Shaylee's warning made his heart race as he held on for dear life.

Feeling the pounding of Aidan's chest prompted Shaylee to sing a song from the Otherworld. Her voice traveled on the wings of the whirlwind, transfixing Aidan's being and calming his heart. Together, they would face their punishment with calm minds and courageous spirits.

She continued to sing until their feet came to rest in the grove of oak and ash trees where Simon had first discovered Shaylee—her night had come full circle. Lights began floating down from the sky, transforming into their physical forms. It wasn't long before Shaylee and Aidan stood surrounded by fairies holding their glowing orbs for light. One by one, they joined in singing the final verse of Shaylee's song in support of their friend. Clasping their hands, Shaylee and Aidan found strength in the choir of voices as they waited for the queen to arrive.

Entering the small clearing from the forest, the fairy queen walked

THE 14TH TALE

toward the young couple. The night had taken a toll on the age-old leader, and it showed in her countenance. The choir of voices ceased with a final tamp of her silver walking stick.

Shaylee fell to her knees and bowed her head in reverence. "Mother."

"Mother?" whispered Aidan, shocked by the revelation as he stood beside her.

"You have betrayed me, child. And for what?"

"For love," answered Aidan, supporting the woman he loved.

Whisperings and chatter rippled through the onlookers, forcing the queen to retaliate. "What do you know of love?"

"All I know is what I feel," replied Aidan, defending his unabashed challenge. "I meant no offense to the rules of yer world. And Shaylee didn't plan to betray her mother." Sensing the spectator's sympathy, Aidan continued his opening statement. "It began with a game of tag on a starlit night." Aidan chuckled to himself as he relived their magical spring. "We were innocent t'what was takin' shape, naive t'the course our hearts were travelin'. With trust came friendship, then love."

The muffled gasps of the onlookers emboldened Aidan. "Each day, I waited for the sun to set, hopin' that Shaylee would be waitin' near the grove of trees. We walked and talked and played games till the roosters crowed. No matter the weather, my feet beat a path through the meadow. Starved of sleep, I met her night after night."

"Leading you to your death bed," inserted the queen.

"Save for Shaylee's help and my father's sacrifice; I would of perished."

"Yet, here you stand," responded Rígan Lár, not a drop of empathy in her tone. Raising her voice, she addressed the other fairies. "A mortal, perfectly healed from the waters of our holy well, defending his actions where he does not belong." Turning back to Aidan, she concluded her argument. "There are rules for a reason."

"I love your daughter."

"You're a child playing a game." Looking back at Shaylee, the knife plunged deeper into her heart. "We care for millenniums."

"Then slap my wrist as ya would a child and let us go."

"The rules of the Otherworld do not apply to you. You are not the one on trial. Your punishment will be to witness what is written in stone." With a *signal from the fairy queen, two male fairies grabbed Aidan by the arms, restraining him from interfering.* "An immortal life will be lost tonight."

"It was my doin' meetin' Shaylee each night," pleaded Aidan, realizing that Shaylee had forfeited her life to save his. "I carry the fault."

"Do not think for a moment that I'm easily deceived. My daughter, brilliant and gifted, has a mind of her own."

"I will speak for myself!" Shaylee's fierce defense silenced everyone in the grove. Rising to her feet, she addressed those present. "It was I who implored Aidan."

"Shaylee, no!" screamed Aidan.

"I defied you, Mother because I love him. Just as you cared for my father."

"I am bound by the laws of our world. You, of all people, know that." Rígan Lár stretched forth her hand and opened it. A bottle magically appeared in the palm of her hand, inciting a second wave of muttering from the rest of the fairies. "There is only heartache in what I must do," she whispered in her ear.

Staring into her mother's eyes, she saw the agony, the torment of a queen's rule. Taking the bottle from her hand, she removed the cork. A mystical smoke escaped the opening, circling her from head to toe.

"Stop, Shaylee! Don't do it," called Aidan, fighting the grip of his captors.

Shifting her glance toward Aidan, she smiled to reassure him, then drank from the bottle.

The queen caught her in her arms and reverently lowered her limp body to the ground. The onlookers stood in silence as Rígan Lár knelt on one knee, supporting her daughter's upper body with her arm. For a brief moment, the queen gave way to mother as she said her last goodbye. Kissing her on the forehead, she allowed her head to rest on the ground.

Sinking to his knees in defeat, Aidan's guards let him fall without loosening their grip. The idea of living without Shaylee was a curse worse than death.

Rising to her regal height, the fairy queen retrieved her staff and faced the circle of mourners. "Shaylee will wake with the sunrise, no longer of the Otherworld. She will be cursed to walk the earth as a human, to live and die as a mortal."

Hoping he heard her correctly, Aidan lifted his wet eyes toward the queen. "Yer lettin' her live?"

"If you consider mortality to be living," she answered with a signal to his keepers. The fairies released their grip on Aidan as their queen commanded. He crawled to Shaylee's side and swept her into his arms. "I'll make her my wife before the sun sets."

But the fairy queen was not finished with them yet. Walking to the center of the circle, she lifted her staff to the heavens. "On this, the fourteenth day of the mortal month of May, the Killian name will be cursed." Slamming the end of her staff on the ground resembled a lightning strike. Turning back to Aidan, she pointed her staff directly at him. "At the age of fourteen, your first-born son will die, except he drinks from the same well that allowed you breathe tonight."

Stunned by her cruelty, Aidan pulled Shaylee closer to his chest. "Why would ya do this t'yer own family?"

"For the same reason a sacrifice is required before partaking of the holy well. The law demands it."

"Ya took my father from me, and now this?"

"I simply accepted the offering."

"What is life worth if gained at such a cost?"

"You will know the answer when you take your own son to the well. As will each father of each Killian son for fourteen generations."

"You will curse our family for generations because we fell in love?"

"I am bound to the duty of law. If it is hope you seek, know this. The curse can be broken but not until the fourteenth generation."

"I'll be the one to end the curse."

"All the cleverness in the world will not break this curse, Aidan Killian."

"Don't be doin' this."

"Tis done!" The sound of the queen's pronouncement ended the assembly. One by one, the fairies turned to light and floated away.

Alone in the grove, the queen stared down at her daughter and future son-in-law. "Each generation will record their tale in the Book of Killian." A large book materialized on the ground next to Shaylee. "This book shall be passed down through the generations, penned by father to son."

"What does it matter?" asked Aidan, humbled to the depths of sorrow.

"I left Shaylee a gift. She'll know what it is," said the queen mother as she transformed into light and disappeared into the trees.

It wasn't long before the break of dawn replaced the darkness. Aidan looked to the East for a sign of hope, but the trees blocked his view. He had a decision to make about the world Shaylee would wake to. They could spend each day downtrodden beneath a gray sky of tragedy or live every minute as though it were their last. He chose the latter and waited for her to wake to a new day.

CHAPTER TWENTY-TWO

Ailee opened her eyes to find herself in the back of the caravan. Living inside Shaylee's memories made the trip feel like no time had passed. In reality, they'd been traveling for hours. Full of questions, she fought the waking process. She closed her eyes, hoping to return to Shaylee and Aidan. The tragedy of their story had touched her teenage heart like nothing ever had. Turning to her great-grandmother, she had to know. "What gift did he leave Shaylee?"

"Her magic."

"Were they happy?"

"For fourteen wonderful years followin' the birth of their first-born son."

"Fourteen." Ailee's place in the long line of Killian generations became clear for the first time. Placing her free hand over her mouth to muffle her gasp, she weighed the role her father would play in the cure. Witnessing Simon's death was horrifying. How could she watch her father make the same sacrifice, to forfeit his life in such a terrible way?

"Whoa, Murphy!" hollered Quinn from the front of the wagon.

The sound of his voice raised Molly from her sleep. Still holding her daughter's hand, she sat up followed by Ailee.

Parting the canvas, Finn poked his head into the back. "Are you ready, Ailee?"

"Turn back!" she screamed. "I won't let you do this."

Surprised by his daughter's opposition, he pressed for answers. "What's got into you?"

"She'll be ready," answered Molly, wrapping her arm around her daughter's shoulders after yanking the curtain shut.

Defiant, Ailee turned to Molly and held her ground. "I won't do it."

"We're doin' it, Ailee," her mother replied as she fought to remove her IV.

Ailee continued her defiance as she crawled to her knees. "I don't want to."

Molly tried to understand her resistance as an unsettled feeling washed over Maureen and the aunts. Looking into her daughter's eyes, Molly cut to the chase. "We're tryin' t'save yer life."

"I can't watch Dad die!" she yelled through gritted teeth, silencing everyone in the wagon.

Surprised, Molly looked to her two aunts for answers about how Ailee knew the curse's details. The wisdom of their years offered only silence as a response.

"I saw what happened to Simon Killian," whispered Ailee, trying to catch her breath after the argument.

"How do ya know about Simon?" Molly asked, trying to properly bandage the portion of Ailee's arm where she removed the needle.

"Shaylee took me there. In my dreams."

The eyes of the Killian women searched each other for answers as Ailee recounted the unprecedented happening.

"I saw everything. From the moment Shaylee and Aidan met to the night they were cursed. I was there for it all." Ailee waited for a response, not realizing the impact her experience would have on her family.

"Shaylee." The revelation fell hardest on Molly, dispelling her belief that she was prepared and in control. For years she laid the groundwork to spare Ailee the painful history of the curse. She never expected to be blindsided by her teenage daughter's mystical connection to her namesake: her twelfth great-grandmother.

In all the years of the Killian line and on all the pages of the *Book of Killian*, they'd never heard of such a happening. A silence fell over the women as they tried to digest the turn of events.

Parting the rear curtain with gusto, Finn caused the ladies to jump out of their skin as he shared the situation's urgency. "We need to go."

"It's goin' t'be a minute," responded Saydee as she closed Finn out on the other side of the curtain and then turned to Ailee. "Yer father's right. We need t'reach the entrance t'the cavern by afternoon."

With her mind settled Molly spoke to her daughter from the heart. "The name, Ailee, was whispered t'me in a dream. Half Aidan, half Shaylee. It makes sense that she'd accompany ya through this final chapter."

"Did you know I'd be the one?" Sliding back against the front of the wagon, Ailee pulled her knees to her chest and wrapped her arms around them as she awaited her mother's answer.

"You were named before the birthmark appeared. I had no idea the curse would fall on yer shoulders." Looking to her family for support, she continued. "We all believed the curse ended with Quinn since he had no children."

Maureen, Gladys, and Saydee nodded their head in agreement, giving validity to Molly's answer.

Believing her mother's words did not sway Ailee from trying to save her dad from certain death. "What happens now should be my choice."

Molly pulled herself close to her daughter. "A beautiful future awaits ya, Ailee."

"Not without Dad," she said, resting her chin on her knees.

Molly recognized that reassuring her about Finn was the only way to get her daughter out of the caravan. "No harm'll come to yer dad."

"I saw what happened to Simon."

"This time's different," said Molly, rising to her knees. "Just think of it, Ailee, the curse'll finally be broken after ya drink from the holy well."

"I have to get through the gate first," she argued.

"You'll get through the gate."

"Not without Dad's sacrifice."

Grabbing her hands, Molly positioned herself in front of her. She looked her daughter straight in the eyes and made a promise she knew she could keep. "Finn'll walk out of the cave with ya."

"How do you know that?"

"It's written in the *Book of Killian*," exclaimed Molly, looking to Saydee for reinforcement.

Saydee weighed the consequences of not backing up her niece's embellishment of the truth. A life was at stake. Two lives. Molly wasn't counting. Finding the words that would suffice, Saydee shared a portion of the truth. "The fourteenth tale's different for certain." It was the best Saydee could do to back up her niece.

"How different?"

"We don't have time for this," argued Molly. Severing the line of questioning, she turned toward the woman who had raised her child. "Tell her it'll be different, Aunt Gladys?"

"Ya want the truth, Ailee?" responded Gladys in true motherly fashion as she worked to divert her niece's thoughts. "Look around this wagon. Look at these women. We've been preparin' for this moment for years. The two men outside: yer father, yer uncle. We're all here for you. At this moment. Yer moment." Gladys crawled to the center of the caravan and reached out for the hand of her mother on one side and her sister on the other. "Trust the people who love ya."

Before Ailee could respond, Maureen took hold of her hand, creating a chain of strong women. "'You'll never plough a field, Lass, by turning it over in yer mind.' Now is the time, Ailee. Your time."

Completing the chain of sisterhood, Ailee took a deep breath and reached for her mother's hand.

Molly accepted her hand with a smile. "Finn'll walk out of the cave with ya. That I promise."

Saydee crawled forward and linked her hand with Molly, closing the circle. "You'll need more strength than ya got to make the journey." Focusing on their magic, the four women closed their eyes and channeled their strength to the youngest Killian. The transfer of vigor felt like a direct beam of sunshine-infused vitamins, permeating Ailee's muscles and settling into her bones. Each individual's contribution came with its own signature strength. Ailee felt her spirits lift to new heights as her capacities woke to a sharper level of function. The combined years of Killian courage ended her fears, strengthened her backbone, and fortified her grit. The power came from their unified magic, induced by their familial love.

Opening her eyes, Ailee looked at each woman in the circle: aunts, grandma and mother. The pride of her Killian Irish heritage penetrated her heart as their strength lifted her wings.

"It's time," whispered Saydee as she opened her eyes and gently broke the circle. With a nod, the others agreed: the moment of action had arrived. True to fashion, Saydee parted the curtains at the back of the wagon with the zeal of an opening night. Finn stood waiting with his arms folded and foot tapping impatiently. Quinn stood behind him, still and silent, staring up the long hill.

Saydee was first from the caravan, her carpet bag of potions in tow. Next came Gladys and Maureen, all assisted by Finn's gallantry. Molly took advantage of the distraction and hugged her daughter for the first time outside the dream spell. "I'll be by yer side the whole way." Needing to move quickly, Molly crawled toward the back to keep the tears at bay. Together, they waited for Ailee to arrive at the tailgate, her father ready to assist. Before crawling out of the wagon, she stared down at her family, no longer strangers belonging to bedtime stories but heroes to a fourteen-year-old girl.

Once her feet touched the ground, Finn feathered the hair from her face as their eyes connected. "It's a bit of a hike. I'll carry you the whole way if that's what it takes." He'd spent his life protecting her and would to his last breath. Finn placed his pack over his shoulders and offered Ailee his arm.

"I've got my second wind," she replied, wrapping her arm around his. "I'll hang on just in case."

Gladys kissed her niece on the forehead, concealing her mixed emotions. "I'll be stayin' with Mum. We'll only slow ya down."

"We'll be waitin' for ya," added Maureen.

Molly approached Quinn and stood beside him as they surveyed the climb. Gently she took her twin's hand in hers as reinforcement. "How ya holdin' on?"

"There are other ways up," said Quinn, sticking to the business at hand as he relived his own trek to the Kingdom of Idir. The numbness he felt from one of Saydee's soothing remedies was helping for the moment. "This be the path we took."

"I'm sorry ya have t'see it again."

"It's still as I remember," whispered her loving brother, barely able to release the words.

"Ya remember too often," she said, bumping her upper arm into his.

"Dad promised everythin' would be all right," he whispered to Molly so no one would hear. "Everythin' won't be all right."

"Dad did what he had t'do," responded Molly, reminding herself of the same thing. "I know how hard this is for ya."

Quinn turned to his sister and placed the palm of his hand against her cheek. "No, Molly, ya don't. But Ailee will," he said with deep sadness. Turning back to the wagon, he dropped her hand as he looked at the climb ahead. "I'll take ya as far as I can. That's where we'll say our final goodbyes." Quinn started up the hill for the second time in his life while Molly considered his words. She had one more thing to do before joining the trek.

Saydee winked at her mother, Maureen, as she pulled the top of the key from her pocket, sealing their secret plan. Molly wasn't the only Killian capable of turning the key, and she'd lived a long life. Lugging her bag, she caught up with Quinn, Finn and Ailee. Molly waited for them to be out of earshot, then turned to her aunt and grandma. "When Ailee returns, help her make sense of it."

"There's no sense to be made, but we'll do our best," said Maureen as she hugged her granddaughter goodbye.

Next in line, Gladys wrapped her arms around Molly, pulling her tight. "Let me do this for ya," her aunt whispered. "Return with Ailee and be the mother you've longed t'be."

For a split second, Molly found herself entertaining the idea. Weakened by the thought, she pulled herself back. "You've done more than enough, Aunt Gladys. Thank ya for raisin' my daughter."

"It's been a privilege."

Taking the first step toward her destiny, Molly physically faced the hill she'd been mentally climbing for years. Without looking back, she hurried to catch up with her daughter.

"One day, I plan t'give the fairy queen a piece of my mind," spoke the matriarch of the Killian clan as she watched her family ascend the rocky hill for the final time.

"Get in line, Mum. A long line."

CHAPTER TWENTY-THREE

The view of the valley was a welcome distraction as they continued their flexuous climb. Finn and Molly flanked their daughter, arm in arm, helping her along. The added strength she obtained in the wagon had made the vigorous trek possible, but she could feel it waning. Her parents continued to take up the slack as she moved her feet, one step at a time. Reaching a rock face camouflaged by native bushes and shrubs, Quinn stopped. He stood in silence as the others waited. "We're here."

"Where's here?" asked Finn, searching the area for an open cave.

Lifting his arm, he pointed at the bushes, his finger shaking. "A crevice lies behind the bushes."

Lovingly, Saydee lowered Quinn's quivering arm back to his side and helped him to a nearby rock. "Rest now. You've done all ya can." Turning back to the others, Saydee took the lead. "I'll find the openin'." Then she disappeared with her bag into the bushes.

Finding a boulder nearby, Finn and Molly gently lowered their daughter to its surface. "Rest while I check on Quinn."

Coach Finn offered his daughter a bottle of water and a protein bar as Molly walked toward her brother and sat down. Wrapping her arm around her brother's shoulders, she reassured him. "Thank you for gettin' us here."

"I can't," he muttered, shaking his head. The tonic Saydee provided had worn off, allowing him to feel the full force of his emotions. "Dad's still in there."

"No part of what happened was yer fault, Quinn."

"Ya weren't there." He'd spent a lifetime shackled by a self-imposed stigma that he could never unchain.

"Make yer way down and wait with Gran," advised Molly, standing up and offering her hand. "We'll figure it out from here."

"I can't leave ya," he responded, refusing her outstretched hand. "You've always been there for me. What will I do after?"

Pulling Quinn to his feet, Molly looked him in the eyes. "I have t'do this for Ailee."

With a change of mindset, Quinn threw his arms around his sister and placed his mouth next to her ear. He had one last piece of instruction to deliver. "The person who approaches the keeper of the gate must be Ailee's escort. The one who'll use the key."

"Keeper of the gate?" she whispered back.

"She's waitin' for ya." Unable to say goodbye, Quinn pushed passed her, retreating from the hill.

Poking her head through the shrubbery, Saydee hailed her family. "I found it," she whispered loudly, as though surrounded by spies. Molly looked at Finn, only to find him staring back. Welding their courage, they helped their daughter to her feet and led her toward the entrance to the cavern. "Wait!" Ailee stopped her parents.

"We can't wait any longer," advised Molly. "The sun is settin'."

"Your mom's right."

"Wait, please." Ailee looked at her parents standing in front of her. A sight she never thought possible. "I don't want to forget this moment. No matter what happens, being here in Ireland with both of you is the best birthday gift ever."

Finn lovingly reached out to his daughter. "In all the hustle, I forgot to wish you a happy birthday."

"We forgot," added Molly, taking hold of her hand. "Happy birthday, Ailee. It's nice t'say it in person."

"It's a start."

Ailee's response sliced through Molly's heart like a jagged shard of glass as she watched Finn lead her toward the cave entrance. Molly wished she had more time with her daughter—more time as a mom to her only child. The 'start' had arrived too late. Shrugging off the nostalgia, Molly focused on the endgame and followed Finn and Ailee into the shrubbery.

It didn't take long to locate Saydee inside the cave's entrance. She was using her flashlight to study the pictographs on the stone wall. Peeling the moss from the rocks gave way to more imagery. "Such history."

"Instructions?" asked Molly, looking at the century's old fairy paintings.

Saydee's response needed no explanation. "Warning'."

"Is this it?" asked Finn. "Are we there?"

"We've only begun," said Saydee, leading the way down the dark tunnel. The lush moss gave way to bare rock the farther she walked from the entrance. The darkness was no environment for plant life. The opposite was true for insects, rodents, and the possibility of wild animals.

Turning on her flashlight, Molly followed, bracing her daughter while Finn took most of the weight. Ailee's need for help gradually increased, as did Finn's apprehension. It wasn't what lay ahead that concerned him but the growing distance from the light at the entrance. His mind grew more troubled with each glance over his shoulder. The splinter of light, as haunting as a crescent moon on a dark night, slowly faded from view. The darkness nipped at his heels, amplifying his uneasiness. He mopped the sweat from his forehead with a swipe of his shirt sleeve. Finn's natural tendency to seek the light was in peril, causing pressure in his chest. Again, he wiped his brow.

Concerned for Finn's well-being, Molly halted their momentum. "Are ya all right?"

"Keep moving," he replied, urging them forward.

"Ya keep glancing over yer shoulder."

"I'm fine."

"Dad?" whispered Ailee, mindful of her father.

"We're going to make it," he assured them, hoping to reassure himself. "Just keep going."

The tunnel continued deep into the hill, leading them down a steady incline; their feet crushing into the wet pebbles. As they continued into the unknown, the air grew damp and cold, settling a chill in their bones. Without stopping, Saydee pulled a tissue from inside her sleeve and wiped her nose. The dampness had triggered the faucet.

"Uh!" A drop of water slid down the back of Molly's neck. Her utterance echoed in the cave's acoustics. It was a nice distraction from the imaginings of her mind as she took a final inventory of her life. The timer on her existence for the past thirteen years had ticked down to minutes. Death was imminent.

Finally, a glimmer of hope sparkled in the beam of Saydee's light, delivering a much-needed dose of relief. "There's somethin' up ahead." Saydee picked up her pace, leaving her team behind. With hope, she watched as the shiny flickers revealed an ornate gate made of precious metal. The silver bars, shaped like leaf-covered vines, ran vertically from the ground to the top of the cave. "I've reached the gate," she hollered back.

Wrapping her fingers around one of the bars, she touched her forehead to the gate, ready to join generations of Killians who made the same sacrifice. The opportunity to give Molly a life with her family was a privilege. Finn and Molly practically carried Ailee to the gate, her strength evaporating with each step. "Time is running out," advised Finn. "Open it." Before Molly could retrieve the key, Saydee pulled it from her pocket and slipped it into the lock. "Saydee, no!" screamed Molly as she watched her aunt do the unthinkable.

With a look of assurance, Saydee smiled at her niece. "It's my turn." Then she attempted to turn the key. It wouldn't budge. She tried again with all her strength. The key refused to turn. A collective gasp echoed through the chamber as their hearts failed them.

In frustration, Molly ripped the key from the lock and examined it beneath the light. She found no clues. With no book to rely on, they looked to each other for answers.

"Look!" Molly pointed through the gate at a light moving toward them. Mesmerized, they watched it grow closer. Once the light reached the gate, it transformed into a fairy holding a glowing orb. "We've been expecting the child." With a wave of the fairy's hand, the gate opened, revealing a lit cave magically concealed by the bars of the silver gate. "Follow me."

Molly slipped the key into her pocket as they entered a large cavern lit by a fire pit the size of a small pond. On closer inspection, the fire was not of wood but of rock containing precious metals and phosphorus. The round cavern funneled into a long corridor that disappeared into the darkness. "Will that hallway take us t'the holy well?" asked Molly, pointing across the spacious cavern.

"I doubt it's that easy," responded Saydee as she walked between the high piles of treasure stacked throughout the spacious cavern. Brushes and ornate combs, keepsake boxes, picture frames, mirrors, and jewelry from aristocrats and royalty were all lumped together with no care or thought. Gold and silver steins, goblets, jugs and platters reflected the glow from the fire pit—hundreds of items, centuries old. Each pile was littered with thousands of gold and silver coins. Saydee found no clues in the piles to help them know what to do next.

"What is this place?" whispered Finn.

"We're somewhere between the two worlds," responded Saydee as she stared in awe at the surroundings. The Kingdom of Idir."

"Is the holy well here?"

"That I don't know," she replied.

"The keeper of the gate will entreat you," spoke the fairy before changing into a light and floating down the long dark hallway at the far end of the cavern.

With everyone's attention on the disappearing globe of light, the keeper of the gate appeared behind them. "Welcome to the treasury.

THE 14TH TALE

In our travels, we encounter many who seek to know what fate has in store for them," said Rígan Lár as she passed through the cavern, keeping her identity hidden. "They pay in many forms." All eyes were on the mystical figure as she made her way to an ornate throne-like chair several steps up from the floor.

"Keeper of the gate and fortune teller?" asked Molly.

"To those foolish enough to seek it," she said, resting in her chair. "Allow the child to rest." She pointed to a settee near the warmth of the fire. "I will speak with the escort."

Once Finn had Ailee situated on the couch, Molly positioned herself on the first step, unaware of gate keeper's true identity. "I don't believe in fate. We write our own futures."

"Something you've been attempting since your daughter's first birthday," she whispered so only Molly would hear.

"We all have a role t'play." Molly took another step, exercising caution as she ascended the steps.

"Does Finn know the price you'll pay for his daughter's life?" she asked, leaning forward on her throne.

"Our daughter's life," clarified Molly as she took another step.

"To twice give a child life is a virtuous act."

"What I do has no root in virtue." Molly held firm with both feet on the third step to make her point.

"Guilt, then."

"Love." Correcting her interrogator, Molly took another step.

"You're the first Killian woman to take her child to the well."

"And the last Killian t'make the trek." Molly's final step placed her on the same level as the keeper of the gate. She waited for permission to approach.

"Are you certain of that?" With the tiniest movement of her finger, the keeper of the gate slid a golden stool in front of her. Pointing her hand toward the stool, her questioner suggested she take a seat.

"She's the child of the fourteenth tale," replied Molly as she sat facing the throne.

"The curse'll end with her."

"Only if she drinks from the holy well."

"Why wouldn't she?"

"You're the one with the plan."

No longer able to contain herself, Saydee made her way to the bottom of the stairs and lowered herself to her knees. "Please inform Rígan Lár that it was me who allowed the *Book of Killian* to be stolen. I failed t'keep it safe. I accept whatever punishment she sees fit."

Rising from her throne, the fairy queen passed Molly and walked down the stairs. Bidding Saydee to rise from her subservient position, she offered a response. "The book will find its way back. As for punishment, you've chastised yourself enough."

"Isn't that for Rígan Lár t'decide?"

"I speak on her behalf."

Rising from his daughter's side, Finn decided to add his two cents to the conversation. "As Ailee's father, I'm prepared to do whatever it takes to save my daughter's life."

Leaving Molly and Saydee behind, Rígan Lár walked toward Finn, standing next to the settee. "You have no idea what that means, Finn Donnelly."

"He knows more than you did," uttered Ailee, recognizing the fairy queen from Shaylee's memories.

With a simple tap of the fairy queen's forefinger, everyone in the cavern became suspended in time. Except for Ailee. "What do you see, Child?"

"You're Shaylee's mother, the fairy queen." Ailee had received the birthday gift she wished for. Not only had she met a fairy, but the fairy queen herself.

Stunned by her knowledge, she lowered herself onto the foot of the settee. "Your powers of observation are strong."

"Your daughter's power. She showed me everything."

"Then you carry a heavy burden."

Finding enough energy to sit up, she struggled to place her elbows behind her for support. "What's wrong with them?"

"They've come too far to be distracted by my true identity."

"You want the curse to end," stated Ailee, sensing the queen's motivation.

Standing up, the fairy queen turned away from the girl's gaze. "That would imply that I care what happens in your world."

Refusing to drop her investigation, Ailee labored to turn her body and place her feet on the floor. "Ending the curse won't bring Shaylee back."

"No, it won't."

"If I don't drink from the well, the Killian posterity ends with my death," said Ailee, reaching out and taking hold of the queen's hand. "Your posterity ends with my death as well."

"It does." The feel of her human touch caused a sensation in the fairy queen reminiscent of holding her daughter, Shaylee's hand.

"That's why you sent all the fairies to protect Uncle Quinn. You were protecting your family as well."

Pulling her hand from Ailee's, Rígan Lár looked down on her young protege' and distant granddaughter. "You've known of the curse for a matter of days. I've watched the results of my ruling for centuries. Don't think for a moment that you know me or the ways of my world. You can't understand the burden I carry."

"A mother's love is a mother's love no matter what world you're from."

"Love cannot bend the law, Child."

"I have a name. Say it."

"You must go."

Rising to her feet, Ailee repeated her demand. "Say it!"

"You're running out of time."

"Say my name!"

"Ailee!"

No longer able to hold herself up, she fell against the fairy queen, wrapping her arms around her for support. Undaunted, Ailee continued her assertion on Shaylee's behalf. "Half Aidan, half Shaylee. You were the one who whispered the name into my mother's ear before I was born."

Offering her support, the fairy queen broke protocol by lifting Ailee into her arms and placing her on the settee. Sitting beside her,

Rígan Lár looked down at the child of promise. "Ailee is a fitting name for the one who will end the curse."

"I'm proud to be their namesake."

"Wisdom beyond years," she said, combing the hair from her descendant's face. "A gift few people have." Sensing evil's approach, Rígan Lár jumped to her feet and released the others from their suspension. "You must go. Now!"

None the wiser, Finn and Molly heeded the gatekeeper's counsel and rushed to Ailee's side. "We're runnin' out of minutes," advised Saydee, sensing the sands of time.

"Before you stands a doorway," said Rígan Lár, pointing at the cavern's rock wall. "Who has the key?"

Reaching in her pocket, Saydee expected to find the key. "It's still in the gate."

"No," said Molly, lifting it for all to see. "It's where it should be."

"I don't see a doorway," said Finn.

"I need you t'stay behind," said Molly as she pulled Finn aside.

"Because I can't see the door?" he protested.

"I'm the one who'll take her."

"I'm her father," he shot back. Sitting beside Ailee, Finn wrapped her arm around his neck for support.

"It's now or never!" With a wave of Rígan Lár's hand, a doorway appeared in the cavern wall, then she turned into a ball of light and disappeared down the long dark tunnel.

"There is a doorway," observed Finn. He placed his hand around his daughter's waist and helped Ailee to her feet. "She can barely stand, let alone walk. You'll never get her to the holy well by yourself."

"He's right," added Saydee.

"I've got an idea," came a familiar voice behind them. "Let's all go together."

In horror, they turned to see Cyrus Boyle and the witch standing at the entrance to the cavern.

Holding the *Book of Killian* in her hands like a trophy, the witch tossed it to the ground. "I'll take that key now." With a flick of her hand, Nurse Brón caused the key to jump from Molly's hand and fly toward her. Molly countered, using her magic to stop the key in midair. With her powers at max, Molly fought for control of the key, but the witch's pull was too powerful. "Saydee!"

Searching her bag, Saydee shoved her pockets full of potion bottles until she found what she sought. Seizing the vial in her grip, she prepared to launch it.

Thrusting his hand toward Saydee, Boyle attempted to grab the vial, but nothing happened. He tried again with no results.

"Borrowed magic only works in our world. Down here, ya need the real thing," Saydee said with great pleasure, then she threw the vial onto the rock floor next to the evil duo. The explosion sent them reeling through the air, leaving behind a smoke screen. The key dropped near Saydee, and she bent to make it hers. As much as she'd wanted to be the one who turned the key on Molly's behalf, she recognized the mission had changed. With a toss of the key in Finn's direction, she hollered after them. "Get Ailee t'the well. I'll hold 'em off!"

"Ya can't fight her alone!" yelled Molly.

Catching the key, Finn shoved it into the lock, opening the door. Leaving the key in the lock, he scooped Ailee into his arms. "Now or never, Molly. You can't save everyone." Finn ran through the door, uncertain if Molly would follow. Forced to choose, Molly looked back at Saydee for the last time. After a reassuring nod from her aunt, Molly pulled the key from the lock and followed her husband into the darkness.

"Hurry, the door is closing!" screamed the witch as she hurled a force at Saydee, tossing her through the air and landing her on one of the piles of treasure. Running as fast as he could, Boyle leaped through the door just before it closed, slamming his head into the rock wall on the other side.

Saydee looked up just in time to see the door shut. She could do no more for Ailee. Dazed, she tried to pull herself from the pile of metal before the witch got too close.

"I've waited for this moment for a long time," said the witch, commanding a broadsword to come to her aid from a nearby pile. The time had come for the two archenemies to face off in a fight to the death. With her hand wrapped around the hilt, Nurse Brón slowly walked toward Saydee, prolonging the threat. "Give up now, and for old time's sake, I won't make your death too terribly painful."

"Not without a fight!" Reaching into her pocket, Saydee tossed a vial onto the large rug beneath the witch's feet. Obedient to the potion, the carpet wrapped tightly around Saydee's nemesis and slammed her into the rock wall. The witch rebounded as though it were nothing. "Your potions are no match for me."

Limping from the pile, Saydee pulled a ceremonial sword along with her. The reflection of light off the silver blade blinded the eye of the witch, causing her to flinch. "Ya know better than to go after the well. It's off-limits to yer kind."

"Soon, the sídhe-folk will live to serve me." Pointing with the forefingers on each hand, the witch propelled objects at Saydee from all points of the cavern.

"Yer war with the fairy queen's yer business," Saydee responded, using the sword like a baseball bat to divert the incoming objects.

"That war includes the Killians," she screamed, hurling a golden harp at her target. "As the keeper of the book, you should know why."

Moving quickly, Saydee avoided being decimated by the weight of the harp. "What did we ever do t'ya?"

Nurse Brón had no intention of destroying Saydee until she laid the charges at her feet. She wanted her to understand the pain she'd suffered at the hand of a Killian. "The witch of the haunted forest was my friend. She took me in when my own kind tossed me aside."

"By yer own kind?" asked Saydee, confused by the revelation.

"I was second in command to the fairy queen of Idir. I carried the key to the well for over a thousand years."

"They must of had a good reason for takin' it back."

"Cowards. All of them!"

"What does that have t'do with the Killians?"

"My friend's health was failing her. No potion or magic would help. We needed access to the healing well. A battle with a Killian left her dead."

"You'll be speakin' of John Killian of the eighth generation," recalled Saydee. "He killed the Witch of the Haunted Forest t'save his son."

"Lies!" Nurse Brón's anger sent a string of objects in Saydee's direction.

Deflecting as many objects as she could, Saydee felt the bruising sting of the objects she missed while swinging her sword. "The Witch of the Haunted Forest should have left the Killians t'their business. Just as you should."

"That healing well's been my business long before the Killian curse."

Unable to withstand the beating from the heavy objects, Saydee hid behind the tallest pile to regain her strength. "All I know is what the book's told me," she hollered.

"I've just as much a right to that well as any Killian. My friend also did."

"The Killian curse ends today. After that, you and the fairy queen can battle it out."

"We'll battle it out but not till after I've destroyed every last Killian. Starting with you."

"Keep yer hands off my family."

"Who will stop me?" asked Nurse Brón. "You won't last much longer."

"Long enough," yelled Saydee before sneaking behind a different pile to hide. There was no slowing the ticking of time. Saydee's only mission was to give Ailee enough time to reach the well. A game of cat and mouse would eat away at the clock more easily than getting battered by flying objects. Saydee was no match for the witch's magic, but she still had plenty of tricks up her sleeve and in her pockets.

CHAPTER TWENTY-FOUR

Prying open his eyes, Cyrus Boyle faced the pitch black of total blindness. Echoes of labored breathing led to long-drawn-out groans as he attempted to get a sense of space or location. His head pounded with the wildness of a child at the drums, unchecked and without mercy. Grasping his head with his hands, he contemplated the self-diagnosis of death. "Am I alive?" The sopping substance, matted in the hair beneath his fingers, confirmed a head injury.

Searching with his hands, he worked to determine the extent of his confinement. The cold, wet rock beneath him allowed for a sigh of relief. He was not in a coffin. His respite was short-lived. The horror of being entombed or buried alive surpassed his fear of death.

"Where am I?" he muttered, trying to piece together the fragments of his shortterm memory. Distorted images of a lofty, treasure-filled cavern flashed through his mind. Was it a dream, or did he know this mysterious place? An uneasy familiarity of people echoed through his mind, settling on one face in particular. "Molly." Her image lingered, rousing feelings of intimacy.

Sifting through impressions, Boyle labored to rewind the film leading to his predicament. A large, well-lit cavern filled with sparkling gold and silver. The warped moan of a helicopter's rotor blades. A bird's view while soaring over the countryside and rushing from his hospital after discovering the location of the holy well from the *Book of Killian*.

"The hospital." Searching his pockets, he pulled out an embossed pen that doubled as a doctor's penlight—a gift from an eager pharmaceutical rep who pursued him as he hurried to his car.

The light gave way to sight as he studied the rock walls rounding into a ceiling. They appeared to be closing in on him. A closer inspection revealed his hands stained with blood. He recalled diving through a closing door to keep Molly and her family from crossing the threshold to the holy well. The road leading to his current predicament had finally been reverse-mapped.

Straining, he rolled onto his belly and pulled himself to his knees. Using the layers of protruding rocks, he leveraged himself to his feet. The struggle to stand caused his blood pressure to plummet. Blurred vision and dizziness accompanied his head rush. Releasing his grip on the penlight, he clung to the rock as the cave swirled about him. "Stop. Stop!" Closing his eyes, he hoped for a reset as he pressed his sweaty forehead against the damp stone.

In the dead of silence, the pounding of his head gave way to a feeble heartbeat coming from the stone wall. "It can't be." Turning his head, he pressed his ear to the clammy stones. He waited for an electrical impulse to trigger another set of thumps. "Someone's in there," he whispered, astonished by the strengthening of the rhythmic beat. The sound continued to contract and relax like pumping blood through the rock. A second beat joined in, a third, and a fourth until he could no longer distinguish between the many pulsing hearts.

"How is this possible?" Bewildered, he searched his medical and scientific training for an answer. The results were inconclusive. Perceiving the mystical nature of his surroundings, he abandoned the attempt to avail himself to science. Growing alarmed by the prospect that the stones were alive, Boyle stepped back from the wall. The racing of his own heart replaced the eerie drumming growing in amplification.

Keeping his eyes on the wall, he bent to the ground and retrieved his light. The beam from the cheap instrument was dimming, limiting his time for escape. Staggering back and forth, he headed down the tunnel, stumbling from wall to wall like a drunk man in a tight alley. He pushed the limits of his strength as he raced the battery life in his penlight. The terror of being trapped in the darkness produced the adrenaline he needed.

No matter how fast he hurried, he couldn't shake the fear of his own heart joining the haunted chorus inside the stone.

CHAPTER TWENTY-FIVE

Rebounding off the cavern wall, Saydee landed hard against the stone floor. The witch's powerful jolt left her lying like a pile of laundry in a crumpled heap. After several brutal rounds, her aging body refused to bounce back. "Get up, ya withered ol' bag of bones," Saydee moaned to herself, attempting to lift her wounded body from the floor. Her elbows gave in to gravity, and she melted back to the ground. Desperate for rest, she allowed the stone to cool the side of her bruised cheek.

The looming threat of the witch's heels striking against the floor grated against her nerves. Reaching into her pocket, she searched for one more potion bottle. "Empty." She was defenseless and at the mercy of her arch-enemy until she spied her bag a few feet away. It had to contain a remaining bottle or two. Reaching toward the scattered pile of treasure next to her, Saydee wrapped her fingers around the handle of an ornate German beer stein. Adding a few more pounds to her punch was the only plan she had for escape.

Resting on the back of her heels, the witch crouched next to Saydee. She wanted to enjoy every second of the final seconds of her enemy's life. Taking a moment, she built suspense as she searched for the perfect words. "Soon, you'll be reunited with the husband you murdered in your own bed."

Her words cut Saydee to the quick. She owed her an equally deep cut in return. Swinging the beer stein at her face, she knocked the witch backward. The witch's shrill squeal drove Saydee to her arms and legs. With haste, she crawled across the floor, reaching for her bag before the witch realized what was happening. Retrieving the last bottle from her bag, Saydee sighed at its function. "An exposin' potion." It was the only weapon left in her arsenal. Whether she wanted to see it or not, the truth was about to be exposed.

Taking advantage of the witch's floundering about, Saydee aimed and landed the bottle at her feet. The cloud of pure white smoke engulfed the witch, leading to a different type of squeal. Rather than pain, it was the sound of heartache and sorrow. There was a reason it was the only potion left in the bag. Saydee loathed the instability of exposing potions. They were precarious by nature, dependent on what the target was hiding. She only had seconds to find a place to defend herself from the unknown. Limping across the cavern, she stumbled up the stairs and took refuge behind the throne at the top. Peering around the side, she waited for the screams to stop. When the smoke lifted, she saw what had been hiding behind the human form of the wicked, Nurse Brón.

A tall and mighty fairy stood in the center of the battle-tossed cavern. The light of the fire pit reflected against her knee-length, fiery red hair as she twisted and turned. She gently rubbed her hands over the soft skin covering her arms and face. It had been centuries since Deora had felt her true form. Her choice to embrace dark magic had twisted and withered her body into a frightening sight. Deora's impossible struggle to balance her evil mind with her fairy form brought a whole new level to the fight. "What have you done to me?" Her deafening scream filled the cavern.

The sight of an age-old fairy who held the power of a magical warrior threw Saydee for a loop. "What have I done, indeed?" Moving to the center of the chair, Saydee was out of ideas. Her only hope was that Molly had enough time to get her daughter to the well. "Please, don't let me fail twice," she said quietly to anyone listening. She would willingly join her Killian ancestors, knowing Ailee and the Killian line would go on.

The tip of a broadsword scraping across the smooth stone caught her attention. Peeking around the side of the throne, Saydee saw the fairy approaching the steps, dragging the sword with her. Her bare feet had replaced the striking sound of heels against the rock. Her brilliant red hair covered half of her face, leaving one eye to guide her up the steps. Lifting the sword above her head, Deora basked in the delight of dealing death to her longtime nemesis. Plunging the blade through the back of the chair, she waited for movement.

The sword missed Saydee's ear by an eighth of an inch. Taking a second to catch her breath, she eased herself away from the sword. A quick analysis of the situation confirmed her fear. There was nowhere to run. Crawling to her knees, she placed her fingers over the throne's golden trim and pulled herself to her feet. "Ya won't stop 'em," warned Saydee, defiantly.

"I already have. Boyle will make certain of that."

"Ya speak with uncertainty in yer voice?"

"Even if he fails, that child won't make it out of this cavern alive," she said, retracting the sword from the chair. "None of you will."

"Rígan Lár will stop ya."

"Let her try," she said, positioning the sword over her shoulder like a baseball bat.

With nowhere to run, Saydee stared death in the face. Courage and honor would be her legacy as she faced the imminent sting of the sword.

Before she could strike, the witch got an unexpected dose of her own medicine. Thrust sideways with a cannonball's power, Deora flew through the air and smashed into the wall. "You've messed with my daughter for the last time, Witch!"

The familiar voice brightened Saydee's heart. The Killian clan had come to her rescue. "Well done, Mum," cheered Gladys, motioning to Saydee to run toward them. Saydee took advantage of her window of opportunity and hobbled down the stairs. Quinn met her halfway, and the two limped toward the others. They'd never been more excited to see each other. Readying themselves for the witch's counterattack, they cut their reunion short and prepared to defend themselves.

Quinn stepped in front of the women, willing to take the first hit. He knew they were no match for their enemy. Scooping the *Book of Killian* from the floor, he used it as a shield.

Rising to her feet, Deora straightened her body as she addressed the last of the Killians. Summoning all of her power, she glowed with fire secreting from her pores. Her red hair blew back, dancing on the force of her wrath. "All your powers combined aren't enough to stop me and you know it."

"Mine are," spoke Rígan Lár, appearing in front of the throne in all her glory.

"You cannot interfere in the breaking of the curse, Braoinín!" she screamed, furious at her intrusion. "The laws of our world forbid it."

"I know the laws of our world, and you will not speak of them."

"I'll destroy you as well."

Before she could unleash the fiery power brewing inside her, the fairy queen lifted her old friend into the air and floated her across the cavern.

"She'll never get to the well in time," she screeched, trying to fight Rígan Lár's constraining pull. "The Killian line will end with that stupid girl's death."

Lobbing a stinging strike at the witch, Grandma Maureen shared her displeasure with a zap. "That's my granddaughter yer talkin' about."

Positioning the witch in mid-air, Rígan Lár liquified the largest pile of gold and silver treasures. Rotating the molten metal in a fiery circle, she wrapped it around Deora's body like a python, squeezing the life from her body—the fire from her pores connected with the molten precious metals penetrating her skin. The magma-type substance consumed her muscles and bones as it enveloped her body. Her ear-piercing shrieks found no sympathy with the Killians or the fairy queen. Deora's end came quickly as the fire of her vengeance and the molten metals became one.

Moving her hands like a conductor directing her final symphony orchestra, Rígan Lár manipulated the precious metal.

The Killians watched in awe as a colossal pillar began to take shape in the cavern's center. The marbling of gold and silver reflected the light, causing them to shield the brightness with their hand. Soon, all the piles had melted and joined the revolving mixture making its way to the high ceiling of the cavern.

Within seconds of forming, the fairy queen exhaled her icy breath, solidifying the soft metals. Lowering her arms to her sides, she surveyed her work. A monumental pillar stood in the center of the cave. The tomb would forever house the remains of Braoinín's old friend.

A large glass urn appeared on the fairy queen's outstretched hand. It was ornate and beautiful. Removing the lid, *Braoinín* summoned the once great warrior's orb of light that had separated from Deora's body. As commanded, the ball of light entered its glass prison, and fire welded the lid tight. Wrapping her arm around the urn, Rígan Lár felt the sting of a decision she'd made so long ago. The pain of judgment had hurt many of those she loved—the price of being judge and jury.

She hid the turmoil ravaging her heart as she looked to the family with whom she shared an eternal connection. She was a queen, after all. The Rígan Lár of the Kingdom of *Idir*. She had a semblance to uphold. "I've been meaning to reinforce the ceiling," she said coldly, feigning indifference.

"That's what you've been meanin' t'do?" Maureen sternly refuted. Standing her ground, she demanded an answer for centuries of Killian pain. Taking the *Book of Killian* from her grandson's arms, Maureen used her gnarly walking stick to cross the floor and climb the steps. Gladys, Quinn and Saydee remained behind out of respect for the matriarch of the Killian Clan.

Reaching the top of the stairs, Maureen stared up at the tall and regal Rígan Lár, unshaken by her majesty. "This book represents centuries of pain from yer curse on my ancestors. Our ancestors!" she repeated, linking their shared history. "What is done is done. I get that. What I want t'know is why? Why such a cruel punishment?"

Placing the glass urn on the small table, Rígan Lár chose to accept Maureen's questioning. Her day of reckoning had arrived. Pointing to the side of her throne, a beautiful chair appeared. The fairy queen welcomed Maureen to rest her weary bones. Out of respect, she waited for her guest to find comfort in the oversized chair before she sat down. "Welcome to my realm. The kingdom of *Idir*."

"*Idir*." She searched for the translation in her memory. "In between?"

"The In-betweens, if you like. You stand at its threshold. It's one of several kingdoms throughout the Otherworld. The laws of the Otherworld are just a few of the precepts that keep our two worlds apart."

"What does any of that have t'do with the cruelty of yer curse?"

"I would like to say that the curse was only about the laws of our land, that it wasn't personal. But I cannot." She spoke with honesty and duty. "I have lived longer than you can imagine time to be, Maureen Killian." The fairy queen borrowed the book from her guest and slowly began turning the pages. "Ages longer than fourteen generations. I've watched many of my kind slaughtered in great battles. I have seen my people sink from the height of glory to the depths of obscurity—from gods to a thing of folklore. I have known more than mortal eyes could ever see. There is no answer to your question about cruelty. All I can do is offer you an olive branch. Or, in our case, an oak leaf."

The fairy queen's answer was candid and abrupt. Not what Maureen was expecting. Sensing her retort was all she would get, Maureen chose the diplomatic approach. "And what might this oak leaf be?"

With a wave of Rígan Lár's hand, the door to the tunnel leading to the holy well opened. "Find out for yourself." While Maureen's focus turned to the secret passageway, the fairy queen picked up the urn and the *Book of Killian*. "Whether Ailee lives or dies, the curse ends today," she said, rising from the throne.

"Our book," cried Maureen.

"The *Book of Killian* belongs in the Archives of the Ages. It's time we look toward the future and leave the past behind." Turning into a giant orb of light, the fairy queen floated down the long corridor, lighting the darkness along the way.

Maureen watched the glowing sphere float away, pondering her final words. She'd spent so many years wanting some form of vengeance for her own personal pain, her family's pain, and her ancestors' pain. At the very least, she wanted to give the fairy queen a piece of her mind.

In the end, she reached a like-minded conclusion. It was time to look toward the future and leave the past behind. The sorrow from loss would always have its place in her heart. Letting go of the anger freed her grief from the indignation that had entangled it for so long. Maureen looked toward her family, standing near the entrance with a hope she'd never experienced.

"C'mon then," said Gladys. "Ailee needs our help." Taking her sister by the arm, she helped Saydee across the floor. Taking one last swipe at her enemy's tomb, Saydee slapped the metallic pillar with her empty carpet bag as she limped past. Her 'withered ol' bag of bones' had triumphed in the end.

Quinn limped across the cavern and up the stairs to offer help to his gran. She happily accepted, and they made their way to the floor. Proudly, Maureen smiled as she watched her daughters approach the tunnel entrance. Their scrappy endurance was a testament to the Killian name. Looking at her grandson, she would never ask him to take that journey a second time. "I'll wait with ya, Quinn."

"I'm done with waitin', Gran," responded her nephew, lifting his flashlight like a banner. Proudly, Quinn escorted his grandma across the floor to the tunnel's entrance.

"Then we finish it as a family," she said, stepping into the darkness. Quinn followed, and the entrance shut behind them, leaving the cavern as quiet as they found it. The gold and silvery pillar stood in silence, reflecting the light of the glowing rocks.

CHAPTER TWENTY-SIX

There seemed to be no end to the rough-hewn tunnel as they forged through the darkness. The damp air intensified the sound of each footstep as their feet crushed against the wet rocks and pebbles. Rogue drops of water dripped onto their heads while other droplets slipped inside their collars. Finn could feel his pace waning as the endurance of his arms and legs dwindled. The pain in his back begged him to stop, but he'd sooner die than fail his daughter. The gradual slope of the rock floor was the only saving grace to the forbidden tunnel.

Finn kept his focus on the circle of illumination radiating from Molly's flashlight. He was grateful for her unwavering hand. A stumble to the rock beneath their feet would be devastating to their progress. Despite his fading hope, Finn gave everything he had to keep up with Molly's pace.

A dim light appeared in the distance as they rounded a bend in the cave. With renewed hope, they pressed forward toward their oasis. Glowing orbs of limestone lit the way through the final stretch to the gateway. The orb's eternal flames highlighted the passageway's dark secret.

Seeing a change in the rock pattern, Molly gradually slowed her stride. The ominous sight of human images engraved on both walls stood as a warning. Feeling her knees weaken, she scanned the walls as they solemnly walked through the corridor of great men. The facial expressions of the effigies were content yet chilling, typifying the two sides of the coin she'd been dealt. Taking a deep breath, she continued the last leg of her journey.

Finn watched Molly study the impressions as he continued his investigation. At first, he marveled at the detail captured by the artist's work. A closer examination revealed a dreadful conclusion. The stone engravings resembled the portraits hanging in the hallway of Saydee's home. He was starting to connect the dots.

Sensing his slower pace, Ailee lifted her head from his shoulder. "Help me stand," she whispered, encouraging her dad to touch her feet to the rocky floor. Hanging on for balance, Ailee found herself in the same cave as the one in Shaylee's memory. Although Simon's effigy had aged with time, she recalled every horrible detail of watching him transform into stone.

She wasn't the only one with a first-hand connection to the stone carvings. A reverence fell over Ailee and Finn as they watched Molly approach her father's image. Tracing the grooves of his face, she recalled the pain of her loss. The sound of a faint heartbeat caught her attention. She fell against the wall and pressed her cheek to her father's stone heart. The pulsations were as clear as if she were using a stethoscope. Pulling away, she cast it off as the imaginings of a temporary delusion.

Thoughts of her teenage brother standing at the gate, watching their father turn to stone, seized her mind. She finally had an inkling of what Quinn had experienced.

Summoning her courage, Molly backed away from her father's likeness and turned toward the gate. The silver bars reflected the light as she walked forward. She found some comfort in knowing she'd be the last Killian to face the gate's cruel toll. Shutting off her flashlight, Molly peered through the silver bars. She could see a light at the end of the tunnel. All that stood between Ailee and the well's healing power was the fateful silver bars. Turning back to Finn, she handed the flashlight to her husband with her final request. "I'll unlock the gate. You get Ailee t'the well."

"Wait!" yelled Ailee, surprising her parents with the forcefulness of her voice. "It's you." Clinging to her father, Ailee stepped toward Molly with an accusing look. "It's always been you." Feeling the life draining from her body, Ailee grabbed onto the gate as she confronted her mother. "You lied to me in the wagon. You said this time would be different."

"I promised you'd walk out of here with yer dad."

"It's not fair," she cried. "I just got you back."

"Please, Ailee," her mother begged. "I'm the only one who can save ya. Let me do this for ya." Pulling the key from her pocket, she took one last look at her beautiful daughter. Caressing her cheek, Molly tried her best to console Ailee. "I'll always be with ya, swimming by yer side."

"No!" argued Ailee, covering the lock with her weak body. "It can't be this way." Turning to her father for help, she pleaded with him to stop her. "Tell her, Dad. Tell her!"

Finn's heart began to fail him as he considered the terms of the curse. He had a cruel choice to make—the life of his daughter for the life of the woman he loved. He knew in his heart of hearts that it wasn't his choice to make. His reunion with Molly had come to an end. "If there were any other way, Ailee," he said, fighting back the tsunami of emotion.

"Tell her you've never stopped loving her," Ailee implored. "Tell her!"

Returning the key to her pocket, Molly wrapped her arms tightly around her daughter, hoping to calm her down. "The only thing that matters is you," Molly whispered, stroking her hair for the last time. "We have t'do this."

Reaching into her mother's pocket, Ailee slid the key into her hand and then pulled away from Molly. Turning her back to her parents, she moved the key toward the lock.

"Ailee, no!" screamed her mother."

"Listen to your mother, Ailee," hollered Dr. Boyle with the force of a coach on the sidelines.

The surprise of a stranger's voice stopped Ailee from inserting the key. Turning back, she saw Cyrus Boyle step into the light. The dried blood on his face and 9mm pistol showed the lengths he would go to for access to the well. "Give me the key."

Stepping in front of Ailee, Molly confronted her colleague. "How did ya find the entrance t'the cavern?"

With a malicious smile and an arrogant tone, Boyle took great pleasure in revealing his source. "The *Book of Killian?*"

"I don't believe ya," argued Molly, stealthily wrapping her hand around Ailee's hand that held the key. "It's impossible."

"Not with your daughter's blood pumping through my veins," he replied, reveling in his power over the woman he'd grown so infatuated with over the years. "I'll be taking that key now."

Taking a moment to consider the biology and the terms of the curse, she turned her head to Ailee and whispered in her ear. "Give'm the key."

"He's not getting that key!" argued Finn.

Molly placed her free hand against her husband's chest to stop him from advancing toward their nemesis. "He'll help us." Turning to Boyle, she softened her voice in an attempt to show her submissiveness. "Won't ya, Cyrus?"

Lowering the gun to his side, Boyle walked toward Molly with reanimated hope. Having her by his side would be the finishing touch he longed for. Although it seemed too good to be true, he dared to dream. "You know better than anyone, Molly. Healing others is my only reward."

"I don't trust him," warned Finn, pushing against the force of his wife's hand.

"Do as I say, Ailee," said Molly, helping her daughter lift the key. "Give Dr. Boyle what he wants."

Pushing Molly's hand aside, Finn moved to intercept the key. Molly jumped between them to stop her husband just as Boyle fired his gun. Falling into Finn's arms, she felt the fiery path of the bullet as it burned through her liver. She watched in horror as blood began to spread along the fibers of her shirt. The unexpected turn of events set her mind to whirling. It wouldn't be long before shock set in from the drop in blood flow. Shaking off the panic, Molly tried to regain focus.

"What have I done?" whispered Finn, pressing his hand to Molly's wound to slow the blood loss. "Hang on, Molly. Hang on!"

Reaching up, she turned his face towards hers. "The curse requires a sacrifice, Finn. It was only a matter of time." Molly's only concern was her family as she faced certain death."Help Ailee."

Boyle backed toward the cave wall, taken aback by what he'd done. He was so close to getting everything he wanted. He could taste the victory till a stranger snatched it from his grasp. It didn't take long for Boyle to shift the blame onto Finn. The feel of his finger against the trigger fed his vengeance. Pointing his gun above Molly, he aimed at Finn's head.

"Cyrus, No!" screamed Molly. The adrenaline rush gave her the energy she needed to use her magic to focus every particle of the cave's light toward the silver key in Ailee's hand. Then she directed the reflected light straight into Boyle's eyes.

Blinded by the brightness, Boyle waved his gun about erratically. The light made it impossible to see his target. Pulling back on the trigger, a bullet fired from the chamber and ricocheted off the rocks, sending Boyle crouching toward the gate. Searching for the source of the blinding light, Boyle saw the key dangling from Ailee's hand. Grabbing the key from her hand, he pushed the weak girl to the ground next to her parents as he rose to full stature. "Nice trick, Molly," he said, trying to regain his composure. "You should have stuck by my side from the beginning."

"I prefer my husband's side," she said, wrapped in the warmth of Finn's arms. She could feel a chill settling into her arms and legs. She knew her body was abandoning her limbs to keep the blood flowing to her heart and brain.

Lifting the key for all to see, Boyle turned to the gate. He took great pleasure in sealing their fate as he slid the key into the lock and turned it. "The Killian line ends today." A terrible howl came from the depths of the dark tunnel as he opened the gate. The unexpected sight of a whirlwind coming straight for them caused Boyle to cling to the gate. "What's happening?"

"Ya should have read the whole book," said Molly with great satisfaction. "Welcome t'the family, Cyrus!"

"The blood!" he screamed as the whirlwind engulfed him and carried him away. His shrieking and howling, mixed with the thunderous noise of the whirlwind, was bone-chilling. Finn wrapped his arm around Ailee to shield her from the horrible sight. He had no idea she'd previously witnessed the phenomena in Shaylee's memories.

They watched in fascination as the whirlwind entered the rock wall, securing Boyle's body apart from the generations of Killian men. After a moment of silence, Molly explained the situation to Finn. "The escort t'be sacrificed must be of Killian blood."

"All these years," said Finn, holding his dying wife in his arms. "You've been preparing for this moment."

"I'm a Killian. It's what we do," she said, trying to turn the dire situation into a regular occasion.

"That's why you stayed," he said, defeated by the truth.

She placed her hand around his head, pulled him close and kissed his cheek. "It was the only way I could have the courage t'save our daughter."

Their tender moment was interrupted by an alarm beeping on Molly's watch. Looking at the time, she returned her mind to the task at hand. "Ailee's got thirty seconds till she turns fourteen. Go!"

Finn gently pulled away from his wife and scooped Ailee into his arms. Reaching for the bottom of the gate, Molly pushed it open as Finn ran through. With the help of the silver bars, Molly pulled herself to her feet. "Twenty-five seconds!" she yelled, looking at her watch. Relying on what little strength she had left, Molly used the wall for support as she struggled to make her way.

Finn raced through the rest of the tunnel toward the distant light. The sound of Molly's resounding countdown increased his speed. He was reliving his nightmare in realtime. One wrong step, one turned ankle, and Ailee's life would be forfeit. The stakes were too high for human error.

"Ten seconds!" Her terrifying words echoed in the cave and his mind as he passed through the greenery and foliage at the end of the tunnel. He'd never relied on his warrior persona as much as he did at that moment. He could hear his mother cheering him on, as well as generations of Killians.

Pushing himself beyond his limits, he ran toward the pool of water at the opposite end of the waterfall. The last thing he heard was Molly's distant voice echoing from the cave. "Two seconds!" Zeroed in on the turquoise pool, he forgot about his fear of water and inability to swim. Desperate to beat the clock, he leaped over the side with Ailee in his arms.

Finn Donnelly's splash was heard throughout the Otherworld as the centuries-old curse came to an end. Its ripple effect stretched far and wide, touching every fairy's heart and mind. Finn had no idea of the epic nature of his warrior feat. The only thought on his mind was his daughter's life as they both disappeared beneath the water's surface.

Stumbling through the tunnel, Molly could see the light but lacked the strength to reach the end. She slowly lowered herself to her knees using the jagged rocks like rungs on a ladder. Knowing her mission was complete, she closed her eyes in peace.

Out of the still of the water, Ailee pulled her father to the surface of the healing well. Then she helped him grab onto the grass-covered earth surrounding the pool. Struggling to stay above the water, he finally found footing at the shallow end of the pond. Coughing from all the water he swallowed, he took his daughter into his arms and hugged her tightly. "You're alive."

"Thank you, Dad."

"Molly," remembered Finn, pulling away from his daughter. Searching for footing against the pond's slick, muddy wall, he tried to pull himself to the bank. Before he could crawl out, they heard familiar voices from inside the cave.

Quinn emerged, struggling to walk with Molly in his arms. Saydee walked beside her nephew, supporting Molly's legs, while Gladys helped support her niece's upper body. Maureen followed behind with a watchful eye. Kneeling at the side of the well, Quinn lowered his unconscious twin sister into his best friend's arms.

Finn received his wife's limp body and kept her afloat as Ailee poured a handful of water between her parted lips. The Killians watched from the bank in suspense.

"Come on, Molly," pleaded Finn. "Come back to us."

"Please, Mom," joined Ailee. "I need you. We both need you."

Maureen wrapped her arms around her two daughter's shoulders as they knelt around Quinn's shaking frame. He was alone the last time he knelt beside the healing well. This time he had the full force of the Killian clan. All they could do was wait for fate to rule.

Pressing his lips to Molly's, Finn kissed his wife for what he feared was the last time. The touch of her soft lips flooded his mind with sweet memories of their years together. Theirs was a childhood crush that became a teenage love that bloomed into a romance for the ages.

Staring into her face, he used his wet hand to wipe a smudge of dirt from her cheek. Looking at his daughter, he saw the anguish he felt mirrored in her eyes.

"Tell her, Dad," whispered Ailee. "Tell her what you should have told her in the tunnel."

"Ailee."

"Tell her you've never stopped loving her," she pleaded. "Tell her!"

Finn released the truth hidden deep in his heart for twelve long years as he lowered his mouth to Molly's ear. "I've never stopped loving you, Molly. And I never will." Believing his confession fell on deaf ears, Finn turned from Ailee to gain composure.

"Spoken like a true warrior," Molly weakly whispered.

Molly's words destroyed his composure as Finn's eyes welled up with emotion. Ailee and Finn smiled at each other in astonishment, then turned their attention back to Molly.

With blissful rejoicing, the Killians roared with excitement as Molly opened her eyes. Still weak from her near-death experience, she gently embraced her daughter as the rest of the family cheered from the sidelines.

Watching the reunion of their little family, Maureen couldn't help but wonder. Had Molly's life been restored by the magical waters of the healing well or the power of her and Finn's enchanting love? Leaving it as a mystery for the ages, Maureen called to her great-granddaughter. "How do ya feel?"

"I feel," paused Ailee, lost for words. "I feel perfect."

"My achin' back could use some perfect," said Gladys.

"My whole body could use some perfect," agreed Saydee as she stood up and followed Gladys around the pool of water toward the stairs leading down into the healing well. "A proper endin' for the *Book of Killian*."

"The Killian Clan's alive and all together," said Maureen as she stared into the eyes of the young family. "There can be no better endin'." Rising to her feet, she followed her daughters to the stairs leading into the pool.

Ailee smiled as she watched her great aunts and great-grandmother enter the healing well. It didn't take long before they returned to their childhood personalities, splashing about and playing games in the water.

Looking up, Ailee noticed Quinn staring intently at the many grassy ridges protruding from the tall, straight hillside next to the waterfall. Looking in the same direction, she saw the past thirteen generations of spirits of the Killian men and women standing in pairs on the different ledges. She watched as Quinn smiled at his father. The healing could finally begin. Making eye contact, Quinn winked at Ailee then jumped into the healing well. The first cannonball he'd performed in decades.

Ailee smiled at Quinn's happiness then turned her attention back to the ledges. Lifting her arm from the water, she waved at Shaylee and Aidan standing near the top of the waterfall. There unfailing love was on full display. Shaylee nodded her head in return, congratulating Ailee on a job well done. Shaylee and Aidan's story had come full circle and the fourteen generations of Killians were present to witness the curse's finale.

The sound of Quinn alerting the Killian women to their ancestors caught her attention. This was a gift beyond the ending of the curse.

The sight of her dad holding her mother in his arms was indescribable. There would never be a birthday gift as great as this moment—a moment Ailee never wanted to end.

Feeling the familiar weight of Ailee's stare, Finn looked to his daughter. "When we get home, you're teaching me to swim."

"I think we're already home," said Ailee.

"Ya won't be gettin' an argument from me," added Molly.

"That'd be a first," smiled her husband.

"Welcome home, Finn." Molly kissed her husband with twelve years of passion behind it. The first kiss of many to follow.

Sensing they could use some alone time, Ailee joined the rest of the Killian clan. "So," she said, putting on her best Irish accent. "Got some luck on my side, but I'm gonna need some teachin' t'make up for bein' gone for so long. Who'll be givin' me a hand?"

"Don't ya know, Lass?" said Maureen, wrapping her arm around her greatgranddaughter. "If ya lucky enough to be Irish, ya lucky enough."

EPILOGUE

Sleep was the order of the day as Saydee waved goodbye to the family. The boost received from the holy well had breathed enough life into her sleep-deprived body to get her home. After removing Murphy's harness, she led the horse to a fenced-in area in the backyard for some water and feed. Returning to the front of the house, Saydee faced the rising sun. Just twenty-four hours earlier, they embarked on a family adventure of a lifetime, uncertain of the outcome. Today, she looked toward the dawn with renewed hope and a blank canvas.

The house was cold and shadowy as she entered the front door. A chorus of *coos* and *caws* alerted her to visitors. The missing window panes in the kitchen allowed the crows to make themselves at home while she was away. Saydee shooed them from the house using a broomstick as she moved toward the kitchen. "B'gone, ya manky interlopers." Standing in the explosion's epicenter, she surveyed the colossal damage. Using her broom, Saydee began to sweep the clutter into a pile.

A muffled ring stopped the stroke of her broom. She waited in silence for the noise to repeat. Again, it sounded. Calmly, she placed the broom in the corner and walked toward the pantry door. She moved a mess of pots and pans tossed askew by the blast and entered the storeroom. She pushed aside small bags of flour, oats, and sugar to reveal a gray, crushproof case no bigger than a woman's shoe box. Carrying it by the handle, Saydee brushed the cluttered mess to one side and laid it on the counter. The double-throw latches on the airtight case released easily. Opening the lid, she pulled a satellite phone from its foam slot and positioned the antenna toward the window above the sink. The country code let her know it was England calling. With a sigh of exhaustion, she answered the call. "It's a wee bit early, even for London."

A calm, low voice replied. "We've got a situation."

"Of course ya do, or ya wouldn't be callin'."

"It requires a stealth touch," said the man on the other end. "Your touch."

"It's been a ferocious week. I'm knackered," she replied. "Can't SAS, UKSF, or MI-6 handle it?"

"You're it," he said. "I'm sorry, Saydee, it can't wait."

"What good is t'retire if ya keep callin' me?"

"I can't be the only one calling," he replied. "You're the best freelancer in the business."

"Yer just lucky my body parts are feelin' thirty years younger."

"Does that mean we can count on you?"

"It's goin' t'cost ya," she said, looking around the disastrous kitchen. "I'm knee-deep in a remodel."

"A helicopter will arrive within the hour."

"I'll pack a bag." The call ended the same as always.

Leaving the kitchen, Saydee grabbed her trusty carpet bag as she walked past her set of travel research books and headed toward the stairs. The gate's iron hinges welcomed her with a long creak. She shook her head at the sticky note next to the entrance that read, "Grease hinges." Walking down the long stairs, she entered her magical workroom—her home away from home. Her magical candles continued to burn. They called to her as she made her way toward the cupboard at the back wall. Turning the vintage door knob back and forth like a safe dial with no numbers, she listened for a familiar click. The small cupboard door opened.

Crouching down, she stepped through the door into a hidden room. Her presence instantly lit the candles. The shelves covering two of the rock walls held hundreds of small containers of prepared potions, magical tinctures and enchanted tonics. Opening her bag, she selected certain bottles that her experience taught may be useful. Framed newspaper articles from countries worldwide covered the wall behind her. The headlines told of kidnappings solved for the past thirty years—Saydee's resume of sorts.

Once her bag was half-full of potion bottles, she turned to her rack of modified tools of the trade. She selected a matching chunky bracelet and necklace made from stones with specific properties, a specially adapted monocular telescope, and a handful of run-of-the-mill zip cable ties. Her modified night vision goggles waited for her upstairs. She took one last look around the room before leaving. "Keep yer shop, and yer shop'll keep you."

All that was left to pack were a few pairs of black culottes with matching turtlenecks, some street clothes for blending in, and an Aran sweater and proper boots. Saydee threw her clothes in a bag and rushed into the bathroom for her toothbrush. Catching sight of herself in the mirror, she stopped and looked at the train wreck before her. The helicopter would have to wait. After fighting the forces of darkness, her family was the only people allowed to see her this disheveled. Taking a second look, she smiled at her reflection. "The older the fiddle, the sweeter the tune."

ABOUT THE AUTHOR

Xann-shapella Smith had the opportunity to study playwriting and screenwriting at Brigham Young University and has brought her plays to the stage on many occasions. Her love for great storytelling has produced scripts that span many genres, including: drama, romance, comedy, fantasy, adventure and science fiction. After years of writing screenplays, she made the decision to broadened her horizon in terms of storytelling and became an author. Xann resides on a small farm where the beauty and solace that surround her provide the perfect atmosphere for creating stories as far as the expanse of her imagination. Writing has been one of the great loves of her life and telling a good story is one of her passions. Xann-shapella's writing is a skill that rewards her in abundance each and every day and a passion she loves to share with audiences everywhere.

For more books and updates:
www.xannsmith.com